THE DOOMSONG VOYAGE

THE DOOMSONG VOYAGE

by

J.G. Harlond

www.penmorepress.com

The Doomsong Voyage by J .G. Harlond
Copyright © 2024 J.G.Harlond

ISBN-13: 978-1-957851-70-9(Paperback)
ISBN: 13: 978-1-957851-69-3(E-book)

BISAC Subject Headings:
FIC002000 FICTION / Action & Adventure
FIC047000FICTION / Sea Stories

Editing . Chris Wozney

Front Cover and Back Cover Illustration by
EMILIJA RAKIĆ

Address all correspondence to:

Penmore Press LLC
920 N Javelina Pl
Tucson AZ 85748

DEDICATION

For Pepe and Minna

Our yellow sun will cease to shine.
No silver moon shall gleam.
A wolf-winter will run until
the black night battle
at Ragnarök.
(Adapted from old Norse by author)

CHARACTERS

Master Odo – The Wanderer

Finn – a young tale-maker

Tait and Augal – Finn's older cousins

Katranina / Kat

Hebden Seavogel – shipmaster of *Guillemot*

Norna Silveryarn

Thorsman – one of Seavogel's crew

Beorn Wolfman – a Viking warrior

Rolfgar – Earl of Heorot

Harold Harp-Legs – Viking voyager

Adeef – Grand Visior to the Barbalus Emir Hammil

Zongolo / Zongo – servant in the High Alcazar

The Mighty Hammil – Emir of Barbalus

Goran Ice-Heart – a pirate

Perla – Ice-Heart's captive

Seren – a British thrall

Troll – one of Ice-Heart's crew

Walrus – one of Ice-Heart's crew

Using the wooden shaft of his crystal-tipped staff, an ages-old Wanderer lowered himself to the ground beside a small lake. It had been a stagnant pond when last he saw it, many mortal generations ago. It was far wider and deeper now. He would need greater will power to raise Doomsong from its depths, unless he had help.

He looked across the pool, studying its circular brown banks, noting wildflowers, pink and mauve among the tufted grass. Bugs dipped and danced over the wind-lapped water. A she-otter popped her head from her muddy holt and two cubs squeezed past her to play in the shallows. As they tumbled in, a male otter rose to the surface of the pool, caught sight of the old man and paddled towards him. Help had arrived.

"Find the sword, Master Otter," the old Wanderer commanded. "Dive deep."

The otter disappeared and stayed gone for as long as he could breathe underwater. He bobbed up again, and dived again – and again and again – until a wider set of ripples told the old man the clever creature had found what he sought.

The otter placed the ragged edged but un-rusted weapon on the grass like a prize salmon, and with a squeak returned to his fishing. The Wanderer stared at the sword, what was left of it, and sighed. "It is a hard task we have before us," he murmured.

Removing his fine woollen cloak, he laid it on the grass and turned his attention to the sword before him. He stared at it, glared at it, willed it to mend, but it lay there, as dragon-damaged as it had been the day it was flung into the pool.

"Doomsong and Truthteller," the Wanderer spoke aloud, giving the sword its full name, "become whole. We have great need of you."

The blade stretched a little. The Dwarf gold in the hilt glinted in the weak sunshine, then slowly, very slowly, began to glow. The meled metals shivered back into a seamless sharp blade until the runes could be read once more. 'I am Doomsong and Truthteller,' the sword declared.

The Wanderer flipped it onto its other side, chanting under his breath until the runes rearranged themselves. Where once they had stated: 'Whomsoever bears me in battle shall triumph', they now said, 'Hear my song True Owner and return.'

The Wanderer gave a satisfied smile, weary from his efforts. Above, a she-eagle screamed into the gentle wind. Tilting back his wide blue hat, the Wanderer searched the sky with his one good eye. "Skiila!" he laughed and raised his ash-wood staff into the air until the crystal quartz glinted in the sunshine.

The eagle hovered, her eyes fixed on her master below. "Seek out Finn of the Volsung, Skiila," the Wanderer instructed. "I have a vital quest for him."

Chapter 1

Finn had never seen a dragonship like this in the harbour before – a sea-going flying serpent, with scales painted green and black along the hull. He gave an involuntary shudder and hurried into the tavern known as The Old Salvation.

Removing his thick woollen cloak, Finn took his usual seat by the fire, concerned by what he had seen and what it might signify. A jolting tray of ale mugs passed by. "Hey!" Finn called out.

"Have you got coin tonight, Tale-Maker?" the tavern maid demanded.

"Maybe. Later," Finn said with a slow wink. "My throat's too dry for story telling at the moment, though."

Grinning despite herself, the girl lowered the tray. Finn grabbed a mug and drank heartily of the warm, golden liquid, then gazed about him to see if any of the dragonship crew were also drinking here. There were a few new faces, but they hadn't reached the rowdy stage yet. He'd have to time it right to try a tale on them. The tavern was busy; some familiar bodies were grouped around a barrel, yarning about their latest voyage. Another group was moaning about the cargo for their next. A shrunken, raggedy old woman perched on a bench near the main door was knitting something long and shapeless. Her wooden-clogged feet barely touched the floorboards. Beside her, a skinny youth in a yellow jerkin was also scanning the smoky room, as if searching for a face.

Finn met his gaze, glimpsed a shred of scarlet red stocking above the boy's scuffed boots, and hastily looked away.

Turning to face the steaming peat fire, Finn noticed a ginger cat occupying a cushioned chair. She – Finn knew instinctively the cat was a she – was curled as if sleeping, but her eyes were open slits. She, too, was watching and waiting.

Finn slurped his ale and peered over the rim of his mug. The dragonship crew didn't look as if they'd be recruiting. He gave a sigh of relief, not wanting to be taken as an oarsman against his will, and sat back in his bentwood chair to enjoy the evening. The next time he looked up, an elderly Wanderer was seated in the chair opposite him, seated so close their knees nearly touched. The man twitched the wide brim of his dark blue hat with a long-fingered hand in greeting. Finn gulped with surprise.

"Do not worry, Finn of the Volsung. I came with the dragonship, but I am not here to entice you away. Not with me, that is."

Finn gulped again, unable to form a reply. Around them, men and women carried on ordinary conversations. Some laughed, some argued. Between Finn and the Wanderer there was an awkward silence. Finn sipped his ale, let the barley malt warm his sudden chill and tried to relax. When he felt he could speak without croaking, he struggled for a polite greeting and then blurted out, "Are you Master Odo?"

The Wanderer inclined his head. "That is what some name me."

"Oh. Erm, well, pleased to meet you, sir, Master Odo."

The Wanderer inclined his head again, this time with a smile beneath the wide brimmed hat.

Finn responded with a nervous grin. "Good day to you. I mean, evening. Not good exactly. Far too cold for springtime.

Mad weather, isn't it? For the time of year. Four months since Yuletide."

"A storm will come soon, then sleet and snow during the night." The Wanderer spoke quietly. Finn leaned forward to hear him better. "Yes," the elderly man said, cocking his head to one side and revealing a single very blue eye. "Is there something you wish to ask me?"

"I don't think so." Finn's mind went blank as he raced through all the snippets of gossip and the warnings he heard about the legendary Master Odo. He was tempted to ask which bits were true. Instead he heard himself say, "Why are you here?"

"Why are *you* here, Finn?" the Wanderer replied.

"This is my island. I stay here during the winter months. I'm planning to move back to the mainland again, when the weather improves."

"Are you? That should please your cousins and their wives."

"Yes," Finn said with a frown, wondering how the stranger knew about his cousins and their wives.

"For you are no great help to them, are you? More of an extra mouth to feed, or so I'm advised."

Finn winced at the truth of it and studied the fire, then looked up, "Advised? Has someone complained about me?"

"What do you think?"

"But why would you be interested in... oh, no! No, no. No. I am not boarding that dragonship."

"Have no fear on that score. I am not here for oarsmen."

"Thank the gods for that," Finn sighed, then realised the old man had repeatedly used his name and spluttered, "How do you know who I am?"

"Inspired guess based on..." the wrinkled features beneath the dark blue hat broke into a wide smile, "...your appearance. I have been looking for you. In the end you were relatively easy to locate, with a little help from my fine-feathered friends in high places." Finn squinted at him, trying to make sense of what was being said. "Oh, for heaven's sake, boy, your Volsung colouring: snow white hair on a young head."

Finn flicked a wave of thick white-blond hair off his brow, embarrassed and hurt by the Wanderer's patronising tone. "Why do you want to see me?"

"I'm beginning to wonder that myself." Master Odo gave a long meaningful sniff. His thin lips disappeared into his chest-long grey beard. After a moment, he said, "Perhaps this will help to explain." Pushing his floor-length grey cloak from his knees, he tapped an arrangement of leather straps lying across his lap. "Unlikely as it may now seem, I – that is, *we* – have need of you. You are to voyage to the Middle Sea Isles."

Finn peered at the straps on the man's bony knees, none the wiser, then with a jolt of fear reacted sharply. "You just said you weren't here to get me on that dragonship!"

"And I spoke the truth. Which, incidentally, I always do. One way or another."

Finn glanced around, trying to calculate how quickly he could get away, and which exit to use, front or back.

Master Odo tapped his knee again. "The dragonship that brought me here is not sailing for the Middle Sea. There is space for you on another vessel, however. The merchant knarr, *Guillemot,* came in on the same tide. She trades in the Middle Sea and Isles. Antler horn, amber and furs from here; wine and spices and cotton from there. Her shipmaster is called Hebden Seavogel; you will like him."

Fearful, yet tempted by the prospect of sailing south, Finn's heart missed a beat. His head told him to refuse point blank, but the chance to escape his cousins' whining and his annual hand-to-mouth existence walking the length and breadth of the Northlands was too good to ignore.

Master Odo studied Finn's changing expressions and nodded his head. "Good," he said. Then, pausing for effect, he added, "You'll need this." Lifting what appeared to be a harness from his knees, he passed it over to Finn. "This is for you."

Finn set his ale mug on the floor and grasped the jumble of leather straps and buckles. "What's it for, a dog sled?"

"No, you ninny, it's a shoulder harness for a back-sheath."

"A back-sheath? For a sword?" Finn's eyes narrowed with suspicion, but he rearranged the straps so they might be fitted onto a body nonetheless.

"You put your arms through those straps there and buckle the wider one across your chest," Master Odo explained.

"Ah, yes, I can see that now. But I don't need it. I don't have a sword."

"You do now." Master Odo pulled a short, bright weapon from behind his own back and laid it across his knees. "You have heard of the legendary Doomsong Sword."

It was a statement, not a question. "Doomsong?" Finn murmured, unsure how to react. "There is a dragon-slayer story about a sword named Doomsong, and – what's its second name?"

"Truthteller."

"That's it. According to the legend it was used to slay the evil shapeshifter, Grafnir, or Fafnir, there's various names for him. It was thrown into a poisonous lake." Staring at the bright, dwarf-forged blade, Finn said, "But this can't be Sigurd's sword. That saga is ancient. I don't believe half of it anyway."

"You do well to disbelieve the popular version," Master Odo replied, leaning back in his seat and folding his arms.

Finn stared at the weapon. "So, this *isn't* Sigurd the Dragonslayer's weapon?"

"Yes and no. Grafnir the Dragon was slain with this sword. But very few know by whom."

"But there was a dragon, and it was slain with *this* sword?"

"Oh, yes."

Finn gazed at the weapon with awe. "It's rather short."

"The dragon-poisoned pool did a lot of damage."

His hands somewhat unsteady, Finn reached out, "May I hold it?"

"Be my guest."

Receiving the sword by its hilt, Finn weighted the weapon in his two hands, then tilted it to the firelight to examine the blade. "There are runes on it. What do they say?" he asked.

"Oh, something apt for your quest."

"*My* quest?" Finn laughed. "What quest?"

"Well, I'm not letting you have the sword without a bargain."

Finn blinked. "It's for me?"

"Temporarily."

"You seriously think I am going to voyage all the way to the Middle Sea with a sword from a saga?"

"I do. That is your quest. To find Goran Ice-Heart and —"

"*Ice-Heart!*"

"Oh, do stop bleating, Finn. Ice-Heart, yes. He's a famous pirate. Infamous, I should say. Either way, he is the True Owner of the Doomsong Sword. Find him and tell him we have need of him. Great and urgent need of him."

Despite his reluctance to credit what Master Odo was saying, Finn's right hand closed around the hilt with a tingle of anticipation. Despite everything his sensible mind was telling him – *no, he did not want to sail on the cargo knarr named* Guillemot *to find a pirate* – the sensation of the sword in his hand was saying something else entirely.

Master Odo, whose one good eye missed nothing, nodded with satisfaction. "Keep it safe. And keep it hidden. The sword is for Goran Ice-Heart, but you may find you have to defend yourself with it along the way. You may also find others who covet it. For this reason, *never* mention its name; keep it with you at all times, but out of sight. There is a glamour upon it to disguise its appearance when it is out of your hands, but you will be a long way from my influence, and it may fade. Do you understand?"

"I think so."

"Hand it to Goran in person, and *only* Goran. He is the rightful owner of Doomsong because he is the rightful leader of your clan. Which is why he should be here, not shirking responsibility, playing at pirates where he is no use to any of you."

Finn ran the fingers of his left hand down the runes, trying to form in his head the words they made.

Master Odo leaned towards him and tapped the melded steel. "This side says, 'Hear my song True Owner and return'."

"True Owner." Finn grabbed his mug of ale with his free hand; his mouth had gone dry. "Does this mean Goran is related in some way to the person who slew the dragon?"

"Direct descendent."

Finn took a swig of ale. "And both the sword and I will return – with Goran Ice-Heart?"

"That is the plan. Give him Doomsong and tell him to bring it to me at the Barnstock Oak. At his earliest convenience."

Finn laughed out loud. "You want me to give a pirate named Ice-Heart, who I have never met, a legendary sword from an ancient saga, and tell him to bring it back, from wherever he is, to the Barnstock Oak – at his earliest convenience?"

"That is what I said."

"Does he know the Barnstock Oak gathering place?"

"Of course he does, he's a Volsung."

"Oh, 'of course.'"

"Don't be sarcastic, boy. That's my prerogative."

"Boy? I'm not a child to be ordered about."

"You're acting like one. How old are you?"

"Old enough not to answer that question. If you know so much about me, you know the answer." Which, Finn thought, made the interview that much stranger. He was still a boy in some ways. Tall for his years, and wiser than many of his age thanks to his travels, he was old enough to choose a wife, but not ready yet for such a venture. He averted his eyes and finished his ale. As he did so, Master Odo turned to the cat on the fireside chair. She stretched her forepaws, flexed her claws, and in one fluid movement dropped to the tavern floor and strolled towards the main door.

The old woman clicking the bone needles watched her. The skinny youth with red stockings watched her.

Taking no notice of the cat, Finn said, "Why, if he's got such a bad reputation, and he abandoned his clan to go south, do you want Goran Ice-Heart to return?"

"Because it is his obligation. Because he can make unpopular decisions and act on them. Because he knows the ways of the sea and commands respect or inspires fear. Either way, people will follow him out of their great danger."

"What great danger?"

"This danger, which your clan and all their neighbours from these islands to the high snows of the mainland mountains are facing: starvation. The North has always been snow-cold, the winters dark and long, but there will be no summer again in your lifetime. Have you not noticed how the weather is changing?"

"Winter lasts much longer, I've noticed that."

"There is worse to come," Master Odo said flatly. "A mountain will explode."

Finn snorted. "And bunnies will fly!"

"Bunnies will *fry*. As will everyone here, unless they are stifled and buried alive first. Which is why you will go south. Find Goran and bring him back. He has the character *and* the hereditary authority to get people away to safety and to a better land."

"What if he doesn't want to return? And he obviously doesn't, because if he cared about his clan he'd be here now."

"That is your quest and task. Find him and make him return."

Finn shook his head. This was nonsense. He was a storyteller, not a voyager or a warrior. His fingers, however, caressed the pommel of the sword. "I am going into danger anyway, though, aren't I?"

"You are, yes." Master Odo's tone softened. "There will be danger, and you will face challenges, that I cannot deny. But you should live to tell the tale."

"I *should live to tell the tale*! What's that supposed to mean? That I *ought to* live, because I deserve to, but there's some doubt about it?"

Master Odo grimaced and tilted his hat a little further over his blind eye. "I am as much at risk as you, and every person in this tavern, Finn. I am also anxious about your safety and *very* keen for you to return. For obvious reasons."

Given that there was nothing obvious in what the old man had said thus far, Finn made no reply.

"I shall hear about your voyage and progress, though," Master Odo continued. "Skiila – my eagle – flies to distant lands each year, and returns. I shall hear news of your travels and travails. And your tests."

"Tests?"

"Challenges, obstacles, minor or greater hindrances, call them what you will, you are bound to encounter them, and I need to know you are up to the task. Apart from being sound in mind and body to continue."

Finn's heart sank. "Tested," he repeated, his voice barely a whisper.

"I shall hear of your success or failure fast enough."

"Fast enough for what?"

"Fast enough to find a replacement. If need be. Unless you want to leave your people to their fate?" Master Odo cocked his head to one side, waiting for Finn to respond. The silence between them drowned out the noise of the tavern. "This is where you are expected to say, 'I shall not fail', boy."

Finn swallowed hard and tried to repeat the words, then said, "Why is a Volsung from the North called Ice-Heart in the South?"

"Because he is a merciless pirate. Did I not mention this earlier?"

"And people here need him *because* he's a 'merciless pirate'?"

"Precisely. For every force of good in this world – and beyond – the forces of evil outnumbers them. There are some, one in particular I could name, who revel in chaos. Watch out for fire-lovers and Loki's sparky followers. They may try to stop you. That's another reason why Goran Ice-Heart is the man we need. He'll have the experience to employ unpleasant tactics to a positive end."

"Meaning he has earned his name."

"Yes. Callous, cruel at times, heartless, but ultimately, for good or evil, he is your Clan Leader. Have your cousins never mentioned him?" Finn shook his head. "Ah, I see. Hmm. Let us hope Goran will correct your ignorance."

"What if we are not welcome in these warmer lands?" Finn murmured, his mind elsewhere.

"That is exactly why you need a leader like him: he is a pirate now, but he was a warrior before."

"But... Master Odo, forgive my rudeness, but why don't *you* take on the task?"

"I have no skills for the open sea, and even if I had, I am not recognised by..." The Wanderer spread his long-fingered hands. "Not everyone sees me as you do – at this moment."

Finn blinked with surprise. Was he imagining this conversation, after all? Taking a deep breath, he said, "So you're saying that our people, here, should cross the sea to other lands?"

Master Odo's hands shot up in annoyance. "Yes, lazy-brained boy, they should! Dwarves are moving out as fast as they can carry their treasure. Fire will reach the sky and the mountain will melt. It has happened before. Long ago in your years, but the Aesir know the signs. The ground here is already too solid and frozen to plant seeds."

Finn thought about his cousins Tait and Augal, how they did nothing but complain about failing crops and thin sheep; how they moaned about their continual hard labour that produced scarcely enough for one meal a day. "Why don't people just go south on their own?" he said.

"Ah, well, now you are referring to common sense: the human mind, planning, organising, working together to improve your lot; but mortals aren't very good at co-operating for the greater good, I'm afraid. Which is why you need a strong leader. Look, Finn, all that you need do is to find Goran and convince him to return. That, I grant you, may be a little tricky. Living with your conscience, if you do nothing, will also be tricky. Trickier still will be having no home to return to. Think on it, but quickly, there's a serious time issue here."

Finn nodded, "I will." What else could he say?

"Well, then," Master Odo said, rubbing his hands together with what Finn felt was uncalled for satisfaction, "*Guillemot* sails on the morning tide."

Finn turned to see if any of the mariners present had overheard the strange conversation. When he turned back, Master Odo had gone. In his place sat a fat leather coin pouch.

Despite all his misgivings, Finn's stomach looped the loop with excitement. Something wonderful – and perilous, but never mind about that – was going to happen. He lifted the fabled sword from his knee and stared at the runes running down the blade. He was being entrusted to take it to its True Owner. A pirate in the Middle Sea. This was better than any tale he'd ever concocted – as long as he didn't have to use the sword in self defence.

He'd spent his life avoiding conflict. He had never even held a sword before. Doubt extinguished his joy. He was going to be tested, challenged, confronted by who-knew-what on a voyage he could barely imagine. "I won't fail," Finn whispered to himself. "Assuming I live to tell the tale." Then he pushed the sword into its sheath as if he'd been doing it all his adult life, swung his cloak around his shoulders, dropped a coin from the heavy pouch on the bar, and made his way towards the door.

The old woman on the bench had gone. As Finn lifted the latch, the gangly youth with the yellow jerkin and red stockings flicked a thumb against a forefinger and produced a blue flame. The small blaze illuminated his sharp features. Finn gaped at him in surprise, and the boy with the burning fingernail winked.

Chapter 2

Finn paused a few paces from his cousins' longhouse. The low roof that nearly reached the ground, the timber and wattled walls, the shrunken main door that welcomed a howling wind top and bottom: the whole structure needed repairing. Built in better times, when three families had come to the island to grow crops and graze their beasts on lush meadows, the house, like its occupants, was in decline. It was not a happy place, and Master Odo had been right to question his welcome here, Finn thought. Despite being family, he did not belong. Would never belong. Not here.

Lightning cracked. Finn counted: one, two, three, four... thunder rumbled. The storm Master Odo had predicted was overhead. Freezing rain began to fall in heavy spatters, forcing him to hurry for shelter. Placing a hand on the door latch, he waited a moment longer. Then, with a damp cloak, a heavy heart and muddled thoughts, Finn entered the gloomy interior.

His cousins were dozing beside the stone-rimmed fireplace. Their wives looked up from their sewing. Nobody spoke. Finn removed his cloak in silence and dropped it on a bench by the doorway to dry. Out of the corner of his eye he saw the brothers sit up. They had noticed the sword strapped to his back. One sister-in-law nudged the arm of the other and pointed in his direction. Smiling to himself, Finn unbuckled the harness across his chest then laid it with the sword beside his cloak, waiting for someone to speak. No one did.

He sat on the bench to remove his muddy boots and rested a hand on Doomsong, knowing he should not leave it unattended, even in the family longhouse. "Why do you never speak of Goran the Volsung here?" he asked Tait and Augal brightly.

"Goran *of* the Volsung," Tait replied with a dismissive sneer, "was a legend before his twenty-first summer, then abandoned his clan to go who-knows-who-cares where."

"Ruined his reputation," Augal added, "and went a'viking to avoid the consequences." He raised a bushy eyebrow meaningfully at Tait.

"That's the truth of it," Tait responded. "What you asking about him for?"

"I heard someone talking about him, that's all." Finn hunched his shoulders. "They say he is our Clan Leader." Finn wasn't going to give his cousins any opportunity to make snide remarks about meeting the legendary Wanderer in The Old Salvation. Not that they'd believe him anyway.

The two men exchanged glances again, then Tait lumbered to his feet and headed for the sleeping area, saying as he went, "Goran left the North years ago. He's nothing to us."

Pointedly ignoring the sword, Augal followed his older brother. They had grown more alike over the years: thick set, heavy-bellied, their dark brown hair long and lank. Pausing at the cow-hide door to the sleeping quarters, Augal looked back at their much younger cousin and then pointed at the bench. "Where did you get that old sword?"

"I told a story for it."

"Must have been a rotten story."

Finn covered the hilt of the sword with his cloak, waiting for Augal's slow brain to form another insult, but Tait got in first. "If you're back at that story-telling lark and you're not sharing our workload, there's no point in you staying here."

"No," Finn said, "I can see that." His tone was light, as if he really didn't care, but his stomach gave a churning dip all the same. This ultimatum would force him to accept – and fulfil – the task set by Master Odo.

The leather screen to the sleeping area flapped down with a snap of finality behind the two men, and the women returned to their stitching. There was silence, save for the crackle of the red-hot embers. Finn tucked the sword and harness under his arm and moved to a vacated fireside seat. He needed to think, to decide what he should do next.

Within moments, there was a scuffling along the rough floorboards. Small children began to gather around him. Larger children emerged one by one from corners of the smoky room.

"Why have you got a sword, Uncle Finn?" a small boy asked.

"I have to take it to someone," Finn replied. Adding silently, *Maybe*.

"Who?" the boy demanded.

"Someone famous. Infamous."

"What's an *infa-mouse*?"

"Someone with a bad reputation."

"Does he have a story?" asked a small girl.

"Tell us the story, Uncle Finn," a smaller boy begged.

"It hasn't happened yet." Finn smiled.

"Tell us about Jormungand the sea-serpent and Thor."

"Again? Can't I tell you something else?"

"Anything," the small girl piped.

"Scary," an older boy added.

Finn shook his head. How often had he devoured tales such as these when he was their age? Repeating them as he grew up, adding to the legends and sagas, inventing exciting scenes, hoping someone would notice the skinny, white-haired orphan. Tait and Augal had teased him mercilessly. He was much younger than they – younger, smaller and different in every way. They had no respect for wordsmiths or skalds, for anyone who couldn't dig a ditch or grow turnips. Yet, here were their children, begging for his stories.

Finn settled back on his seat, gathered his thoughts, then began. "On nights such as this, when storms crash through the stars and the rain beats on rooftops…" He cast a glance at his audience, gathered cross-legged around him. "On nights such as this, Odin gallops across the sky in the wildest hunt for the wildest beasts; monsters and creatures that never show themselves in daylight but lurk in the dark, waiting for… what?" Finn asked in a whisper. "What are they waiting for?"

"Naughty children," the small girl said with a solemn gulp.

The younger ones grasped each other's hands as if afraid, but not really afraid, for they had heard all this before. Even so…

"In his right hand," Finn continued, "Odin carries his spear, Gungnir. Once he takes aim, Gungnir never falters, never fails."

"Does he kill the children?" lisped a voice.

"No, not children."

"He kills men," declared an older boy. "I've heard it told. He takes warriors for his Ghost Army in Valhalla."

"Odin takes only the bravest and best," Finn said.

"How does he take them?" asked the same boy.

"It is said that he appears in battles and chooses the bravest warriors. You have heard tell of Sigmund and his sword, yes?"

"Yes," came a lisping chorus. "Doomsong."

"And Truthteller," Finn murmured.

The sword belonging to Sigmund that was broken in two and remade for Sigmund's posthumous son, Sigurd. The sword was used to kill Grafnir, the evil dragon, but not by Sigurd. Could it be? Finn ran a hand over the short blade on his lap; he had related this saga to weary crofters on the mainland and weary mariners on the islands for years. Was it a trick? Was Master Odo playing games with him? Or worse, had he started believing his own stories? Was there *any* truth in it? Finn's mind raced back over the weird conversation in the tavern, but a high-pitched, demanding voice interrupted his thoughts.

"Finish the story, Uncle Finn."

"Yes, sorry, where was I?"

"About the *un*dead," a boy prompted.

"Oh, yes, the slain warriors. At *Ragnarök*, the battle at the End of the World, Odin will lead his Army of the Undead and..." A roll of thunder shook the low-roofed dwelling. "Listen. Listen to the storm, my dears, tonight Odin rides out. Listen. Hear him. He is our master, for he has the most powerful weapon of all, and..."

"That weapon is called *maa-gic*." Two of the older boys sitting near him chorused, dodging the blow they knew would follow their insolence.

"You laugh at your peril, do you hear? At your peril!" Finn was genuinely annoyed.

"But..."

"But what, you snivellers?" Finn reached out and hooked the nearest boy by the ear.

"Ow!" cried the lad, trying to twist out of the vice-like grip. Despite his lean and mild appearance, Finn was surprisingly strong.

"I'll give you 'ow'. Out! Out of this room, out into the night, disbeliever." The boy was released and sent spinning across the floorboards.

"But...

"'But, but,' what are you, a goat? Go on. You don't want to hear our tales, so go and do something useful. Chop some wood for your mother. She's done enough work for you today. And you," Finn pointed at the other adolescent, "go with him."

The youth stared in horror. "Outside? But there's a storm."

"And not a star in the sky to light your path. And who knows what might be lurking out there, waiting behind the wood pile, waiting to catch a juicy boy for supper? Who knows?" Finn reached out his arms to the younger children in a gathering gesture as if to protect them, whispering, "Who knows what might be out there? It might be a slithering Grendel come for its supper."

At this, Tait's wife threw down her sewing. "That is enough, Finn. We shall have a night of screaming children the way you go on." Lifting the youngest child into her arms, she poked a foot at the others, "Come on; bedtime. Shift your shanks."

Augal's wife blew out their stubby candles and joined her. Lifting a toddler, she spoke to the older boys hovering by the doorway, "Finn is right, you avoid your chores. Get the logs in to dry, then get to bed."

The mothers and youngsters disappeared behind the smoke-blackened hide curtain and Finn was left in peace to gaze into the warm ashes of a dying fire and reconstruct his interview with Master Odo.

Sometime later, the two older boys returned with armfuls of damp logs. "Were you scared then, out in the storm?" Finn spoke but did not turn to look at them.

"No," they said, too fast for truth.

Dumping their logs, they sat cross-legged at Finn's feet. For a few moments there was nothing but the sound of cinders and distant thunder. Eventually, the older boy whispered, "Is it really true about Odin?"

"What is true is what you see with your own eyes. Or what you must believe because someone you trust saw it with *their* own eyes," Finn replied, thinking of Master Odo's words: *the Aesir know the signs.* Could he trust Master Odo's words?

"But these stories you tell, are they true?" the younger boy persisted.

"Someone began them for a reason, so there must be truth in them somewhere."

"Have you ever actually seen Odin?" the younger boy challenged.

"Yes. No. I'm not sure," Finn replied. For this was the truth.

"You only tell these stories to scare us," the older boy sneered.

Finn nodded, "In part, yes. Most tales have a warning in them. It is not safe for young children to be out at night alone, for example. I learned this for myself."

"Papa says you ran away from all your chores when you were small."

"More or less." Finn admitted with a grin, then blinked as a spark lit the darkness. 'Sparky friends and followers': whatever could *they* be?

"But you haven't seen these things with your own eyes, have you?" a boy's voice insisted. "Not really? There's no real truth in them."

"There may be. There could be..." Finn was about to tell them what had happened in the tavern, but his hand closed over the sword on his lap, and he stopped.

"Tell us about the sword," the boys demanded together.

Suddenly Finn was weary. The truth of how and why he now had the sword, *if* this was the genuine Doomsong, was too strange to tell. "Tomorrow, perhaps," he said. "Go to bed now."

Finn waited until he was sure he was alone, then pulled the sword out of its sheath and held it over the remaining firelight. Despite the poisoned water into which it had been thrown, the pommel was still a golden rising sun, the cross-guard a silver half-moon, the grip still held the pink and reds of burnished copper, the blade was Dwarf-forged steel. He tilted it sideways to read the magic runes. "Shall I find him, and return?" he whispered to himself. "Is that my destiny?"

"Only Frigg knows that. And Frigg does not tell. No person can predict their destiny," said a soft voice.

"I suppose not," Finn sighed.

There was a movement behind him. He turned to see a girl with wild gingery hair pulling a sleeping fur in front of the hearth.

"You should be with your sisters," he said.

"Kat has no sisters," the girl replied.

"Well, off to bed anyway."

"Kat sleeps by the fire."

"On the floor?" Finn studied the girl. She had thick reddish hair and a round face. "I've seen you before somewhere, but not here. Who are you?" he asked.

"Katranina. You may call her Kat."

Call her...? "And whose daughter is Katranina?"

"The Kat's mother's, of course."

Chapter 3

Taking only Doomsong, the fat coin purse and a spare shirt and trews, Finn left before dawn, wearing an old seal-skin cloak to keep him dry. The dragonship, he noticed with a mixed sense of relief, had already sailed. Moored nearby was a much larger trading knarr. Standing on the quayside beside it was a short, stocky man with a completely bald head. He was counting barrels being loaded into the hold.

Finn gazed about him; Master Odo was nowhere to be seen. Nevertheless, with a distinct sensation of being pushed, Finn made his way through the crowded wharf and spoke to the square-set man. "Shipmaster, good day. Is this *Guillemot* bound for the Middle Sea?"

The shipmaster turned. His face was weather-beaten leather, and he had seen battle or met pirates, for his left cheek was scarred from ear to lip.

"Hebden Seavogel, master of the *Guillemot* I am, young sir; and you will be Finn. Your passage has been paid, past the Pillars of Hercules to the Balearic Isles. If that is agreeable to you, and you are willing to lend a hand on the rowing benches when required?"

Finn took a deep breath. His experience of the sea had been crossing from one island to another or to the mainland; he had never been required to row. He took a surreptitious glance at the soft hand holding the oiled-leather travel pack balanced on his shoulder. When he looked up, Hebdon Seavogel gave a crooked smile. "You'll manage, lad," he said. "It'll put some muscle on you."

That meant he'd definitely be required to row, Finn realised. He studied the vessel that would take him far from all he knew. It was a sturdy trader, much larger and far wider than any he had seen before. A round-headed, long-beaked guillemot was carved onto the prow, and there was a tiny hut-like structure set beside the mast. Various mariners were running up and down steps to the raised bow and stern decks, others were manhandling barrels into the hold. *Guillemot* was big and probably hard work in heavy seas.

"A fine vessel, no?" demanded the shipmaster, following Finn's gaze and grinning with satisfaction at what he saw.

"It is, master, it is," Finn replied, and with an inward sigh of resignation, he shook the captain's meaty hand and agreed to take an oar as required.

As Finn's feet touched the deck, he heard a woman laugh. Less a laugh more a cackle, it sent a chill down his spine. A thin woman dressed in layers of night-coloured clothing appeared in the open doorway of the hut-like cabin. She reached out a long-taloned hand and beckoned to him. Finn made his way toward her with Hebden Seavogel behind him.

"This is our ship-mother, Norna Silveryarn," Seavogel said as an introduction.

Trying to hide a shudder of repugnance, for close up she resembled an old crone from a children's tale, Finn greeted her with a polite 'good day' and a bow of the head.

Norna Silveryarn squinted at him from under hooded eyelids. She had a face like a wizened apple with an owl's beak nose. Something shapeless consisting of tangled threads hung from two bone needles grasped in her left hand. A vast dish cloth, the start of a fishing net? Then Finn noticed her fingernails; she had a rune symbol scored into each yellowed talon.

He looked up and caught her staring back at him with a gaze that would pierce a warrior's shield. *She can read my soul*, he thought.

"I can, boy. And never forget it," she whispered.

"What do you see?" Finn asked her.

Norna Silveryarn gave another screech of something like laughter and thrust out her hand again. This time with the palm flat. "Pay your way, boy, and I might tell you."

"His passage is already paid," Shipmaster Seavogel said.

"And you, you fool, have *already* told him that," the woman grunted. "How am I supposed to fill my coffers, eh? Eh?" Turning back to Finn, she pointed at his waist. "What's that tied to your belt, boy?"

Finn blinked. His cloak covered his entire upper body, hiding the purse Master Odo had left him. "My..." He turned away, annoyed and embarrassed, and was surprised to find the girl Katranina at his side.

"Ahh, here you are," sighed the old woman, pulling Katranina towards her, "Good girl. This one is mine, Seavogel; no payment required."

Katranina smiled an over-sweet smile at Seavogel. "Kat may voyage with you, Shipmaster?"

"She already is," Seavogel huffed, indicating the quayside. "See how the land moves away from us."

Finn swung around, trying to see how far they were from the shore. Was it too late to change his mind? Could he get back? No, because he couldn't swim. Waves slapped against the ship's hull and panic engulfed him. This was a mistake. A huge mistake. He had walked onto a floating trap.

Hebden Seavogel tapped him on the shoulder; the old woman was speaking to him. "Leave your pack and purse with me, boy," she said. "And the sword under your cloak."

"You won't need a weapon on board with us," Seavogel added. "Unless we meet pirates, at any rate. Then we'll need every blade we've got."

Finn looked at him with a mixture of shock and surprise. "Pirates? Before the Middle Sea?"

"It happens. Unstrap your sword, there's a good lad. It will be safe here with Norna Silveryarn."

Safe? With this old crone? Finn wanted to refuse, but he dropped his travel pack inside the hut and his hands started fumbling with his cloak of their own accord. Reluctantly, he unstrapped his sword harness and was delighted to see the hilt of Doomsong had lost its lustre. The rainbow-melded, rune-enchanted blade had become a blunt old weapon in a cracked leather sheath. Even so, Finn couldn't bring himself to place it in the woman's hands. "I'll put it in my travel pack," he said.

Norna Silveryarn pushed her needlework into Katranina's hand and silently prised the sword and harness from his fingers.

Finn slapped a hand over the heavy pouch at his waist. In the space of three heart beats, they had organised him under their control, but they weren't getting his coin as well. He turned again to see how far the ship was from land, thinking to risk jumping overboard, but it was too late. Why had he never learned to swim?

Katranina touched his arm. "Finn will be all right."

"How can you know that? What are you doing here, anyway?" he demanded, but received no reply beyond a tilt of chin.

"Come, my pretty cat," Norna Silveryarn said, beckoning Katranina, "come and find your place with me."

Katranina gave Finn a smug grin and sidled through the narrow cabin door.

Before the midday sun was high, Shipmaster Seavogel was at the mast, checking the huge square sail as it stretched taut in a north westerly wind. Finn watched the ten crewmen going about their tasks, trying to assess how often he might be called upon to row. As if divining his thoughts, Seavogel called out, "That'll be your bench with Thorsman." He pointed at an oarsman with arms like tree trunks.

Thorsman was resting now, but Finn could easily imagine the length of his reach and pull, how the man's muscles would ripple as the heavy oar cut through the water, and tried to hide his sense of inadequacy, causing the shipmaster to laugh out loud. "Don't fret, lad, I'm only pulling your leg, Thorsman can manage on his own, unless we meet raiders. He's got the strength of two and more, but we don't carry useless passengers, except her up there. And she'll have her uses, I don't doubt."

Finn looked towards the prow and located 'her'. Wearing a boy's buckskin tunic and trews, Kat was leaning over the bow rail watching the water break against the hull. She turned, pushing a mass of gingery hair from her face and – exactly as if she knew he was watching her – stared back into Finn's grey-eyed gaze.

"What are her uses?" Finn asked.

Hebden Seavogel shrugged. "Norna Silveryarn knows."

Finn closed his eyes and sighed. How could they possibly benefit from a tiresome girl who spoke about herself as if she were someone else? Unless she'd been sent by Master Odo to report on him.

But how would she relay her information? It would take weeks to reach the Middle Sea, and when he got there (*if* he got there), he had a very specific matter to attend to, which did not require a weird girl tagging along.

"Look," Kat called out, pointing upwards.

Finn squinted into the weak sunlight. "Sea birds," he shouted back. "Guillemots, gulls."

"Long necks for gulls."

"Geese, then. They fly north to south and back again over these islands."

"Wide wings for geese."

Finn rolled his eyes and started to move away, but a flapping sound drew his attention skyward. "Dragons," he gasped.

"Well done, Finn," Kat replied as if he were a four-year-old.

Finn ignored her. Two young dragons had begun to circle *Guillemot*. "They've come for me," he whispered to himself. "Obstacles, challenges, hindrances…" One of them sent a spurt of blue flame into the air. Finn's heart began to race. "They've come because of the sword," he murmured. "Revenge for the death of Grafnir."

No, that was a foolish thought. The tale of Grafnir, the shapeshifting, gold-hoarding dragon, was from ancient times. No, these dragons, if they were dragons – he squinted into the sunlight – they couldn't have anything to do with him.

Unless – obstacles and hindrances – they'd been sent to prevent him leaving the islands? And if they had, who had sent them, and why?

There was another burst of blue flame. "Fire lovers and Loki's followers," Finn whispered, repeating Master Odo's warning.

"Pull!" Seavogel yelled, as he scuttled as fast as his bandy sea-legs would go, into Norna Silveryarn's hut.

"That won't save him," Kat said, skipping down the prow companionway to the lower middle deck. "Another puff from them and the sail will go up in smoke, and us with it. Finn must do something!"

"Me! What can I do?"

"Get over the side and into the water, hide under the hull, idiot. Out of sight."

"I can't swim!" Finn yelled, rushing for the gunwale anyway. Tripping in his panic, he tumbled onto a rowing bench and scrambled underneath it beside a sweating oarsman praying to his gods.

Tucked behind the oarsman's legs, Finn didn't see Norna Silveryarn emerge from her cabin. He heard her, though. Everyone for a hundred leagues could have heard her. The two dragons came lower, circling like vultures for carrion, and the old woman began screaming words Finn did not recognise but which sounded like appalling abuse. One of the green-scaled beasts approached the mast, its claw-tipped wings almost close enough to rip the sail to shreds. Norna Silveryarn shook her wrinkled fists and hurled vicious curses until it backed off.

Finn peeped out of his hiding place just as a double blast of blue flames filled the air. For a moment there was absolute silence, and then the rhythmic beat of the flying serpents' wings as they slowly flapped northwards towards their ice-capped homeland. Finn watched them go in grateful disbelief. They had come and gone, and the laden cargo knarr and its passengers and crew were safe. Why? Why had they come? Why had they gone?

Because, he thought, they were only trying to locate him, or the ship, to convey the information to someone. Master Odo had warned him about Loki's followers.

Unless they were two of Master Odo's 'friends in high places', like the eagle, Skiila?

Were the blue flames a signal or a warning? He'd seen something similar recently. Where? Who else knew of his task, and why would they want to hinder or prevent it? Loki, because he was a semi-mortal fire-god who loved evil mischief? His followers, because they would love to see a mountain explode? If that was possible? If that's what was really going to happen?

"Nooo," he sighed, as what he considered to be common sense calmed his panicked mind: Master Odo was only making sure he was aboard *Guillemot*.

As his breathing returned to normal, Finn's thoughts turned to his clan's favoured seeress, the goddess Frigg, who knew their future. Frigg, who could ask the All-father Odin to grant requests and boons no mortal dared ask; Frigg, who watched over the safety and well-being of every Volsung – he hoped. "Earth Mother Frigg," he whispered into the wind, "have you found me on this water? Shall I live to tell the tale?"

One knock for yes, two knocks for no. It was a stupid thing, even to think. Nevertheless, he waited for a signal, a sign she had heard. The sail gave a single sharp flap and stretched in a strengthening breeze. Taking that as a 'yes', Finn got to his feet with a smile of relief on his face and went to the gunwale to watch the last of his island archipelago disappear, then made his way to the communal area in the stern.

Kat was there, sipping from a bowl of milk. In the sunlight now, Finn noticed her hair was a thick, wavy, honey-coloured ginger. And she was older than he had assumed in his cousins' longhouse. She glanced up, smiled her particular smug smile.

Settling down beside her, Finn accepted a hunk of rye bread and a lump of hard cheese from the cook. They ate and drank in companionable silence, giving Finn time to study her more closely. She was definitely older than she had seemed the night before, with broad cheek bones and a small, pink mouth, an almost button-like chin, and green-gold eyes that darkened when she looked at him.

"Who are you, Katranina?" he asked.

"Finn will see."

"Did Master Odo put you on the ship?"

The girl's lips twitched.

"Why?"

"Perhaps Kat is the ship's cat," she replied and sipped her milk.

Chapter 4

Two days out from the islands, Seavogel's trading knarr ran into a strong westerly wind. The sea churned, lifting and twisting each clinker-lapped oaken plank as if intent upon separating them. Shipmaster Seavogel shouted orders about the sail, the ropes and pulleys, while the crew secured their shipped oars. Not knowing what to do except keep out of their way, Finn crouched under Thorsman's bench. If they went under, he reasoned, Thorsman was the most likely to stay afloat. Wind screamed through the rigging. Waves surged over the side and thrashed across the deck. Loose cargo swam in a soup of spilled ale and whale oil.

"Carrying passengers always brings trouble," Thorsman grumbled. "We should stick to the old ways."

"What old ways?" Finn gasped.

"Sacrifice. In the old days we made a sacrifice to Rann of the Coral Caves, and Aegir, father of the Nine Wave-women,, before a voyage." Thorsman said, clinging to his useless oar.

"What sort of sacrifice?" Finn asked, hoping his first thought was wrong.

"Last on, first off, used to be. Depends. Times are changing."

Whatever Thorsman was going to say next was lost as a huge wave shifted Finn backwards. He righted himself and caught hold of the end of Thorsman's oar while the barrel-chested oarsman continued as if uninterrupted. "Seavogel used to take better care of his crew; hated losing anybody. Once, in a bad gale coming back from Hibernia, he let us sacrifice an old-timer who'd lost his teeth. He was in a bad way all round. Couldn't pull his weight."

Grasping the slippery oar, Finn edged closer to Thorsman's body. Who or what might they sacrifice if the weather got worse? Who was expendable on this voyage? Katranina, or the ship's cats — two mangy, blue-grey creatures that lived in the hold? Or the passenger who couldn't manage an oar on his own? *Yet*, he told himself. Yet.

The wind squealed at them and howled at them and snapped at them for what seemed like an entire day; then it got worse. Much worse. Every mariner aboard viewed their worst nightmare. "It's Jormungand," they cried in horror.

Jormungand: a tale Finn had told many times of a vast sea-serpent that grew and grew until it could crush Midgard in its coils. Another tale told of Thor, the slow-witted but mighty-in-strength Aesir champion, who threw a bull's head into the sea as bait and slew Jormungand when it rose from the deep to snap it up.

Except he didn't. The ending was obviously not true: neither Jormungand nor the Midgard Serpent were dead. It looked and felt exactly as if a vast creature was coiling and uncoiling beneath them, creating a whirlpool that would swallow the *Guillemot* and every soul aboard.

A woman Finn had not seen on board before suddenly appeared at the bird-carved prow. Silver hair fanned out behind her like a silken banner. Raising her hands, she shouted into the sea, then turned and cried out, "Show your silver, mortals!"

"What is she saying?" demanded Finn.

"Show her a silver coin! To pay your way to safety!" Thorsman yelled, tugging a small pouch from around his neck and extracting a coin no larger than his fingernail. "See! We must pay her to release us from the Great Sea Serpent or be trapped forever by Aegir and Rann. Or worse."

Finn couldn't imagine anything worse, but he understood the meaning: pay the silver witch to save the ship. Slipping back under the bench he crouched in the swirling water, scrabbling to open the sodden purse tied at his waist without losing its contents. Wondering, as he did so, if its weight would hasten his sinking.

Guillemot listed heavily once more, sending Finn and a crate of hysterical hens crashing together against the mast. The crate cracked apart like a breaking eggshell. Sea water rushed over them and washed the birds overboard. It was a small sacrifice to a vast monster and had no effect. Thorsman tried to come to Finn's aid, but he, too, was sent sprawling.

Jormungand's glistening green coils rolled over *Guillemot*. White water surged around them. Thorsman slid into Finn. Wood began to splinter.

Sensing the sturdy knarr was about to break in two, Finn fumbled again at his purse. Finally extracting a coin from the sodden leather, he stuffed the purse inside his trews then popped his coin into his left cheek, saying in his mind, *Frigg, goddess of Destiny, let this not be my Fate*, then coughed out the coin so he wouldn't choke to death before drowning.

Tucking the silver into his left fist, he groped his way towards the mast, hoping that that, at least, would remain afloat. Just as he reached it and flung his arms around it, just as he was certain *Guillemot* was going down, he saw Jormungand rear up, spitting venom. Then, with its vast head and upper lengths in mid-air, it paused, stared straight into his eyes and reared away from the vessel.

Finn shut his eyes in terror. When he opened them again Thorsman was standing upright with his arms in the air; the silver woman was balanced on the prow beside the carved bird's head, and the waves had ceased churning.

Guillemot settled onto an even keel in calmer water, and the crew all stared about them. Someone started to laugh. A silly, nervous laugh. Others joined in, slapping each other on the back. This was a tale for the tavern that would last to their dying days. Everyone was in a high good humour. Except, for some reason, the silver woman at the prow.

"Hand me your silver, weaklings!" she screamed, gliding down the steps to the main deck and holding her soft skirts out to catch their coins.

Without a word, each man dropped a coin into the hollow.

Finn retrieved his silver dirham and dropped it into her skirt as she passed, trying to identify the face hidden in thick silver tresses. He turned to Thorsman to ask who this strange and beautiful woman was, for she had appeared out of nowhere and there was no place for her on board. As if guessing Finn's thoughts, Thorsman put a finger to lips. When Finn turned back, she had gone.

The crew began shifting loose crates and untangling ropes in an eerie, frightened silence. Seavogel set some to baling and some to retrieve and count oars. Thorsman and Finn went down into the hold to check on the cargo.

As the giant oarsman shifted Seavogel's crates and barrels back into place, Finn tried to make knots in broken ropes. "That was the strangest and bravest thing I've ever seen, tackling Jormungand," he said, as if it were a casual comment. "You are *very* brave."

"Me?" Thorsman looked up in surprise, bumping his large head on a low beam.

"You had your arms in the air."

"Did I? Ah, well, that wasn't Jormungand," Thorsman replied flatly. "That's only a tale to keep kiddies out of deep water."

"But I saw something come out of the water. It coiled itself over us. I know it did. If it wasn't a monster sea-serpent, what was it?"

"What was what?" Thorsman asked with a grunt as he shoved a pile of sodden furs back into place.

"What happened to us, just now."

"Maelstrom. Happens in these waters. When the wind's strong."

What is true is what you see with your own eyes. How often had he said that? Finn wondered. "But *what* was it," he insisted, adding more quietly, "if it wasn't Jormungand?"

"I just told you, a *maelstrom*. Makes a whirlpool."

Finn slumped down against a crate. Had he imagined the worst because he was expecting the worst? Or was he a victim of his own tale-making – again? Or was Thorsman trying to calm his nerves? "And the beautiful woman on the prow? Who was that?" he asked.

"Norna Silveryarn."

"Nooo!" Finn laughed, shaking his head. "Can't have been, she was beautiful. Had long, flowing silver hair."

"Trick of the light," Thorsman replied.

"But we gave her a coin for what she did."

"Yeah, well, last resort when it looks like the Deep will get you. You can't risk offending Norns and *disir* nature witches. Here, give me a hand with this and stop asking daft questions."

"Yes, but I saw—"

"Look," Thorsman said, straightening up as much as he could in the low-ceilinged hold, "you've got Luck with you. That's all that matters. If you hadn't, you'd be in Aegir's Deep by now."

"Does that mean I won't be sacrificed if we get into bad weather again?"

"Nah, not you. Norna Silveryarn won't have it."

"You asked her?"

"I asked her."

"And Katranina?" Finn's voice cracked on the K.

"Her? No, never. Too precious. We could throw in Grey Tom instead. Won't be the same, but it might help."

"Grey Tom?" Finn tried to recall an old mariner called Tom.

"The mangy cat that lives down here. He's not worth saving for a cap, if that's what you're thinking? She can manage mice on her own," he jerked a thumb at a skinny she-cat perched on a bale of smelly fleeces. "Here, let me do that rope, or we'll be here all night."

When everything was ship-shape, Katranina appeared on deck. Her hair was perfectly dry, her tan buckskin tunic and trews without a sign of dampness. Sauntering up to Finn, who was lying, exhausted, on Thorsman's bench, she stood still in front of him and gave him her silent green-eyed stare.

"What?" he asked. Kat responded with a small shrug of her narrow shoulders and her special grin of smug satisfaction, then tip-toed back to Norna Silveryarn's cabin without a word.

Finn watched her go with suspicious unease. Kat never got wet. Waves tossed spray over the sides, seawater sloshed under their feet, but Kat stayed dry.

Chapter 5

As morning lit the sky, Shipmaster Hebdon Seavogel announced they would put in at a nearby harbour to repair storm damage. The port consisted of recently built wooden huts and a fishing jetty. Frames had been constructed to dry herring, but the place still smelled of freshly cut pinewood. This was a growing port with sturdy dwellings and new warehouses under construction. As *Guillemot* was rowed in, merchants gathered to watch her dock. A few stall-holders called out their wares, a pie-man with a wicker tray of pasties and a baker with a basket of delicious-smelling loaves jostled each other to reach the new arrival first.

Once the knarr was tied up, Seavogel told the crew to fill their bellies with fresh food and then to check the hull, strakes and decks for damage. Eight burly oarsmen scrambled onto the wharf, eager for a decent meal. Seavogel watched them go, like a benevolent father, then began selecting goods to trade ashore. Katranina and Norna Silveryarn stayed out of sight.

Pleased he had managed to keep his coin pouch safe, Finn tightened the cord to his damp woollen trews and climbed over the side to stuff himself with pies and pickled herring. When his stomach was full, he sauntered into the village in search of a tavern to ply his own trade. There was no tavern, and it was too early in the day to encourage people to sit around in the open for a tale that might or might not result in a few coins, so he went back to *Guillemot* to lend a hand.

Most of the crew were busy caulking weak areas with greased wool, pitch and flax, or double-checking for loose nails. "Here, Finn, give us a hand," Thorsman called.

Finn was so engrossed in poking wax into cracks he didn't notice a group of armed men arrive on the jetty, but turned in time to see the first man climb aboard. He was a tall, dark-haired young Northman wearing a boiled leather breastplate with a battle-hammer at his waist and a sword at his hip. Ten well-built warriors followed him over the side and then crowded together in the confined space between the upper stern deck and the open hold. Each man had a leather satchel of belongings, a battle hammer, and a long dagger, known as a whinger, which doubled as an eating knife. Each wore a sword tucked in a sheepskin sheath.

The crew eyed the newcomers suspiciously and exchanged meaningful glances. Nobody called out a greeting. A short time later, Hebdon Seavogel returned with a local trader, carrying a small iron-hinged chest in his arms. They climbed aboard, passing the heavy casket between them carefully. Seavogel raised a hand in greeting to the tall Northman and then disappeared into the hold with the trader and the casket. Once their deal had been concluded below, the merchant re-emerged, minus the casket, and two oarsmen were instructed to deliver a bale of furs and a box of amber to somebody with a cart on the wharf. Seavogel accompanied the merchant ashore, taking no notice of the new passengers, and went about his business again.

Returning a good while later, Seavogel sought out the tall Northman and accepted a bag of coin. Finn watched the transaction carefully, noting how Seavogel said nothing about his rule against weapons on board.

The warriors, for that was obviously their calling, sat around the deck talking together. The Northman caught Finn watching him. "I am Beorn Wolfman," he said raising a smooth hand. "You may have heard of me."

Finn gave an apologetic smile. "Sorry, no. Beorn Wolfman: it is a good name. Why are you named for a bear *and* wolves?"

"I am Beorn for my mother's clan, and Wolfman because I once owned a pack of wolves."

"You 'owned' them?" Finn queried with narrowed eyes. Nobody 'owned' wolves. He had been told that by a man who related the saga of the legendary Davor, who had travelled the Cold North for years in the company of a white wolf and could converse with animals. The wolf was loyal only to Davor, but never tamed like a dog.

Beorn Wolfman gave him a hard look, then joined his companions' banter about who would be the first to throw up, once they were at sea. Finn returned to stuffing a superficial crack in the deck. Out of the corner his eye he noticed Katranina dressed as a boy, with a hood over her long hair, watching Beorn Wolfman from the door of the tiny cabin. Her gaze shifted to Finn and their eyes met. She shook her head; a slight, slow movement meant only for him. Finn nodded, catching her meaning: let Beorn Wolfman boast, *you* know the truth of this matter.

"So," Beorn Wolfman continued, moving closer to sit by Finn, "what brings you aboard Seavogel's old tub?"

"I'm going south, to the Middle Sea."

"Are you now?" Beorn's eyes widened. "And what takes you there?"

Finn tilted his head, "Why do you want to know?"

Beorn flicked lank brown hair off his eyes and turned to look at the grey horizon. "I travel; I hear things. I may be able to help you."

Finn met Kat's gaze again then replied vaguely, "Thank you, that's good to hear. Is there something I ought to know?"

"Not especially. Warm sun, fresh fruit. Good wine. You know who's living on one of the small islands, I suppose?" Finn shook his head. "You never heard of Ice-Heart – the pirate?"

"Oh, him. Yes. Is he – er – important?" Finn asked, keeping his head down and staying focussed on filling the crack in the wooden deck.

"Important? He's a living legend!"

"And not for good reasons, I suppose, if he's called Ice-Heart?"

"You suppose right: cold-blooded, ruthless, violent, and very successful – as a pirate."

Finn swallowed hard, trying not to show any emotion, then said, "He may be gone, when we get there. If we do. Unless he goes for Seavogel's cargo."

"That's a strong possibility, I'd say." Beorn leaned over and placed a firm hand on Finn's shoulder. "Forget the voyage; it's a long way to go to get injured, *or worse*. How about making a lot of money with me instead?"

"With you? How?"

"Hired sword. Very well-rewarded, hired swords are. You do have a sword, don't you?"

Finn became very wary, remembering Master Odo's instruction to never mention Doomsong. Forcing a laugh, which sounded false even to him, he pushed back his shoulder-length white hair and retied the black leather thong at his neck, saying, "I'm a tale-maker, Beorn Wolfman, not a warrior."

"A skald, what westerners call a bard?"

"No, a skald makes poetry and tells the sagas, they are skilled at kenning. I only recount legends and tell made-up stories to entertain folks in taverns and mead halls. Sometimes I turn important news into a yarn, to pass it on. That's all. I'd be no use to you, unless you wanted a bedtime story after your slaughtering?"

"That's not such a bad idea."

"Well, if we're both still alive when I return, try me again. Just ask for Finn the Tale-Maker and someone'll know where I am."

"You're not staying in the Middle Sea, then?"

It was a simple enough query, but Finn sensed there was more to it, and much as he wanted to know about the islands and the pirate named Ice-Heart, something warned him to keep his plans to himself. The conversation was brought to halt by Seavogel taking Beorn up to the prow for a private conversation.

Guillemot sailed on the afternoon tide. There was a good wind and they made fast going, heading due south. Beorn Wolfman and his companions passed their time gambling with walrus ivory dice and throwing predicting bones, joking and teasing and laughing. Finn kept his distance. Norna Silveryarn remained in her hut. Katranina sat against its closed door whittling a sharp point to the end of a stick.

Later, during a quiet stretch, Shipmaster Seavogel joined Finn, who was hunched in his salt-stained cloak against the starboard strakes on his own. Seavogel pulled a soft pouch from inside his greasy jerkin and began stuffing dried leaves into the bowl of a long-stemmed pipe. "It's a bright, brisk day. What you looking so glum about? You feeling all right, boy?"

"Yes and no," Finn answered. "Why?"

"Just asking. You were proper shook up yesterday."

"Yes, well it was a... frightening..." Finn searched for a better word to describe the strange and terrifying event and failed.

"Happenin'. That's what it was. These things happen at sea and I call 'em 'happenings.'"

"Because they don't always have an explanation?"

"That's it. 'Cept yesterday was a whirlpool in a crosswind storm."

Finn studied the man's weather-worn face. "That's what Thorsman said. More or less. And the dragons? Was that a 'happening'?" he asked, grasping the opportunity to find out how much Seavogel knew about Master Odo and the task he'd been set. "Were you expecting them?"

"Dragons?"

"Yes, the whole crew saw them."

"Did they?" Seavogel paused, sucked on his pipe and then said quietly, "It's a funny thing about seafarers; we weather the storms and we appear to take the dangers of the deep as we find them, but in truth, most of us have got too much imagination. Comes of bein' at sea for so long; from watching the beasts of the water race alongside us, seeing whales blow their tops, and the winds and the weather, and the sky and the stars. You start to see things and believe them. But there are some things you couldn't even invent. Not even a tale-maker like you. I've seen fish with eyes on stalks like bull's horns jump straight out the water, flap their wings – proper wings – then flip themselves backwards like it was a game. I've seen, and you might not credit this but 'tis true, for I've watched it with my own eyes: small whales, doll-fins some call them, with mouths like beaks, going round and round." Pointing a fat finger upwards, he described a spiral, "sending fish into the air like it was an Iceland geyser, then catching them in their mouths. A rare skill they have, working together to catch their supper."

"What's an Iceland geyser, Shipmaster? I've heard of trolls there that turn into boulders and go green in summertime, but I don't know what a geyser is."

"Hot steam bursting up out the ground like the Earth's farted. Hot pools amid ice and snow. Strange place, it is. Mountains there even spew fire."

Finn sat up straight. "Is that true, about a mountain spewing fire?"

"So I've heard tell, I never seen it myself, but like I say, it's a strange place. Why you asking?"

Finn gave the shipmaster a sideways glance: Master Odo had paid for his passage on *Guillemot*; did Seavogel not know why? Or was he fudging? Well, two could play that game. "I like to know things, for my tale-making," he said, gazing out at the green-grey ocean to avoid eye-contact. "I like to know strange things that are true, to slip into my stories. Like the silver lady on the prow."

"Hmm." Seavogel sucked on his pipe, then said slowly, "Like I say, there's things that are real and true, and things that *look* like they might be real, but aren't, and things that can't be real at all. Oftentimes, our eyes are playing tricks."

Finn thought about this. "Yes," he said. "I can understand that. But if they weren't young dragons that I saw, what were they? There were two of them. I *saw* them."

"Cormorants, I 'spect. They got long, snaky necks and hooked tips to their beaks."

Finn wanted to ask why the crew had screamed about dragons, then doubted himself. Had they? Or was it one of their jokes? Oarsmen used special words in their ragging and private jokes. He knew that from the hours he'd spent listening to their yarns in coastal taverns, where many of them recounted tales wilder than any he could ever invent. Then another doubt hit him: he'd spent most of his life traveling through the Cold North, walking from tavern to tavern and entertaining folk at festivals and weddings, and he'd never heard a word about a pirate named Ice-Heart. So how come Beorn Wolfman knew about him?

Misunderstanding Finn's expression, Seavogel gave him a generous smile, "You'll get the hang of us soon, lad. Now, if you're all right, I've got things to do."

As he moved away, Finn reached up to catch his arm. "No, please, about the silver woman, I need you to explain something."

"And I will, but you'll pick up your sailing skills along the way."

"Not that, I mean..." Aware Seavogel was ignoring any reference to the woman, Finn jumped to his feet, but instead of asking about her again, he blurted out, "Is Beorn Wolfman bound for the South as well?"

"He said he might be. Said it depended on a job he's got down the coast. I've hired him as protection, if he returns – as far as the Middle Sea."

"Protection?"

"For my cargo. We need trained swords with us after what I've just put in the hold, and for the furs and the amber we've still got."

"It's going to be a bit cramped. We won't sink with the weight, will we?"

"Sink? Oh, no it'll be just him that stays with us. If he can. His men are contracted to fight somewhere."

Before Finn could extract any details, Seavogel was swaying across the main deck about his daily business.

Chapter 6

Finn stayed at the ship's rail enjoying the chilly breeze. Katranina, still attired as a boy but now with a warm sheepskin jacket, was sitting beside Norna Silveryarn's little shed with her arms around her knees. She looked as if she was dozing, but Finn could feel her eyes on him. Not just him, though. She was watching and listening to the warriors clustered together in the stern. Katranina's eyes and ears missed very little.

Guillemot's pilot, an ancient mariner with a face like a cracked leather cushion, steered them alongside the low-lying coastline southwards as the sky turned an ominous grey and the breeze grew into a strong easterly wind, conniving with the current to strand them before they reached their next port of call. At the first hint of sand dunes, Seavogel's crew lowered the sails, and the oarsman went to their places, waiting for Wolfman to indicate where they should pull in.

The crew worked hard to keep *Guillemot* out of the shallows. Finn moved to the landward rail and noticed a lone rider, a watchman or coastguard on a sturdy pony, following their progress from the dunes. Beorn Wolfman in his studded battle-sark joined him at the side.

"Friend or foe, do you think?" Finn asked.

"Probably only a look-out," Beorn replied. "Nobody needs fear *Guillemot;* she's a cargo knarr, not a Viking longship."

"Trading vessels attract wreckers like gulls to fish guts. Mariners in The Old Salvation tavern are always talking about wreckers."

"That's partly why I'm here. Did Seavogel mention it?" Finn nodded, "So you've nothing to fear. Hired swords, cargo protection, settlement guards... that's my line of business. You pay, we slay." Beorn laughed then, and waving to the rider on the dunes, he said, "No need to panic, Finny lad, they're expecting me here," and called to Seavogel to put in at the next landing stage.

Seavogel yelled to the pilot and oarsmen, and *Guillemot* soon approached a rickety-looking jetty. The crew shipped their oars and Beorn Wolfman jumped out before Seavogel had even tied up, waiting with his arms folded across his broad chest for the rider to arrive.

Katranina appeared at Finn's side. "Is Finn going with him?" she asked.

Finn turned, "Where?"

"Where Beorn Wolfman goes."

"It's nothing to do with me."

"Is it not?"

Finn gave her a long look. "What do you know that I do not?" Kat gave him her irritating shrug. "Go on," Finn snapped, "tell me now, if there's anything to tell. Why are *you* on board, for a start?"

"Kat is here because she is here."

"And?"

"Kat travels at sea with Norna Silveryarn and Shipmaster Seavogel."

Finn wanted to press her for more, but the man on the shaggy pony had reached Beorn, and a group of riders led by a burly man on a wide-rumped bay were trotting towards them. The look-out signaled with his free hand at *Guillemot* and shouted, "They are here!"

As the man on the bay horse joined them, Wolfman called out, "Greetings, Earl. I am Beorn Wolfman, bringing fine warriors to be of service to you."

"Greetings," replied the earl, looking not at the young man before him but at *Guillemot*. "Where is your army?"

"Warriors! I bring warriors. Ten brave, battle-hardened companions."

"Ten! Ten men are no use to me."

"I was not told you were at war. Was I misinformed?"

The old man studied him. "At Heorot we are always at war."

Heorot! Finn's eyes widened. According to rumours running throughout the North, Heorot was plagued by swamp monsters called Grendels. Some versions circulating the taverns said they had a taste for human flesh. Here was a tale to bring him hot food, mugs of ale, and good silver coins.

Curious to see what was going on, Finn climbed onto the landing stage then looked back at the knarr. Norna Silveryarn was standing on the prow deck watching them. Her shrunken body looked frail beside the black-varnished bird's head, but Finn knew the eyes in her wizened apple face were as clear as his own. "You should pray to Idunn," he murmured under his breath. "Ask her for a fresh golden apple."

"Norna Silveryarn is a *disir*. She has no need of Idunn's apples of eternal youth," Katranina said softly behind him.

Finn wasn't listening. Holding up a warning hand, he said, "Get back on board. These men, this place… it's no place for a girl."

"Finn may have need of Kat."

"I'm not going anywhere, and I don't need a servant."

"Kat is no servant."

Finn blinked. "No. Sorry."

While they spoke, Beorn Wolfman's companions disembarked, and the earl and his horsemen moved off. The warriors gathered behind Beorn to follow on foot. Before leaving, however, Beorn turned back to look directly at Finn. He waited a few beats, as if expecting Finn to react, then shrugged, raised his left hand and marched off into the dunes.

Finn was tempted to follow, very tempted. "I wish I could go, just for half a day. To see if it's true about the green-dell creatures. Just to see what it's like. For my tale-making."

Visiting Heorot, discovering whether the swamp creatures actually existed – it was so very tempting. And he'd be at Beorn Wolfman's side, with the warriors, in case anything nasty happened. They were trained fighters, battle-ready. And Wolfman had said he was returning to *Guillemot*. Finn felt a shiver of fear, excitement and anticipation run down his spine, then something caught his attention. High above, a speck in the pale sky, an eagle screamed its strident call.

"Skiila," Katranina murmured.

Finn gazed upwards. Skiila, Master Odo's she-eagle. She was keeping track of him from above.

The eagle called again, circling on a thermal. He was definitely being observed. Finn felt a surge of anger. Master

Odo didn't own him; he was free to go where he chose. "I'm going with Wolfman," he said.

"Course you are," a gruff voice replied, making Finn jump. Shipmaster Seavogel was behind him now. "We sail on the morning tide. You'll have time enough to get there and back, if you're curious – and you've got the courage."

Finn was too wrapped in his own thoughts to take note of the last comment. "I'd like to see the place," he said. "I'll come straight back."

"Make sure you do," Seavogel replied, slapping a calloused hand across Finn's narrow shoulders.

Finn's mind was finally made up by Beorn Wolfman. Standing now at the top of a dune, he called out, "Are you coming, boy?"

"I'm not a *boy*," Finn huffed, and set out to follow the Northman, to prove it.

The eagle circled once more, then flew off, back to the land of ice and snow.

Earl Rolfgar and his men set off up the sand dunes at a trot, slowing only to form a single file along a narrow track further inland, where they had to cross a wide marsh before entering a forest. Beorn's men jogged behind them with ease, despite being on foot. Finn, with Kat tagging along behind him, found it much harder to keep up. Rolfgar's mounted troop were easily visible, though, until they entered the trees. After that, Finn could neither see nor hear anyone. The forest became denser, the trail narrower, and eerily quiet.

The trail became narrow, harder on the feet and harder to follow, and – Finn realised with growing unease – blacker. Like the black flint path in a story he'd been told, about the boy named Davor, who left a stranded dragonship to seek help and followed a black, shiny road straight into a troll's kitchen. "It's only a story," Finn told himself.

"What says Finn?" Kat asked, skipping up behind him.

"Nothing. Just talking to myself," Finn replied.

It wasn't exactly 'nothing', though. Winding his way through trees that were surely getting denser, Finn revisited the doubts he'd had about Wolfman on *Guillemot*. Why was he so anxious to be with him now? Where was he going, if not into danger? Everyone in the North knew the rumours about Heorot. But what a story, what an exciting, compelling story he could tell if he knew Heorot at first hand.

The dark forest trail was barely visible in the gloom now. It would be very easy, Finn thought, to get lost here. To not arrive at Heorot at all. The sensible thing, his mind told him, was to turn around, return to *Guillemot* and stay safe. He turned around, and the bough of a tree smacked him in the face. "Kat," Finn whispered, "are you there?"

"Kat is here," the girl replied, appearing from behind a silver-barked tree trunk. "Why do you call Katranina Kat?"

Finn thought it was strange question, considering where they were, but then Kat was a strange sort of girl. "Sorry, *Katranina*."

"Katranina is also called Kat." The girl's ginger hair shone gold in a sudden ray of sunlight between the dense pines, the birch, larch and ash.

Ignoring her silly name game, Finn stayed silent, but then said, "Can you hear anyone?"

Kat tilted her head. "Yes."

"What? Who?" Finn strained his ears for voices but all he could detect was the gentle rustle of leaves above. Then something else. Something like a man breathing hard with exertion, one of Beorn's men hurrying to catch up, perhaps.

He turned his head to speak to Kat. Kat was no longer with him.

The breeze no longer rippled through dry leaves. Fine grasses no longer whispered around slender tree trunks; the forest glade was completely noiseless. Finn felt the hairs on the back of his neck stand on end. He was being followed, and he was certain – quite certain – it was not by Kat or one of Beorn's men.

With a rush of relief, he caught a glimpse of ginger between tree trunks *ahead* of him. "Wait!" he called.

Catching up with Kat, he said, "This is a mistake. I should have stayed on *Guillemot*."

"It was Finn's choice."

"I know."

"Finn can return."

"Yes, which way, though? I can hardly see my feet."

"Oh, dear, dearie-dear," Kat replied, and skipped out of sight again.

Backwards or forwards? Standing amongst so many tall trees it was hard to tell which way they had come. Finn pushed a branch aside, "Kat – Katranina – where are you?" he called in a hushed whisper.

"Here is Kat!" she replied. "Finn should look beneath his feet. There is a path."

Finn followed the path until the edge of the trees. Free of the forest's strangling sensation, he looked down into a lush valley and a green dell that was surely below sea level. As he moved forward, the ground under his soft leather boots began to get soggy. Soon, he was facing another stretch of open marsh. Running across it were rough-hewn planks leading to a high wooden palisade and tall, iron-clad gates. Heorot. And the gates were open.

Finn hesitated, wondering whether to enter or return to *Guillemot*. Assuming he could find his way back. But really, he realised, he was waiting for Kat to join him.

There was no sign of her, so he called her name again. "Katranina!"

But neither Katranina nor the irritating girl-woman-child he now thought of as Kat, responded.

"You coming in or what?" a guard called from a sentry post above him.

"Um, coming in," Finn replied, and slowly entered Heorot on his own.

Once he was inside the high, spike-topped palisade, four large men-at-arms, two to each side, closed the gate and barred the exit behind him.

Chapter 7

Beorn and his men were in the Heorot mead hall. Built on a platform above the damp ground, it had a high ceiling and timber walls ornamented with painted shields and smoke-stained tapestries telling woven tales of long ago. Oil lamps hung from chains and rush lights cast shadows from wall sconces. A long trestle table laden with wooden platters of roast meats, rosy apples and crusty loaves ran the full length of the hall. Earl Rolfgar was seated at the middle of the table, his lady beside him.

Finn sidled around the room to get nearer Beorn Wolfman, but servants ferrying food to the table and refilling ale jugs got in his way, so he found a quiet space to stand with his back to the wall, intending to nip across to the table as soon as he could. Despite the poor light and general chaos, he had a good view of Earl Rolfgar. The man looked worried. More than worried. Folds of skin fell from his chin, his cheeks were sunken, his eyes red-rimmed. A once bold, brave leader had aged badly before his time. His lady had fared little better. Her brightly coloured gown and carefully arranged, plaited crown failed to disguise how life at Heorot had treated her. Finn watched the earl and his wife exchange worried glances and suddenly knew that the rumours, the shocking tales of flesh-eating marsh-men, had to be true.

The thought made him realise the foolishness of his actions. He had no need to be here. "Curiosity killed the cat," he murmured to himself and began edging his way along the wall towards the open doorway. But the table was laden with good food and his stomach was rumbling, so he perched on the end of a bench near the exit to grab a bite to eat before he left.

As he sat down, he caught Beorn Wolfman's eye on him. Beorn gave him a broad grin and winked. The gesture first pleased and then worried Finn. The grin suggested Beorn was happy to see him, but the wink suggested they were in something together. Finn's empty stomach gave a lurch of fear: was Beorn expecting him to join his mercenary warriors? That could not happen, even if he had known how to use a sword.

Trying to stay calm, Finn lifted a hunk of bread from a wicker basket and then tried to find an unused beaker for ale. Small children scrambled in and out and under the table, squirming up between booted legs and linen skirts to snatch what they could. Dogs thrust damp noses under the elbows of those seated at the table, hoping for a juicy morsel, or joined the children under it in food raids. Cats warmed themselves by the great fire at the far end of the hall, taking advantage of a respite from canine hostilities. A large ginger she-cat sat to one side of the hearth with her back to the flames, upright and alert, watching what was happening at the table.

Flasks of honey-mead and jugs of barley ale began to circulate faster. Beorn's men became jovial and boisterous. Earl Rolfgar's men stayed quiet. Quiet that was, until a short, hunchbacked figure carrying a crumpled cow's horn appeared beside the great fireplace. He blew the horn once, long and loud. The hall fell silent.

The Doomsong Voyage

"Welcome, Beorn Wolfman and warriors. Welcome to the hall of Heorot, the scene of red spectacle," the hunchback declaimed. "Welcome and join with us in the stringed song of suffering souls, here in the home of the Grizzly Grasp."

Finn nodded his appreciation. 'Grizzly grasp' would fit nicely into his tales.

"Welcome, Northmen," continued the twisted skald by the hearth. "Your hero-histories are known in this mead-hall. Tonight, you must prove them right and truthful. Your brave actions will, we truly trust, save us from our suffering."

"Oh, we do 'truly trust,'" sniggered a mercenary in his cups.

"Let us witness your valour and value, Beorn Wolfman *and warriors*." The hunchback challenged, lowering his voice for effect. "Show us how you will destroy our undying torturers. Then – if you prevail – we shall sing of how *you* defeated our swarm-scum, slaughtering foe and damming the red river of Heorot's life blood, *if* you succeed, where we and others have failed."

Beorn Wolfman got to his feet. Placing his ale mug on the table, he took in the fearful gazes and disbelieving stares around him as if it were a wedding party, then, folding his arms and ignoring the courteous tradition of acknowledging and thanking the host for his hospitality before speaking, he declared, "The sap that flows through my warriors' veins is strong and red. Though I doubt you will see it. Fate goes as it must, but it shall not bleed us dry. Skald, you shall celebrate with song in the morn, for we shall prevail." Beorn then turned to the earl, "These creatures, they only come when darkness has fallen?"

Rolfgar's deep voice boomed across the laden table, "When the moon slides across the sky we must stay silent. Music is forbidden. A quiet melody, a lullaby hummed to a babe in a cradle, any tune brings the creatures scrambling to our gate, swarming over rampart and palisade, grasping and gobbling any living being their path."

"And if you hide, do they find you?"

"Heorot does not hide, Beorn Wolfman."

Beorn gave a small shrug. "Maybe not. But maybe that is not so wise. It seems, from what I have learned on my travels and since arriving here, that the Grendel brood is re-claiming their land. Was Heorot not built on their terrain?"

There was a rumble of grumbling around the table. Beorn Wolfman had just made a number of enemies.

"Well," Beorn insisted, "is this constant struggle not a question of land-rights?"

The disgruntled murmuring around the table became louder. Earl Rolfgar's lady whispered in her husband's ear — words he flicked away like an insect. Rolfgar got to his feet and faced Beorn across the wide table. "This may be as you say, Wolfman, but no swamp-monster will send us from our home now."

Rolfgar's men cheered and thumped the table with approval. The women and a few old-timers remained silent. Taking his cue from them, Beorn Wolfman said, "Why not let my men help you create a new settlement at a safe distance from this fenland? Go up into the hills, away from this misery."

"And let those creatures prosper?" the earl shouted. "Never!"

"In that case," Beorn replied, raising his ale mug and waiting until he had the attention of everyone seated in the hall, "let us discover how swamp-dwellers bleed." Gesturing to his men around him with one hand, he continued, "Let us hear a lively jig and watch my fine warriors do their dance of death for, my frightened friends, they will destroy your slimy beasts once and for all."

The hall exploded with cheers and whistles. Fists punched the air or thumped the table. "To success!" someone cried.

"Or your final night," sighed the grim skald, as a fiddle and two cheery flutes filled the dark air around them.

Finn slumped down on his bench, noticing how the children ran to cling to their mothers and fathers, how dogs were slinking through a side door. The ginger cat by the fireplace had disappeared.

"Animals know better than us," he said, knowing he should have listened to his inner voice and returned to *Guillemot* when he had the chance. *I knew there was an evil presence in the forest. I should have turned back then.*

"Aii!" he squealed, as Katranina grabbed his shoulder. "How did you get here?" Kat ignored the question, so he continued with his own thoughts and fears, "There was something following us, you know."

"Kat knows," she replied, gently kneading his shoulder with a hand. "Finn should not be here. Finn has a task to fulfil, and it is not here."

"Who told you that?" Finn snapped, cross because she was right.

Kat shrugged and tilted her heart-shaped face to one side. "Kat has no place in this story, either."

"It's not just a story, though, is it? I thought it was. I didn't really believe these green dale creatures existed, and there's dozens – hundreds – of them according to what they're saying here."

"That is what Kat means. Come, Finn must leave."

Finn began to move, but one of Beorn's warriors grabbed him by the other arm. "Scared, boy?" he jeered.

"No!" Finn retorted. Then, sensing Kat's tension, he added, "Yes, all right, I am."

"Ha!" laughed the mercenary, pushing a cup of mead at him. "Here, get some of this down you. It'll put a few hairs on your chest."

"He don't have any hairs to grow," another laughed, stroking his bushy red beard meaningfully. "Look at him, face as smooth as a baby's bottom."

Kat tugged Finn's sleeve. Shaking her small hand from his arm, he stood up, reached across the table for a jug of ale, filled an empty beaker and tried to look as if he were there for the night. Kat gave him one of her shrugs and left without him.

Finn bit his lip. He wanted to stay; he wanted to leave. He wanted to know what happened at Heorot when there was music during the night. He wanted to get away as fast as possible. Finally, drinking as much as he could in one go, he slipped off the end of the bench and sauntered casually towards the open doorway. As he turned to take a final look at the infamous mead hall of Heorot, a bright blue flame flickered above the table. It could have been someone using a tinder box to light a pipe; it could have been a dry twig or spark pluming into life in the hearth. Whatever it was, it sent Finn scurrying out of the hall.

Kat was waiting for him outside, sitting on the edge of a rough wooden step with her arms around her legs, her red hair spread over her knees. Just another girl trying to avoid her chores and stay out of harm's way.

The minute Finn reached her, though, she was on her feet, down the steps and running across the courtyard. Kat was light and fast. Then she suddenly stopped, and Finn skidded to a halt behind her. "Does Finn have second 's?" she asked.

Finn met her green-eyed challenge. "No, you are right. I have a task to fulfill, leagues from here across the sea. Let's go."

Kat nodded and they crossed the muddy yard towards the tall gates.

"Open up, please, gate-warden," Finn called. "We must leave."

"Can't do that," the gate-warden replied.

"But we have to go."

"You can't do that. Not till morning," the man said.

"But we have to return to our ship."

"Not until mornin'. Gates stay closed dusk to dawn, that's our rule."

"You closed it after I came in, and it wasn't dark then."

"Can't be too careful," the man responded and folded his arms to show the conversation was ended.

Finn looked about him. A thin, waning moon barely lit the sky, and no stars shone. "We'd better go back inside," he said.

As he spoke there was dull thud behind them as the main door to the mead hall was closed and barred. Finn raced to a side door, but that had also been closed and barred from the inside. "We can't get in," he gulped.

"That is good," Kat replied. "Finn must hide his human smell."

"Smell? Oh, yes! Grendels hate the people here."

"This way, come." Kat began hurrying towards the stables. Once inside, she grabbed Finn's arm, "Help me close the doors." Together they shoved shut the swollen wood, each knowing they could be pushed open again from the outside, because there was no bolt or heavy wooden bar to prevent it.

The rush and panic had set Finn's heart racing; he stood still for a moment, trying to catch his breath, but Kat was tugging at his arm again. Pulling him into an occupied stall, she pointed beneath the legs of a fat pony munching oats. "Lie down. Finn must pull straw over himself and stay still."

"Here?" Finn replied. "I'll get stamped on."

"Horses only stamp on rats. Normally."

Finn edged around the pony, sat down, and with Kat's help started layering smelly straw over himself. "Lie flat," Kat said.

"What about you?" Finn said.

"Kat has ways to stay safe." Stuffing a hollow stalk in his mouth so he could breathe, she added, "Finn must keep still. Completely still."

Hoping he was clear of the pony's platter-sized hooves, Finn curled onto his side and became aware of an absence. Of a sense of nakedness. The Doomsong sword was in Norna Silveryarn's cabin; he'd forgotten about it in his excitement to get to Heorot. His heart skipped a beat: supposing Shipmaster Seavogel sailed without him. He might never see the sword again, nor hand it to Goran, leader of the Volsungs, to fulfil Master Odo's task. He wished he'd brought it with him.

Not that he knew how to use a sword. Tale-maker's lives were rarely at risk. *I'd better learn,* he thought.

"At last, Finn remembers he has no weapon," Kat said, pushing another layer of pissy straw over his legs.

Finn pushed the stalk to the side of his mouth with his tongue. "I didn't say anything. What do you know about my sword, anyway?"

"Finn must lie still, or they will smell and hear and see him."

Finn wriggled down and for a while remained silent. Then he realised Kat had made no attempt to hide. "What about you?" he mumbled.

"Sshh," Kat hissed. "Listen."

Under the soiled bedding, beneath the pony's four large feet, Finn listened, then pushed the straw from his face and watched, not the pony's hooves, but Katranina.

She must have heard something – a green dell creature – approaching, for the hair on her head began to fan out. Or so it seemed in the poor light of the dark stables. The hair on Finn's own neck bristled. But it was Kat, not he, who was ready for action. Tense, poised, ready to leap up onto the stall's wooden partition or into the low rafters, if necessary, she stayed perfectly still, waiting. "Is Kat safe?" she whispered.

Finn spat the straw from his mouth to answer, but what could he say? They were both at risk – great risk. Would this night to be the last of their lives? Finn scrambled to his feet to hold her, to keep her safe – as best he could. She pushed him back down. "Finn is stupid," she hissed. Sending the pony skittering across the narrow stall with the sound of her voice. "Finn must cover himself. Fast!"

Finn did as he was told. The pony also stopped moving, standing as close to the stall partition as its fat belly permitted. Then it snorted, nostrils flaring, ears laid back.

A foul odour was oozing through the crack between the double doors. The pony snorted again and tugged at its tether. Kat may have been right, saying a horse rarely trod on a living creature deliberately, but if it panicked...

Kat reached out to the pony, murmuring something under her breath, then leaned over Finn and whispered, "Do not move, speak, cough or sneeze."

Finn wanted to say, "What about you!" but didn't.

Gradually, Kat moved closer to the pony's shoulder. Murmuring, purring softly to calm it, she untied the rope and gently backed it out of the stall, keeping a warm, firm hand on its neck for re-assurance, which calmed the gentle beast until there was a sudden loud screech followed by a crash.

The doors to the mead hall, Finn thought. They've been ripped from their hinges. Then began the wailing and squealing. The Grendels were attacking, of that he had no doubt.

Rigid with terror, the pony snorted again. "They do not come for yours or mine," Kat whispered.

Finn wasn't sure if she was speaking to the pony or him, then decided it was meant for the pony, because Kat removed its halter and let it loose to shuffle into another stall or barge about as its temperament dictated.

What happened next, Finn wasn't sure, for he could not see and was too focussed on trying to control his trembling. Kat must have run from stall to stall untying the other horses, doing what she could to reduce their panic, for there was the sound of anxious shuffling and barging, of frightened horses snorting and neighing.

Finn hoped the scent of their fear would mask his own, because now the stable was filling with the stench of a stagnant marsh, and something he could not name but knew to be the reek of swamp creatures.

Coming closer. Closer.

Finn scrambled to his feet, intending to protect Kat, but she was at the stable doors, squinting at the outside yard through the slit between them. Finn joined her. A large elkhound padded by with something dangling from its jowls.

"Ssss," Kat hissed. There were more dogs milling around. Three terriers were squabbling over a bone. "Ssss," Kat hissed. The dogs moved on.

Finn took a step backwards but stayed close to Kat, watching, waiting, fearing. Focussing all his senses on the creatures that had swarmed over the Heorot fortifications until one came into view.

There was a Grendel outside now, wounded. Crawling on its belly, dragging itself across the yard by a single arm and long-fingered hand. Getting nearer and nearer.

Could it smell them the way they could smell it? Finn turned his head and looked up at the air-vents in the wall above the stalls. Could they get in through there? Yes. Easily.

Something, or someone, scratched at the stable entrance, trying to get in. Something, surely not human, was breathing with rasping breath through the gap between the doors. Kat stepped backwards, bumping into Finn, who stepped backwards against a warm flank. A pony swung around, knocking him to the ground.

"Get back under the straw!" Kat snarled, kicking Finn's backside. "Away from the door, stupid!"

Finn did as he was told. Again.

What Kat did, how she saved herself, *and* him, Finn was never sure, because she disappeared. He was pleased she had got him into the stables, though. The heavy-hoofed ponies would surely trample a crawling Grendel for the outsized vermin that it was. Or run for freedom if the Grendels broke in, and cause a distraction. Either would do, but Kat had been right; it was safer for them here.

Unless the crawling human-haters got in and *didn't* get trampled... Finn rushed into the end stall, into the farthest, darkest corner, and wriggled like a rabbit under the bedding.

Motionless, curled under the straw, Finn gave in to the animal instinct to sleep deeply in a time of stress, and settled down to wait – hoping for the best, fearing the worst.

Chapter 8

Finn jolted awake. He could barely see and couldn't move. Something was pinning him down. Then he remembered where he was, and what Kat had ordered. He squeezed his eyes shut; tried not to breathe.

Pink light flittered across his eyelids. Was it morning? Had he slept through the night? How was that even possible? Perhaps the danger was over. Perhaps the weight on his body was the straw Kat had piled over him. The alternative didn't bear thinking about. He closed his eyes again. Tried to stay absolutely still.

His eyes snapped open: Kat! Where was she? Levering himself onto his elbows he nearly shouted with joy, for there was sunlight and he was alive... and the annoying girl named Katranina was lying on top of him.

Or maybe not. Two yellow-green, not quite human eyes blinked.

"Katranina," Finn whispered in a panic, "is that you?"

"Mmm?"

"Kat, wake up."

With a deep sigh, Kat stretched her arms, flexed her fingers, yawned and gradually crawled off his body. Finn pushed the straw off his face and stared at her. Her buckskin tunic and trews were barely dusty, her hair was as golden and wavy as usual, but she looked....

"You look..." he paused, "... different."

"That happens sometimes," she replied, tilting her head. "When Kat comes and goes."

Finn sat up and nodded as if he understood. He *felt* he understood. Not about the 'coming and going' exactly, but the way one could suddenly feel younger and smaller, or in this moment, a lot older. He sensed it was happening to him, but Katranina definitely appeared older.

"We need to get away from here," he said, getting to his feet.

"Kat knows this."

"Yes, of course. What I mean is..." Finn brushed straw off his head then stood still, listening hard. "It's horribly quiet out there."

"Yes," Kat replied.

"Where's the pony?"

"The pony is in another stall."

"Ah, good. The people in the hall, do you think they...?" Finn's mouth went dry.

"Kat does not know. Kat has stayed with Finn."

Finn wasn't sure how to respond so, flicking dry manure off his filthy clothing, he said, "The thing is, I think these Grendel creatures are a breed that's adapted to living in a swamp. Which explains why they have such strong, long arms, like people say in the taverns. The accounts I've heard, anyway. From paddling log boats across the lakes and fenlands hereabouts." Kat stayed silent. "So, I think Beorn was right. They want their land back and will do whatever it takes to frighten the Heorot clan away. It's worked with me, anyway. We need to get out of this place *right now*. If it's safe enough to go out there, I mean." Finn pointed a rather shaky hand at the stable doors.

He left the stall and walked on stiff, aching legs towards the doors. Peering through the slit between them, he tried to see who or what was in the yard. "Seems quiet enough," he said, trying to smile. Katranina's face told him this was no joking matter. "Too quiet. Yes."

The silence was frightening. Before he could say anything else, Kat pulled a door open a fraction, placed a warning hand on Finn's chest, then closed her eyes and sniffed.

Ignoring her warning hand, Finn leaned around the door. There was no need to sniff to identify an odour; the smell – the stink – was appalling. The yard between the stable and the hall had been churned into knee-deep, gory mud. He tried not to look but couldn't help himself. The yard was littered with bits of... Finn took a deep breath and regretted it. There were bits of tattered clothing; whitish, snake-like, fleshy bits that could only belong to the marsh monsters, and bones. The dogs, at least, had survived. Many were gobbling down a disgusting feast. Some were rooting around in the mud. Some were snoozing in the sunshine, as if it were a perfectly normal morning. Kat gave a sudden hiss.

"What, don't you like dogs?" Finn laughed. It was a silly thing to say at a stupid moment. He felt a hysterical laugh bubble up inside him and clamped his mouth shut.

Swallowing hard, he eased his shoulders then whispered "D'you think Beorn Wolfman is still here?" He tried to look across the yard at the hall without seeing the gore. "D'you think they survived?"

Kat gave an elaborate shrug. Of Beorn and his men there was no sign. Nor any of the people who had so unwisely made Heorot their home.

In the old sagas and tales told of battles fought long ago, this was called the aftermath, when the hero and survivors counted their dead and buried them, according to custom, with their swords and valuables, or else placed them in a ship to float out to sea in flames.

He was a survivor, but no hero. He had hidden – and lived unscathed to tell the tale. Possibly thanks to Kat, though he wasn't sure how.

Kat hissed again, loudly, and turned to look inside the stable.

"Now what?" Finn demanded, but he already knew. There was another odour wafting towards the open door from inside the stables: smoke.

Finn shoved the door wide to let the snorting, sweating ponies scramble out before he and Kat were trampled to the ground.

"How could a fire have started in here?" Finn shouted above the clatter of hooves.

Kat looked up at one of the gaps between the roof and timber walls, "From up there," she said. "Come, Finn, we must get away!"

Kat hastened across the yard towards where the iron-clad gates had once stood. Head held high, Kat looked neither right nor left, nor hesitated. Not until they had passed in single file over the marshy terrain and reached the forest that lay between Heorot and the harbour.

Finn followed, saying nothing until Kat halted in a sunlit woodland glade to catch her breath. Doubled over, pulling fresh air into his lungs, Finn waited until his breathing returned to normal and then looked up at the clear blue sky. "If this was meant to be some sort of test, I think I must be a coward for hiding in the stables," he said.

"Finn is not a coward," Kat replied. "But he must learn to question his actions. Think about consequences. If Finn wants to live to tell the tale."

"Who told you to say *that*?" Finn demanded.

Ignoring him, Kat stepped lightly through the glade. "Come; Finn has a ship and crew waiting. That is why Finn had to stay safe."

"*Guillemot* might have sailed on by now."

"It has not," Kat replied. "Seavogel would not dare."

Trotting along soundlessly on small, neat feet, Katranina led the way through the forest until Finn halted, clutching his side with stitch. Rubbing a fist under his ribcage to ease the pain, he noticed a fallen tree trunk, a big comfortable log where he could sit for a moment to recoup his energy. "Over there," he said, pointing, "that log. Let's rest."

Kat looked at where he was pointing and froze. "That is not a log," she said.

As she spoke, a huge brown bear rose from eating berries to stand on its hind legs, as tall and wide as a house.

"Yell! Sing!" Kat shouted. "Wave your arms! Finn must look big and noisy and dangerous. It might be a real one."

"Of course it's real!" Finn yelled, swinging his arms like a windmill.

The bear dropped onto four paws and started towards them. Kat jumped on Finn's back, her ginger mane flaring from her head. Gripping with her knees, she began screeching in a language Finn vaguely recognised. He had no idea what she was saying but didn't need to, because the crazy, noisy, two-headed people monster did the trick. Branches creaked and twigs snapped as the beast lumbered away through the undergrowth to safety.

Kat laughed and slipped down onto a mossy patch of ground between brambles. Finn stayed upright, anxiously looking about him. "How can you sit there?" he snapped. "It might come back."

"It might," Kat said, "but it won't."

"How can you know that?" Finn demanded.

Kat gave one of her impatient huffs. "Finn must think *how* himself. Finn does not listen precisely to what he is told. Finn is too simple-minded."

"I am not simple-minded!"

"Finn is a simple young boy with a sword he forgets to wear, and no skills to survive without it."

"I am not a *young* boy, either. I'm past my coming-of-age. There was no celebration, but there could have been." *If Tait and Augal had allowed it*, Finn added silently to himself. "And I do have skills."

"That is good. Can Finn name them?"

"Yes! I've been looking after myself since I was a *young boy*. I am a tale-maker. That's how I make my living and find somewhere to sleep each night. My particular skills are...." Finn paused, wincing at a moment of truth. "I admit, I was scrounging off my cousins, and I play up to nice farmers' wives to get a hot meal sometimes, but I've travelled the North from one side to the other since I was old enough to get abouit, so I do know how to survive. In normal circumstances."

"Finn knows many people in the North?"

"Hundreds. Most villages, all towns, some farmsteads. I've slept and been welcomed in shepherds' huts and woodcutters' cabins. Ah, of course...." Finn gave a dry laugh. "*That* is why I got this task. Because I know so many people.

He wants me to take Goran the Volsung to them personally, to convince them to get away."

"Probably," Kat replied. Not, Finn noticed, asking the obvious questions – who, or to get away from what? "But Finn will not find Goran of the Volsung Clan this way."

"You know about this." Finn peered at Kat through narrowed eyes.

"Perhaps," Kat stuck her nose in the air. "Perhaps that is why Kat saved Finn's life last night."

"And Finn shall be forever in her debt," he replied, grimacing at the truth of it.

His heart still racing with fright after being so close to the bear, Finn walked on a few paces then turned and looked back. Katranina had taken charge at Heorot, that he could not deny, and she'd known what to do with the bear. She was only a girl; she barely reached his chest; she was small and slender, yet she had almost certainly saved his life – twice. "Was this planned?" he asked. "Was this excursion to Heorot a test of some sort? Is that why you followed me? To see how I'd...." Finn swallowed the word 'fail.' "...get on?"

Kat met his gaze. "Perhaps. Perhaps someone else is following Finn's progress. Testing his abilities."

"Someone else!" Did she mean Master Odo? "Who?"

Kat tilted her head. "If Finn does not know, Finn must find out. Or not. This is Finn's life story. Not a Kat tale."

"Ha-ha. Come on then, show me how to get back to *Guillemot*. You seem to know the way."

Kat set off at a trot once more, and Finn followed, his mind awhirl with conflicting thoughts and feelings. He was glad Kat was with him. He wanted her gone. He wanted a companion. He did not want to be observed or controlled.

He didn't understand any of it. Not the voyage with *Guillemot*'s strange skipper and stranger female passengers. Not the visit to Heorot. Why was he even there? Was he really being tested – by Master Odo?

And if he was, was he succeeding or failing? Did failing matter if he lived to tell the tale? Finn grinned; either way it made a cracking good story.

But it was the first and last time he would ever be separated from the Doomsong sword.

Cresting the final dune, *Guillemot* came into sight. "Oh, thank the gods, Seavogel's waited for us," he gasped.

"Kat said he would."

"She did," Finn laughed, slithering down the sand to jog the final stretch to the jetty.

As they reached the wooden walkway, Finn halted. "Kat, stop a moment. Before we go back on board...." He had another question nagging at him but wasn't sure where to start. "What you were saying earlier, about Heorot – what do you think I was doing – going there?"

"Kat thinks that is the wrong question to ask."

Finn's grey-blue eyes darkened. "What?"

"Exactly. 'What' is not the right question."

"Eh? Who? What? Where? When? Why?"

"That is the right question." Kat's mouth twitched into what might have been a smile.

Finn flung up his hands in despair, but then remembered what it was he wanted to ask. "In the forest – what did you mean when you said, 'It might be a real one'?"

A gust of wind blew Kat's thick hair across her face, masking her expression and reply. Holding her mane back with clean, pink-nailed hands, she said, "The questions Finn asks should begin with 'why.' *Why* did Finn go to Heorot? *Why* did Kat say that?"

Then, not waiting for a reply, Katranina skipped down the jetty ahead of him.

"Girls!" Finn huffed. "You never get a straight answer."

Later that day, safely aboard the sturdy cargo knarr, Finn woke from a much-needed nap with a dull throb in his forehead. *Guillemot* was pushing through choppy water, the big square sail snapping and cracking in the wind. Shipmaster Seavogel's rotund belly loomed over him. "You're awake, then," Seavogel said.

Finn blinked in the bright sunlight. "Where are we?"

"Heading south. Sit up."

Norna Silveryarn appeared beside them. She had a thick woollen shawl tied across her shrunken body and she smelled of sheep dung, but she was holding a bowl of something that smelt like food from the gods.

"What is that?" Finn asked.

"Food from the gods," she wheezed, and returned to her hut.

Finn drank down the honey-sweet liquid and felt better, and then better than ever, and jumped to his feet. The empty bowl bounced across the rough deck. As he bent to pick it up, he noticed someone sitting splay-legged, with his back to upper prow deck. The man waved a hand.

Finn gaped. It was Beorn Wolfman. He looked haggard, exhausted. A thick brown beard covered his chin.

"Beorn returned!" Finn said to Seavogel. "How?"

"Ask him yourself," Seavogel grunted. "See what excuse he gives you. I contracted all ten of them to protect *Guillemot*, and only he comes back."

Finn made his way down the rolling deck to the prow. "What became of your men? What happened at Heorot?" he asked.

Wolfman wrinkled his nose; his mouth twitched. "They were mercenaries. They knew the risks."

"But you got away safely."

"As did you," Beorn said, peering at Finn through small, dark eyes. "You found a way out?"

"At dawn, yes."

"You were hiding during the night, and they didn't smell you out?" He sniffed again. "Ah. The stables."

"I didn't have a weapon. Nor am I a trained warrior like you." Finn wanted to know what had happened in the mead hall, and more importantly, how and when Beorn had got out. But as he started to speak, he noticed Katranina leaning against the tiny cabin. Ignoring her, he continued, "Beorn, would you show me how to fight with a sword?"

The Northman rubbed his bearded chin. "D'you have a sword?"

"Yes. I mean, no. It's only a broken old thing. Could I use yours?"

"Better to use what you have got. Where is it?" Beorn was on his feet as fast as a trained wrestler. "We can start right now."

As Beorn spoke, a huge wave pushed the fat-bellied trading vessel up into the sky and then plunged her down a steep watery cliff. Finn grabbed the rail. The Northman joined him in trying to stay upright as seawater gushed across the deck. Katranina scampered into the cabin.

"I don't think this is the time for swordplay," Finn shouted above the sound of the tumult.

"The next time we go ashore. Take it with you," Beorn shouted back. "Where is it?"

"In Norna Silveryarn's safekeeping."

Beorn muttered something in reply, but the wind whirled his words into the air.

Chapter 9

The sky turned the colour of bone-deep bruising, the sea an oily black between rolling yellow slopes. The watery kingdom of Aegir's Deep beckoned daily during the next stage of Finn's voyage. Seavogel constantly adjusted the square sail to stay a safe distance off the coast of Frankia, until, as exhausted as his crew, he told *Guillemot*'s aged pilot, Arg, to steer them into shallower waters and find somewhere to rest. Thorsman and the crew, including Finn, took up their oars until Arg found a sheltered spot with pine trees growing down to the tide line, where they could hunt for fresh meat.

It was a welcome respite for everyone. They lit a big fire on the beach, dried out their sodden clothing, and rested for two days, but the hunting was poor and on-board supplies too precious to waste, so Seavogel chivvied them back on deck to race through the treacherous Bay of Biscay and then along the coast of northern Hispania. Arg and Seavogel kept them from being battered into sheer cliffs and jagged rock-ridges, but the weather was still against them, and after another week of fighting the elements, Shipmaster Seavogel decided they should put into a safe haven he remembered from a previous voyage. Katranina and Finn were tasked with watching for the mouth of a river between tall cliffs, like a fjord in the Cold North.

The Doomsong Voyage

The storm eased and bright sunlight lit their way into the channel, but Seavogel's safe-haven proved a perilous place to approach. While the narrow estuary offered some protection from the wind, the tide did its best to crush them against rock walls. Seavogel was planning to go further up-river, but he was delighted to find a man-made jetty, newly built into a rocky recess. After guiding the trading vessel alongside, the pilot, an old mariner, let out a boyish cheer of relief. They tied up, intending to take a much-needed rest and carry out repairs.

The shipmaster's joy was short-lived. They had been observed from a green meadow above. "Oh, no," he moaned.

"What's the problem?" Finn asked climbing onto the jetty.

"Viking raiders. This must be one of their new camps."

"But Vikings are from the North. We're from the North. Why are they a problem? They set to sea to go a'viking, they're only trading like us, aren't they?"

"No, Finn, not like *Guillemot*," Beorn Wolfman said, joining them. "They trade with the blade of an axe and take by force these days."

"It's a good job Seavogel has you on board then," Finn replied.

Beorn Wolfman gave Finn a suspicious sideways glance. "I offered my services as a deterrent in ports. To prevent thieving cockroaches from getting his precious wares, not to fight single-handed against crazy odds." He paused, looked about him then added, "It's not entirely a disaster, though. In fact, we may be in luck."

"How's that?" Seavogel demanded. "They raid, not trade, nowadays. Worse than common pirates, most of them. They'll cut us down and take everything we've got if we don't get away fast enough."

Finn recalled tales he'd heard about the men and women who left the freezing North, seeking, in principle, goods to exchange, but who had turned to raiding for gold, silver and slaves for the thrill of it. Seavogel was right; *Guillemot's* hold would be a fine attraction. And it was too late to get away.

Tattooed warriors and women with rat-tail plaits tied with shells were running down the cliff path, swarming over the jetty like lemmings in summer. Deliberately trying to shove Finn, Wolfman and Seavogel into the water, they scrambled aboard the low-lying *Guillemot,* whooping and joking, to remove anything of any value, starting with the cook's store-boxes. Until Norna Silveryarn appeared on the upper bow deck.

Raising her rag-layered arms, saying nothing, she commanded silence. Finn stared in amazement as everyone halted to focus on the old woman. He tried to remember when he had last seen her in daylight. She had suffered during the past weeks at sea, looked smaller and even more wrinkled than when he had first met her. Norna Silveryarn had the appearance of an aged witch-woman, a *disir*. And nobody dared cross a *disir*.

A bow-legged Viking stepped forward and placed a fist over his heart. "Harold Harp-Legs, at your service."

Norna Silveryarn inclined her head. Harp-Legs clicked his fingers, and his followers scuttled back onto the jetty, as fast as the cockroaches Wolfman had mentioned.

The bow-legged Viking waited until his raiders were all off *Guillemot* and then followed. Seavogel pushed his way forward to confront him, but before he could speak, Harp-Legs clapped him on the back, saying, "We have food and shelter to share, old friend. Come up to our camp and be welcome."

Seavogel looked at Norna Silveryarn, who nodded her head, once. *Katranina uses the same gesture*, Finn thought, watching the silent exchange between the shipmaster and the old woman. What power did she have? Why was Seavogel even consulting her? And why did a seasoned raider with the absurd name of Harp-Legs obey her?

Wolfman was supposed to be protecting Seavogel's cargo, but it was an old woman these Viking raiders feared, not him. And Wolfman hadn't put a hand to any of the weapons he carried on his person.

"We are grateful," Seavogel said, addressing the Viking leader. "Fresh meat will do us all good. But I have a cargo destined for the Middle Sea; can your people be trusted not to steal it?"

"Hah!" Harp-Legs laughed. "No. But with your shield-maiden here," he waved a hand at Norna Silveryarn, "I doubt any of them will risk it. There might be one or two newcomers who are less familiar with our ways, they might try it. Leave an armed guard, just to be sure."

Seavogel nodded, "We'll be up later; first we have repairs to carry out." Adding meaningfully, "I like to be ready to sail at a moment's notice, in case we get unwelcome visitors."

Harp-Legs laughed and clapped him on the back again, nearly sending the old mariner into the water. "Come up and feast with us. You're safe enough for now."

Seavogel waited until Harp-Legs's rabble were climbing the winding cliff path back to their camp, then organised his crew into a repair team and a rotating guard. Finn went to collect his sword from Norna Silveryarn's safekeeping. Pulling it from his damp travel sack he was both shocked and relieved to find it had lost its lustre, and badly needed sharpening. It would be of little use in a fight, even if he knew how to use it, but it was better than nothing, and even though it wouldn't attract attention in its present condition he couldn't risk leaving it on board. Strapping on his shoulder harness, he shoved the ugly blade into its sheepskin sheath against his spine, just as Norna Silveryarn returned to her hut. Finn backed out to give her space to enter, "I came for –" he started to say.

"Course you did," she replied. "You know how to use it?" Finn shook his head. "You'd better learn then, hadn't you?"

Finn smiled. He started to say he'd asked Wolfman to help him, then realised they'd been on dry land in Frankia and he'd done nothing about it.

The old woman stared into his eyes, then gave her sharp, harsh laugh. "Listen to your inner voices, Finn. Trust is a precious gem."

Finn wanted to ask what she was referring to, but she gathered something from her sleeping cot and moved back onto the deck to sit on the low stool outside her cabin, where, using her long bone needles, she continued hooking an unending length of string-like thread into something wide and shapeless.

Checking the hull and carrying out essential repairs had started the moment Harold Harp-Legs's gang of Vikings reached the top of the cliff, just in case, as Seavogel had stated, they needed to make a quick getaway. Finn and even Katranina joined the crew, testing nail heads and ropes until the sunlit afternoon became evening.

Finn eased his shoulders in the harness and studied the cliff path. A goat came into view, clicking on tiny hooves from one rocky outcrop to another. Finn laughed and called out to Katranina, "Look up there!" as a group of long-horned goats stuck their heads over the cliff top to watch the people below, surprised, perhaps, as much as he.

"Goats!" Katranina scoffed, as if they were the commonest, ugliest creatures she knew.

"But look how they move," Finn said, pointing again as they skipped down an almost-sheer rock-face to nibble on tufts of grass and pink flowers.

"It is what goats do," Katranina huffed again, and returned to her place beside Norna Silveryarn.

Eventually Seavogel went up to the stern deck and, standing legs apart, arms folded across his wide chest, he said, "All right, you're free to go up to their camp if you like, in turns and at your own risk. We sail at dawn, if the gods are with us, so don't get drunk and fall asleep up there. Rounds of six can go up while six stay on deck. I want four on guard on the jetty. Two in the hold with Wolfman. Fill your bellies but stay alert." He then began naming who could go up to the camp first.

When he'd finished, he turned to Finn and with a meaningful glare and said, "Go up if you if you want, but watch yourself. Make sure you get back in one piece, understood?"

Chapter 10

A tall, well-constructed palisade had been built around the Vikings' camp to protect against strong sea winds and intruders. Entering through a gate that reminded him unpleasantly of Heorot, Finn decided it was more like a permanent village than a temporary camp, probably due to good fishing and hunting.

Harold Harp-Legs's followers had made their home in a settlement abandoned by a long-gone native tribe. Round, stone huts set in a circle had been re-thatched. More dwellings had been erected, using wood, a material people of the North understood better. Pigs and chickens rooted for scraps, and the usual campsite curs wandered about, seeking food or somewhere safe from children. A large bonfire blazed in the open space at the centre of the circle. Women of various ages and a few children were grouped around two separate fire pits set up between huts, one for roasting a fat wild boar, one for a bony goat.

Harold Harp-Legs welcomed the crew of *Guillemot* as the sun drowned in the wide ocean behind them. Some of his men exchanged slaps on the back with Seavogel's crew as if they were old comrades, and young boys handed them mugs of cider. Finn, watching, sensing it was a hollow welcome, not trusting their host or his band, stood apart until Harold

Harp-Legs beckoned them to sit near the scorching hot campfire in the starlight.

Finn was handed a lump of stringy roasted goat and sat chewing quietly, listening to how Harp-Legs had raided along the coast of Friesland and then crossed the whale road to raid the east coast of Saxon Britain. Where, he said, every village had an unprotected place of worship to the White Christ, full of gold and silver and theirs for the taking. His dragonship fleet had then looted southern Saxon ports and crossed to Frankia, where they'd found a small island inhabited by men whose only occupation was praying to the White Christ and planting beans. The monastery had yielded more treasure than they could carry.

They had then sailed south-west and found this settlement. Despite all the gold, the precious objects, jewels and silver they had taken from the Saxon churches and the Frankish monastery, they were still raiding 'now and then, from here.'

The 'now and then' comment made Finn sit up and take note of what was actually being said. These raiders were, as he had first thought, establishing a permanent base. Exactly as Master Odo had suggested. Not that this Viking band were about to become full-time fisher-folk or farmers again.

"Sometimes," Harp-Legs said, "we go a'viking for a full lunar month. There's some busy harbours along the coast, and market towns inland. Lately, we've being going further inland, looking for these monastery places. Easy pickings, they are."

"Always good for a raid, religious houses are," a grey-beard sniggered over his ale-horn. "Treasure for their god, and treasure for us, eh?" He gave a sly wink. "Proper silver and gold, and pretty bead-stones for my old wives into the bargain."

"What do you want all that for?" Finn asked, tossing his meatless bone to a hopeful puppy. "Can't be much use in a camp like this."

The old man gaped at Finn, his rheumy eyes wide with disbelief, "For our graves," he replied slowly. "Obviously."

"Obviously?" Finn repeated the word as a question, unsure how to react. In the Cold North, loved ones were buried with the everyday possessions, cooking pots and eating-knives, that they would need in their next life. "Do our gods require payment and gifts nowadays?" He'd meant it as a joke but it fell flat.

"Where are you from, boy?" the old man demanded. "Some farm at the back of beyond? Have you never been in battle?"

Finn shook his head, "I'm a tale-maker." Then added, "My family are farming folk," and instantly regretted it.

"A plough-pusher wimpling, that explains it. Well, young clod-hopping tale-maker, if warriors like us," the old man waved a gnarly hand in the direction of his feasting companions, "don't die in battle at our All-father Odin's command, then we must pay tribute for our way into the Hall of the Undead. How can you not know that?"

"Oh, I do. I do. It's only that I can't see why... no, nothing. I mean, if gold and silver can be used in graves... Well, why not?" Finn tried to smile an apology, wondering why he had never given any thought to acquiring precious objects himself. He'd heard men and women talking about grave goods, about how gold did not tarnish; he'd seen people passing around items to be admired. A golden bowl encrusted with precious gems was used as a drinking vessel in one Baltic port tavern and he'd never given it any importance. "I've just never thought about collecting valuables," he said.

"Well, you should," the elderly Viking replied. "You'll need grave treasure sooner or later."

Finn nodded, his mind drifting back to his meeting with Master Odo in The Old Salvation and then to Heorot. Living to tell the tale was turning into *surviving* to tell the tale.

His thoughts were interrupted by a burly raider with a greasy blond moustache that dangled down to his chest. Leaning across the old man he said, "Where you from, boy?"

"Minnaholm. It's an island, but I travel on the mainland mostly. Selling my tales, passing on news and –"

"You've the look of a Volsung."

"Do I?"

"Don't see that white hair without white lashes very often."

The old man next to him squinted into Finn's face. "You're right. He's got the eyes. Black lashes with white hair on a young head, that's Volsung. Not all of them, only..." Somebody nudged him from behind and his toothless gums shut like a clam.

Finn wanted to laugh – battle-scarred Vikings peering at him like grandmothers over a newborn's crib. Then he remembered how his brown-haired cousins had taunted and teased him about his appearance. He was jolted out of it by someone pushing in between them. Finn shifted to make room for a stocky warrior with a serpent tattooed up his arm and around his neck. The creature's head, mouth open, fangs ready, appeared on his right cheek. Finn shuddered, but the Viking was too busy exchanging earnest whispers about Volsungs with his companions to notice.

More men and a few shield-maidens clustered behind them, listening in on the conversation. Finn tried to stand, to escape the crush and pressure of too much interest, and caught sight of Beorn Wolfman moving away from the fire into the darkness.

Hushed words were running through the gathering now. "Ice-Heart!" someone gasped.

"That's what he said. The boy's looking for Ice-Heart."

Finn closed his eyes. Who had revealed that? Surely not Seavogel, or Katranina. Who else could know? Wolfman?

Although, was this a bad thing? Was there a connection between the absent Volsung clan leader named Goran Ice-Heart and this Viking gang?

"Ice-Heart!" a woman's voice repeated loudly. "You mean that wimpling's looking for Goran Ice-Heart?"

The old man began to chuckle, the chuckle turned into a guffaw. The guffaw grew into a communal belly laugh. It ceased as soon as it had begun. Everyone fell silent. Something had been said that caused women to clap hands to their mouths or pull their children closer.

"Rather you than me, boy," someone muttered.

Finn grimaced. This was not the response he wanted to hear. Certainly not from a tough set of brutes like this. Struggling to edge away, he said, "Too hot here for me. I hank you for the meat, but I've got to get down to *Guillemot*."

He'd barely got three paces through the jumble of bodies when Harold Harp-Legs grabbed his arm and dragged him into the shadows. Leaning in close, he said, "There's a few of us who'd like to meet Ice-Heart face to face. Friendly like. If you know where he is? No harm intended."

Finn didn't believe a word of that. "Why?" he asked.

"Ah, well, let's say he's got something that belongs to us." Harp-Legs cleared his throat and started again, "Let's say he owes us. You're a brave lad going after him, I'll give you that."

Finn wanted to say he didn't have any choice in the matter, but Harp-Legs grasped his arm tighter and leaning even closer whispered, "You can call me Harold. 'Cept in public."

Reeling from Harold's bad breath, Finn tried to show an unfelt gratitude at the honour. "Tell me about Goran," he said.

"Ah, umm, *Goran*... Well, now then, where to start?" Harp-Legs tugged Finn deeper into the shadows. Checking to see who was watching or listening, he said, "He came south with us, to start with. Years ago, that was. Had a girl who was somebody's wife on an island, then had to get away quick, due to the usual consequences." Harold closed an eyelid Finn could barely see. "Proper old billy goat, Goran was. Anyway, we traded and raided westwards and then took our loot and new merchandise back to the North. The first time, that was. Second time, we came this way then went further south, raiding mainly. Third time we went all the way round Galicia and on down along the Death Coast," he gestured behind him over the palisade. "We reached the Middle Sea that way. Then Goran says he isn't returning. Sneaks off on his own one night, *in my boat*! Stole it while we was drunk on grape wine in some fisher-folk place. That was a bad thing to do – stealing my boat. That caused bad feelin'. And problems. Like finding a boat good enough to get us back North. Not to mention all the tasty bits we'd lost, stuffed under the benches. Shiny, bright, tasty bits. Oh, yes, that was a terrible thing, stealing from your mates and *loyal* companions. Wasn't right. Wasn't proper for a man of his standing, neither. Did you know he's the rightful Volsung clan leader?"

Finn nodded. "Yes," he replied, taking note of Harold's choice of words: *a man of his standing*. This was what Master Odo had been trying to convey. But this also made

Goran a blatant thief who stole from his shipmates. Borrowing knives or trinkets from companions was one thing, stealing a boat from a brother-in-war was something far worse. "You didn't go after him?" Finn asked. "Didn't try to get your boat back?"

"Oh, we did. Oh, yes. To start with. Then we got a bit side-tracked by what we were finding around the Middle Sea. There are rich harbours and towns near the coast there, you see. Places with proper streets. Big stone-built houses with clear glass in their windows. Furniture to sit on and eat off, and pretty things *ev-ery-where*. And the wine and the food... ah, the food."

Finn adjusted his position to breathe clean air, then, trying to sound casually curious, he said, "So, what happened to Goran? Did you ever find out?"

"By the gods over the Rainbow Bridge, we heard, all right. Wherever we went, Goran had got there first. We started hearing as to why people were calling him Ice-Heart, as well. Enough to make your blood freeze if it weren't so blazing hot in summer there. He was raiding reg'lar around the Middle Sea *in my boat*, then he sets up camp on one of the Pitiusa Islands. Then we hear he's got pirates from the Levant sailing with him"

"The Levant?" Finn queried.

"That's the eastern end of the Middle Sea. Pirates out of the Adriatic Sea as well. Uzcocks or Buzcocks they call themselves. Their boats are sleek and bonnie and fast, and they're thieving rats, every one of them. All pirating *under his command.*"

"Are they still sailing out of the island? Is that their base camp?"

"Camp! Ice-Heart sleeps in a bed with silk hangings, eats off gold plates; got a slave for every ruddy finger, he has.

Camp! Some camp, that. He trades thralls now. Any age, any skin colour – nobody's safe. He's a proper pirate king now, and so rich and strong that he's got *con-nections....*" Harold Harp-Legs pronounced the word with ill-disguised awe.

"Connections?" Finn repeated. "What does that mean?"

"Knows rulers: Ándalus, Barbalus, emirs and sheiks and African princes. Buys and sells for them, and steals things back, right under their stupid noses."

"You mean he tells them he's a clan leader of the North and they respect that and trade with him? Or they give him commissions?"

"Commissions!" Harp-Legs laughed until he nearly choked.

The news gave Finn hope: it would make Goran easier to find. But then his heart sank. Ice-Heart had no reason to return to his clan in the freezing, hungry North.

"So," Harold said, stepping away to get a better look at Finn, "you're sailing with old Seavogel to find the rotter. For trade, or what?"

Finn grinned. The perfect reason, or excuse. "Yes, for trade."

Harp-Legs eyed him suspiciously, "You one of his brats? You've got the same white hair, same look about you, I'd say. You one of his?"

Finn shook his head. "No." He was about to add, 'not that I know of,' but refrained because Harold saw Goran Ice-Heart as an enemy who 'owed him.' Changing the subject, he said, "When we docked at your landing stage, Harold, how did you recognise – I mean, how do you know – the old woman, Norna Silveryarn?"

"Norna Silveryarn: oh, yes, I recognised her." Harold gave a lopsided grin or grimace. In the poor light Finn wasn't sure which. The stocky Viking ran a hand over his smooth skull, uncomfortable at the question. "She's on your boat – been with you since the start of your voyage?"

"Yes."

"Did you ever see her before?"

"No." An image passed across Finn's mind: an old woman sitting in The Old Salvation, knitting or nalbinding. "Maybe. I might have done."

"I expect you have. She'll be keeping a watch on you."

"A watch on *me*?"

"Well, you or someone else on board." Harold shrugged. "It's what she does. When she's not doing the opposite."

"The opposite? You mean the opposite of watching out for someone – to protect them?" Harp-Legs waved his hands as if it were a reply. "So," Finn persisted, "you know her?"

"I know *of* her. Most of us know what she is. That's all. You never met a *disir* before? No witch women where you come from?"

Finn bit his lower lip. He knew about *disir*. Had heard accounts of their power and actions. *Disir* were to be feared, but some also acted for the good – occasionally. "D'you think it's a good thing, having her on board?" Finn asked.

"Pff! I can't answer that. You might be lucky. If having her around can be considered luck." Harold Harp-Legs started back towards the fire. "Seavogel's accepted her for a reason. You should be safe enough."

"Harold, wait!" Finn said reaching out to him. "There's something I need to ask you. It's terribly important. If someone asked you to bring your boats back to the North to help people leave their freezing fields and come here, to this green land, for example, to a warmer, more fertile place, would you do it?"

"What's in it for me?"

"I can't say, at the moment. Something, I'm sure."

"We don't want more people coming here," a voice snapped behind them.

Finn turned, realising others had gathered in the shadows to hear their conversation.

"This camp is a good place. For us. I'm not sharing it. Not the land nor the treasure we're getting," a woman said.

The man with the chest-long whiskers pushed his way to Finn's side. "What d'you want to go bringing people here for, stealing our land and our gold?" he demanded.

Trying to move back into the firelight and noting the blade hanging from the man's belt, Finn said, "There's plenty of green land here. We need new places to live, to grow crops and feed cattle." He swung out an arm indicating the grassy plateau beyond the huts. "I don't think farmers will bother with your gold for their graves; you can't eat it or feed it to your cattle, so I can't see anyone trying to take it."

"Girls want gold," the woman said, coming closer. "It shows we've got..." She searched for a word. "Value," another woman supplied. "It shows her family's got wealth. And it'll go in our graves for the Afterlife."

"But our people are farmers and fisher-folk," Finn replied. "We only need good land, a warm springtime and rain instead of snow all year round for a better life."

"Farmers!" another voice scoffed. "We don't need farmers here. Let 'em find their own place to dig turnips or stay where they are."

"But the weather is making it impossible. Land is frozen nearly all year. And a mountain is going to explode and that will kill them."

Everyone laughed.

"That's their look out," a woman shouted. Turning to Harold she added, "Make sure this namby-pamby doesn't tell anyone about us, all right? Or I'll do it for you."

Finn looked around, hoping to see Thorsman or even Beorn Wolfman. Fearing they had already gone back to the boat, he said, "I'd better go. Thank you for the meal."

Pushing his way through a barrier of iron-muscled chests and naked thighs he started to leave the camp area, then paused. Seeing the place now by moonlight, he realised he'd been right, this was a permanent settlement. The hens and pigs scavenging on leftovers by the fire pits were fattening themselves for the pot.

As Finn reached the gates, he saw Beorn Wolfman and one of Harp-Legs's younger raiders standing under the pointed stakes of the palisade. They were deep in conversation and neither of them noticed him. He had seen Wolfman earlier, too. Wasn't the paid mercenary supposed to be protecting Seavogel's cargo?

Wolfman clasped the Viking's arm and leaned forwards to whisper something. Finn gave a shudder, knowing a deal had been struck. A secret deal neither Shipmaster Seavogel nor Harold of the harp-shaped legs need know about.

Chapter 11

Pretending he had not seen the men conspiring beside the palisade, Finn moved through the gateway and waited for his eyes to adjust to the dark. Tapping the hilt of the sword behind his neck, he waited another few moments to hear if anyone was nearby; then, weary and wary, he made his way back to the steep track that led down to the tiny new harbour.

As he began the zig-zagging descent, an animal brushed past his legs. Too small for one of the local goats or camp dogs. A local fox, perhaps. Just a night-walking animal going about its nocturnal business. He gave it no importance and continued his moonlit descent.

Slipping and sliding on loose pebbles, Finn grabbed at clumps of grass to prevent himself tumbling onto the rocks below. When he reached what he thought might be the half-way point he pulled himself onto a flat-surfaced boulder to catch his breath. Hugging his knees to his chest, he gazed out to where the river met the wide ocean, listening to waves slapping against rocks and the calls of nightbirds, and began to relax.

He sensed, rather than saw, the animal again. Definitely not a goat, nor a lonesome puppy looking for a friend. Something in between. And very close. Two amber-gold eyes. Staring straight at him. Did they have lions here? He'd heard tales of big yellow cats with huge jaws and lethal claws. How big was 'big'? Or was this a lynx? Yes. A wild cat. Dangerous? Possibly. Unnerving? Certainly. The creature's eyes closed. Opened. Turned away.

There was a shuffling noise behind him. A large, hot hand grasped his neck, as someone tried to pull Doomsong from his shoulder harness.

The amber-eyed creature growled.

The hands stopped moving. Fell away. Soft boots scrabbled over rough ground.

There was a blood-curdling howl. A young man screamed.

Pebbles rattled over the rock-face into the river far below, as someone – a person, not an animal – scrambled back up the path towards the gate.

Finn slowly, silently, pulled Doomsong from its sheath and waited for whatever it was to attack, knowing he would fall to his death if he tried to run, because his leg muscles had cramped with fear.

He waited for the worst. The worst did not happen.

He began to shiver with cold; knew he needed to move, yet stayed where he was. Another man approached, huffing and puffing, cursing as he lost his footing coming down the track. "Shipmaster, is that you?" Finn called into the dark.

"Shipmaster I am and shall remain 'til the All-father calls me. Boats are where I belong... not climbing cliffs. This climbing palaver... is not for sea-folks." Seavogel had taken a drop too much strong cider. "I'm staying aboard from here on."

A shower of stones scattered behind Finn. "I'm here, Shipmaster," he called loudly, hoping to scare away the yellow-eyed night-cat. "Can you see me?"

Hebden Seavogel came alongside Finn's boulder, his chest heaving with exertion, and heaved himself onto the smooth surface. Finn reached out to steady him.

"That's it, I'm up now," the rotund seafarer huffed. "You all right, boy?"

"No. Not really. There was a creature – a big cat, I think – here. It attacked something."

"It did. That cocky young fella with the snake tattoo. Scratched him good and proper. Wouldn't be surprised if he didn't wet his pants," Seavogel chuckled. "Budge up, my backside's wider than yours."

Finn budged up. The two sat in companionable silence until Seavogel's breathing returned to normal.

"So," Seavogel began again, "you're doin' all right?"

"Yes. Bit scared, though, to be honest. Why?"

"Gave me a bit of turn, it did, seeing that fella running into the camp in tatters, like, knowing you'd come this way. I had a bad feeling about him from the start. Seeing him bleeding like that... Knowing Harp-Legs is a lying, two-faced snake himself and they're after my cargo. But you're still in one piece, so that's all right. We better get down to *Guillemot*, before anyone else tries to have a go at you. Ready?"

"Have a go at me? Why?"

"Why, boy! Why? Because you've got a mouth like a basking shark and you open it before you think. Didn't nobody ever warn you not to talk to strangers?"

Finn laughed. "Hardly; that's how I make my living, talking to strangers. Telling them tales."

"Well, that lot up there didn't like the tale you were telling about wanting their land."

"But it's not their land!"

"That's not how they see it. Right, you ready?"

"Ready," Finn replied. Then, his voice cracking slightly, he said, "Shipmaster, the man who got attacked by the wild cat – if that's what it was – was he coming after me?"

"I'd say so."

"He tried to get my sword –"

"You should've left it with Norna Silveryarn," Seavogel huffed. "You can't be too careful, Finn. Not with that ol' sword."

"But how could he..." Finn stopped. Seavogel and his ancient muse knew about the Doomsong sword. Of course they did – Master Odo had paid for his passage.

Before he could say anything more, Seavogel put a warm hand on his arm. "Look, young Finn of the Volsungs, you've gotta take more care of yourself. You're making your voyage more difficult every day, and it's difficult enough for all of us without you adding complications. Whatever possessed you to go to Heorot, boy? That was a mad thing to do."

"But you said I could go. More or less. Why didn't you try to stop me?"

"Ah, well, there's an old woman who's got other ideas to me. She said as to let you go. To find yourself."

"Find myself?"

"That's what she said, and that's what you gotta do, boy. Find yourself. And the quicker the better for Hebden Seavogel. My heart's not up to all this worry and tramping about. I made a promise to a powerful person, and I gotta keep it, or I'll lose my boat."

The words were barely out of Seavogel's mouth when something arced over their heads and descended like a shooting star towards the harbour below. The fire arrow landed on *Guillemot*'s main deck.

"Gods and worms!" Seavogel screeched as a second arrow flew over their heads.

"What's happening?" Finn cried.

"They're trying to set fire to my *Guillemot,* and Norna Silveryarn's on her!"

Finn turned to look upwards. A row of blazing arrows illuminated the edge of the cliff.

In unison, a dozen arrows flew through the air. Some to fizzle in the water below; others to die on damp jetty planks; too many to land on *Guillemot*; one to set Norna Silveryarn's little roof ablaze.

Hebden Seavogel slid off the boulder and lumbered down the path as fast as his seaman's legs and loose pebbles would let him. Finn stayed where he was, looking upwards to where, in the sudden dark, a single, small, blue flame flickered into the night.

And then was gone.

Fire! The evening had all been to do with fire: the huge campfire, the roasting pits, and then the fire arrows; *Guillemot*'s funny little cabin going up in smoke.

And then a single blue flame.

Loki? Was that possible? Here?

Loki was a fire-fiend. He loved the heat. Was he present in these warmer lands? Or was he using an agent or his followers to create havoc for him?

No. This was nonsense. The Vikings were trying to frighten them away from their new territory, that was all. And that was enough!

Keeping his body as low to the ground as he could, Finn tobogganed on the seat of his trews down the rough slope and sprinted across the jetty.

Hebden Seavogel had done well to keep some of his crew on board. Thorsman had already returned. Some were hurling buckets of river water onto the flames, closely observed by Norna Silveryarn, holding a ginger cat in her arms.

"You here, boy?" Hebden Seavogel yelled, looking around for Finn.

"Here!" Finn cried reaching the side of the knarr.

"Untie us then. We're leaving. All hands to oars!"

"But Shipmaster, some of them are still up on the meadow."

"That's their problem; we're getting out of here. Those left up there will have to stay and you'll have to take an oar, boy!"

Finn struggled with the heavy ropes to cast off, then jumped aboard.

Guillemot was a yard from land when a voice yelled, "Wait!" And Beorn Wolfman leapt onto the deck.

Finn looked from Beorn to the smouldering roof of Norna Silveryarn's cabin and gave a short sigh of relief. If they'd been trying to scare her – or worse – that surely meant she was acting for the good on board *Guillemot*. Didn't it?

He needed to ask Kat. "Where's Katranina?" he yelled, but nobody knew.

Chapter 12

Finn and Beorn joined the oarsmen to row out of the cliff-walled estuary in the dark until they reached open water, where Seavogel raised the sail. There was no sign of Katranina or Norna Silveryarn until the following morning, when both appeared on deck as if nothing had happened. Finn had a dozen questions to ask but said nothing.

The tiny cabin was patched with cow hides, and Katranina resumed her daily catnaps beside it, until they rounded the western tip of Galicia and put in at a busy port on the perilous Coast of Death. It had taken all Shipmaster Seavogel's skill and experience to keep them from crashing into the jagged cliffs, and by the time they reached the sheltered Tagus estuary Finn was well on the way to becoming a competent oarsman and seafarer. He was also a lot stronger, a lot braver, and utterly exhausted.

They stayed for two days in Lisboa, a trading port for the Cordoba Emirate, watching new customs of behaviour and enjoying sweet-tasting Moorish delicacies. Finn had seen a few Moorish travelers in Baltic ports but had never imagined the variety of wares they traded: aromatic spices and exotic elixirs in curiously shaped glass bottles, silks and soft muslin cottons and bulging sacks of grain that made – he was told – perfect white loaves.

Seavogel traded some of his heavier goods and took on two barrels of a thick local wine under cover of darkness, and on the third day *Guillemot* resumed her voyage. Once they were heading eastwards for the Middle Sea under sail, Shipmaster Seavogel told his crew to get some rest.

Taking his salt-encrusted cloak and the Doomsong harness, which he hadn't returned to the smouldering cabin, up to the poop deck, Finn curled into a ball and slept through a full night for the first time in weeks. Next morning, he was awake at the crack of dawn. As were Katranina and Seavogel, who were standing in the prow behind the carved seabird, watching the sunrise. They turned as Finn approached.

"See those?" Seavogel said, waving a fat finger between two distant land-towers forming a great sea-gate. "Beyond them is the Middle Sea and the Isles. If you go far enough east, there's another narrow gateway and a smaller sea called the Black Sea, and beyond that, another. Two big rivers run into those waters. You can travel up either of them in your own boat then get portage to cross overland back to narrower waterways and back home into the Baltic. Traders have used those routes for generations, picking up all manner of strange merchandise to sell back home."

"Is that what you're going to do?" Finn asked.

"Me? No fear. I did it once from the Black Sea. Never again. Dangerous place, that land is. Brigands, bears, weird folk telling you to clear off after stealing your goods. You have to move your boat out of the water to avoid rapids, then put it on wheels or sledge it over snow to get through leagues of forests and open land. Ruins your feet." Finn grinned, remembering his own travels on foot in the Cold North. "And the food," Seavogel continued with a gap-toothed grimace, "they cook everything, barley cakes, eggs, mutton, you name it, in *fish* oil. Everything tastes and stinks of fish. And they stink worse."

Finn pulled a similar face, as was expected. "So where are you planning to trade?" he asked, watching low-lying grey-green hills and broad sandy beaches slide by the port rail.

"Some of my furs are for our next stop, here at Berjer. Gets cold in winter up on those mountains." Seavogel pointed at a range of mauve-coloured mountains. "They have good fruit and fresh vegetables here for us to buy, though. Once I've off-loaded the furs and whale oil, and some of the amber, I'll take on fruit and olive oil and fresh meat. Right now, though, I've a busy day ahead." Seavogel touched a finger to his forehead and made his way to the hold to supervise his cargo.

A warm breeze ruffled Katranina's hair. Finn marveled at how it appeared to change colour with the weather. Today she had a reddish-tinted, auburn mane. Sensing his scrutiny, she pushed it off her face and ran a small hand around her left ear.

"What happened to your fingers?" Finn asked, noticing her nails were torn to the quick.

She instantly hid her hands. "Kat's fingers are not Finn's concern."

"Only trying to be friendly," Finn shrugged and changed the subject. "It's getting hot already. I can't imagine anyone needs furs here."

"Does Finn never listen?" Kat sighed, pointing at the high peaks rising above pine green slopes. "There is snow and ice up there in winter."

Finn squinted in the sunlight, "How do you know that? Have you been here before?"

"Kat travels."

"That's what I've been meaning to ask you. If you sail with Seavogel, who do you belong to in my cousins' farmstead?"

"Kat belongs to nobody."

"So, what were you doing there?"

"Visiting." Kat gave him an evasive smile and wandered back to Norna Silveryarn's hut.

Finn stayed at the prow until *Guillemot* turned into the mouth of another wide estuary, making for the trading port. This time, there was a purpose-built harbour full of high-sided galleys. Seavogel and the pilot tucked the fat cargo knarr in a gap between a sleek, low-railed galley with bright hangings, and a huge triple-deck galley, its prow towering over them three storeys high. Finn had never seen such a majestic vessel.

"Watch out for yourself," Thorsman said, following Finn's gaze. "Wave-wagons that big need hundreds of oarsmen, be they slaves or war captives. Understand?"

"Ah, yes," Finn said, "I'll take care to avoid that happening. But what a magnificent ship! I wonder who she belongs to?"

"People looking for trouble. She's a trireme war galley. See the way her prow is reinforced into a pointed wedge? They use that for ramming into other ships. Pirates use the same technique with smaller galleys. I've seen it myself in these waters. Like I said, watch yourself. Rowers live and die at their benches on those things. Some don't last a week."

Finn wanted to know more, but they were too busy tying up, and Seavogel was shouting at the crew about his bales and barrels. Thorsman was eager to go ashore but the cargo took priority.

"Coming for a stroll on solid ground?" Beorn Wolfman asked, sauntering down the deck as if he owned it.

Finn shook his head. After weeks of enforced proximity on *Guillemot*, Finn was not keen to be in Beorn's company. "Maybe later," he said. "When I get my land legs working."

"Suit yourself," Beorn replied, striding down the gangplank as if he had somewhere to go.

"Wait!" Finn called out, remembering Thorsman's warning about galley slaves. "No, nothing. I'll probably see you later, in the town."

"Maybe," Beorn shouted without turning, and swung away in the direction of taverns, cool wine and warm-skinned girls.

Waiting until Beorn was out of sight, Finn sought out Seavogel. "I thought you'd contracted Wolfman to protect your cargo. He's first off. Who is he, really?"

"A chancer, lad."

"A 'chancer'? Meaning he takes a chance at different – what – challenges?"

Seavogel pulled a face. "Sort of, I s'pose. He's latched on to you, good and proper though, so watch yourself. Anything for a coin in the palm, that one."

"That's the second time I've been warned to take care this morning. The galley, I understand, but why should I be careful with Wolfman if you're employing him to protect your ship and your cargo?"

Seavogel pulled a face, "Let's say he made *me* an offer of protection for his own reasons. He's prob'ly after a share in my profits."

"So, you don't trust him?"

"Trust is a fair-weather friend, Finn. Do I trust Wolfman? No reason not to. Yet. But remember where he joined us, and why."

"I do. I also remember him leaving his men on their own at Heorot, and how he didn't stay aboard when we went up to Harp-Legs's camp."

"No, but..." Seavogel cleared his throat. "Having a trained sword arm at the ready to protect my valuables is useful."

"We needed that with Harp-Legs, and look what happened. I'm glad I've got nothing of any value for him to 'protect'."

"Haven't you?" Seavogel raised a bushy grey eyebrow. "Happens you're wrong about that. Given what you've got to do."

Finn gave the shipmaster a suspicious look. "You do know why I am here, then?"

"I do. You going ashore or what?"

"Yes. Unless you want me for something?"

"No. Go and learn a bit about the place. We're in part of an independent emirate belonging to the Barbalus Moors, here. They speak a sort of Arabic. Locals speak Andaluz Spanish. Pick up some of the lingo if you can. It's used a lot in the Middle Sea. It'll come in handy later."

"Ah, yes, I hadn't thought of that."

Finn pulled Doomsong and its harness from under his filthy seal-skin cape where it lay on the deck and started to strap it over his shoulders. Checking to see he wasn't being watched, he pulled the blade from the sheath to see if it had been damaged by salt water, and was saddened to see the legendary weapon had no shine. Gold, they'd said at the Viking camp, never lost its lustre, which meant the metals he'd seen on the hilt when Master Odo had given it to him were nothing more than bronze or copper. Master Odo said he'd put a glamour on the blade to disguise it, but surely, it should glint or glimmer a bit for him while he was on his own, the way it had before.

Finn strapped it to his back and, avoiding Katranina because he didn't want her tagging along criticising his every move, and also Norna Silveryarn, because she made him nervous, he skipped down the gangplank onto solid ground, then stopped to take stock of his new surroundings. The quayside was a riot of noise and colours: local merchants peddling their wares, wide-hipped women in bright skirts carrying baskets of fruit on their heads, brown-skinned fish-wives screaming the morning's catch for sale while their menfolk mended nets; scurrying rag-clad children begging or thieving, hucksters and hawkers pushing through the crowd with wicker trays of curios, and long-limbed, black-skinned youths with lengths of shiny fabrics hanging from their shoulders. A small girl-child was selling tortoiseshell combs; another stood by a mound of oranges. At least, Finn guessed they were oranges. He'd heard tell of juice-filled fruits, but he'd never actually seen an orange before.

A large woman with a birdcage on her head and smaller cages hanging from her waist swung around him, the trapped birds chattering in distress. A handcart with rolls of brightly patterned cotton was tugged onto the cobble-stoned wharf, where skinny boys in nothing but loin cloths begged for the chance to load its contents onto a sleek vessel, already lying low in the water. Tall men in white turbans, loose white tunics and pantaloons wandered in twos and threes, talking among themselves. Each wore soft red boots and carried a curved sword at his hip.

Finn gaped, slack-jawed, about him, trying to take it all in. Over the years he'd heard mariners' yarns of ports such as this, but he hadn't visualised the exuberance and busy-ness of it all. As the thought struck him, he caught sight of a single, brightly-clad youth juggling flaming torches. Up they went, and over and across and down and then up again and over and across and down. Fascinated, Finn edged closer. Close enough for the juggler in bright red and yellow to catch his eye – and wink. With a sudden flourish, all the torches were in the air, and then extinguished. The youth caught them in both hands, and with a whoosh of blue flame from his mouth, set them alight once more.

Finn gaped. "How does he do that?" he asked, as if Katranina was at his side, because she usually was.

But Kat was not with him. She was nowhere in sight.

"Master Finn," Shipmaster Seavogel called, waddling through the crowd to pull on his arm, "go back and collect your pack. We've got *scraelingar* foreigners comin' an' goin' with new goods. I can't be responsible for personal stuff left aboard."

"It's only a change of clothing, Shipmaster," Finn replied.

"Oh, well, if you got plenty of other packs of clothes, it won't matter if a cockroach nabs it then."

"No, no, I'll get it," Finn responded. "When should I be back?"

"We'll be here two days, at least; I've a cargo to load and the spare sail to mend or replace." He beckoned Finn closer and whispering urgently in his ear, he said, "Remember what I told you, boy. It's not just oarsmen who get taken. Good-looking lads like you are valuable merchandise here and across the water." He waved a hand, out to sea.

"That would be a joke, Viking slavers taking me back North," Finn laughed.

"It's no joke." Seavogel scrunched up his weather-beaten features and stared into Finn's eyes. "I wasn't referring to Vikings, but now you mention it, maybe I should."

"I know about the slave galleys," Finn said. "Thorsman warned me."

Seavogel raised an eyebrow. "Good, so watch yourself. Apart from anythin' else, your white hair is a screaming invitation to Ma-gravy slavers. You'd fetch a pretty silver dirham across the water. I'd keep it covered, if I were you."

Finn blinked and began scraping his thick, wavy hair off his tanned face and re-tying it into a knot with his black leather thong. Vikings raided for thralls: it had never occurred to him that he could be a victim. Following Seavogel back onto *Guillemot* in a much more subdued frame of mind, he caught sight of Kat sitting on a pile of rope, hugging her knees.

Finn hurried towards her. If his white hair was an invitation to local slavers, her wild auburn locks would be, too. "Katranina, you shouldn't be here on your own. Let me get my pack and we'll get something to eat together. You'll be safer with me."

"Safer with Finn!"

Finn had never heard Kat laugh, and she didn't laugh now; her scorn was worse. Tilting her heart-shaped face from one side to another she said, "Kat walks alone, sleeps alone, eats alone, and this day, Kat has other things to do – alone."

Finn huffed with impatience. Kat got stranger by the day. "As you wish. But I'll get us something different to eat for when we're back on board. I'm sick of dried fish and oat biscuits."

"Finn will like oranges and lemons and figs and…"

"What are figs?"

"Fruit with sugary flowers inside. Get cinnamon and almond cakes."

"You *have* been here before!" Finn snapped and jumped aboard *Guillemot* to collect his belongings. When he returned to the jetty, Kat was in exactly the same place, hugging her knees.

"Does Finn have everything with which he began his voyage?" she asked.

Finn tapped his shoulder to check Doomsong was safely tucked in its leather scabbard. "Yes," he said, shading his eyes to study the mountains. He could just make out a sort of white castle and village on a conical hill. It was enchanting. He felt excited again, glad to be alive. Glad that he had been forced on this voyage of danger and discovery. "Come along, let's find something good to eat," he said, wanting someone with him to enjoy the day. Katranina ignored him. "Oh, as the little queen wishes," Finn said, and hooking his travel pack over his shoulder, he strolled off towards the striped awnings of the harbour market.

As he walked, he was jostled, first by a small boy with thick brown hair flopping over his face, then by two men wearing baggy white pantaloons and white turbans. It was a crowded marketplace; he thought nothing of it at the time.

Chapter 13

Finn wandered between market stalls, tasting new foods and examining unknown objects. Pleased to discover traders would take his coins, he bought a sturdy round basket, hooked it over his arm like a breadman, and filled it with fruit and almond cakes, a brush for his now-long hair and an embroidered cotton shirt, then turned back for *Guillemot.*

He was grabbed from behind; his travel pack wrenched from his shoulder. The basket tumbled to the ground, its contents spilling among the sandaled feet of men and women who made no attempt to help him. A sack was pushed over his head. His feet were lifted from under him. Blind to what was happening, he was thrown over a brawny shoulder and carried away.

Carried away from the noise of the harbour, away from the market stalls, into an alley that led uphill. It was only a sensation; he could see nothing and could barely breathe through the rough sackcloth.

A door creaked open, and he was thrown into a musty smelling shed or dwelling place. For a moment there was a scuffle, a shuffling of feet and muffled whispers. A voice he thought he recognised snapped out an order. Then silence as he was rolled onto a cool dirt floor.

The hood was removed. His captors had white muslin covering their faces. They tied his ankles and hands together in a sitting position with a rope and knotted it at his back. Somebody cut the purse from his belt. Nobody spoke. The door was shut and bolted.

Finn waited a while, trying to recover his balance and decide where he might be. He tried to kneel, then to get to his feet, but fell sideways and eventually gave up. The knot pressed into his spine with every move. Gradually, very slowly, he managed to shuffle around the small space on his backside, rubbing a shoulder around the walls until he found the door. There was no handle, and it was bolted from the outside. He leaned his shoulders – his empty shoulders – against the wood. They had taken his sword. Trying not to weep, trying to ignore the hard knot against his spine, he shoved with all his weight against wooden planks.

Fury that Doomsong had been taken gave him strength, but the door would not budge. He leant his head back and swallowed hard. He needed to calm down. He needed to think. He wasn't dead, and hadn't been thrown in the sea, meaning they would probably return for him. Meaning Middle Sea slavers had got him. He should have covered his white hair; he had been warned.

At nightfall the door was opened. A torch blazed outside. Three men entered, their faces swathed in white muslin pulled from their turbans. As they conversed quietly in a guttural language, one pushed the sack back on his head, another adjusted the rope between his hands and feet so he could stand, then lifted him from the floor, took him into the alley and threw him into a cart.

The cart jolted down the cobbled street. Finn fell against another human body. He closed his eyes inside the hood and tried and failed not to cry. He'd been warned by Thorsman and Shipmaster Seavogel, and now it was too late.

A few moments later, his head was jerked backwards and the hood pulled off. Two occupants of the cart had their hands tied like he did but were managing to release their fellow captives from their blindness.

Finn tried to identify his companions. "Where are we?" he asked, not expecting anyone to understand.

Before the boy at his side could speak, a white-robed guard rode up beside the cart on a small horse and glared in. He said something in an angry tone. The words were strange to Finn but their meaning was clear: no talking.

As his eyes grew accustomed to the dark, Finn tried to see where they were being taken. To one side of the cart, in the distance, the sea glinted in the moonlight. On the other side was a horseman. The sound of hooves on dry ground suggested there were many more behind them and that they were out of the harbour town, going into the countryside. The cart moved onto a track between trees and started to go uphill, tilting the captives backwards, but not enough for anyone to fall out.

The track got rougher and steeper. Were they being taken to the white town on the hill? Would he be able to get away and return to the port, and find *Guillemot* without being captured again? More importantly – more important than the purse no longer at his waist – who had got Doomsong?

The cart halted at a set of elaborate wrought-iron gates flanked by lanterns the size of buckets. Clear glass protected bright blue flames. Beneath each lamp stood two white-garbed guards. Each guard wore a fat round turban on his head and carried a thin curved sword at his hip. Each held a long spear across his body. They were young, clean-shaven and silent.

The backboard of Finn's cart was unhooked, and the captives hauled out like sacks of turnips. A strong wind buffeted Finn as his feet touched the ground and he nearly toppled to his knees. Before he could get any sense of where he was, the gates were opened from the inside and a troop of turbaned guards marched out in pairs. Nobody spoke. Weapons glinted in the moonlight.

Accepting there was no possibility of escape, Finn turned to his fellow victims, three sturdy boys and three much younger girls. One girl wept, the second stayed quiet. The third began jabbering in a language Finn didn't know. A guard smacked the side of her head. She fell to the ground and was yanked back to her feet and then pushed through the open gates, where the girls were met by a group of women wearing white head-coverings and knee-length tunics over pantaloons. The girls were led away.

Silently, expertly, the boys were tied in a line with a lightweight rope, which was then attached to a burly guard's waist. Finn, the first in the boys' line, was tugged through the gateway into a wide cobbled square, illuminated by lamps hanging from stunted trees in round pots. The gates closed behind them with an ominous clang. Then began a steep, uphill trek, with the horsemen clattering behind, until the burly guard halted at a flight of low steps. Two new guards appeared from the shadows and set themselves on either side of the roped boys. The horsemen clattered back the way they had come. The lead guard resumed their climb, up well-worn steps, until they reached a terrace and a set of sliding, smooth-surfaced iron doors which opened, then shut with a horrible thud behind them.

Onward and upward they went, the burly guard pulling them, up broad, worn steps that seemed to curl around the hill. Now and again, Finn looked up, trying to identify their destination, but on each occasion lost his footing, causing one of the accompanying guards to curse and slap the back of his head.

Eventually, with leg muscles aching beyond pain, throats dry and breath coming in chest-racking gasps, Finn and the three boys were tugged into a wide patio where two sets of curved steps converged. The guard yanked them to the right, then there were more steps, then a short walk through an alleyway between houses with lantern-lit doorways, then more steps and an archway.

Open doorways gave brief glimpses of domestic life, of tiny interior patios planted with sweet-smelling night flowers. A small child called out and was answered by a kindly voice. An old man taking the evening air watched in silence as they trooped past his home. Someone behind him asked what sounded like a question; nobody answered.

Then came a series of wider shallow steps, then a moonlit terrace with fruit trees growing in deep pots, then into a tunnel under a building and out the other side, up more steps and another terrace. From here on, the route was lit by lanterns hanging from the curved walls. Everywhere, doorsteps, walls and rooftops were white. Except for the cats. Grey and tabby, butter-cream and black, they sauntered along the tops of walls, monitoring the captives' ascent, or slunk out of sight as if hastening to pass on the news. Noticing the cats perched above them as they went by, Finn realised there was not a single straight wall. Everything, including the tunnels, was curved.

At this point, Finn gave up trying to see where they were going; he was so thirsty and in such agony he no longer cared. As if finally sensing his distress the burly guard halted and said something. Finn hoped it meant, 'we're here' or even 'soon be there,' but he jerked them forward again, up more steps to an open space surrounded by drooping vines on sturdy wooden frames. A few strides on the flat and up more steps. A door opened as they passed, and shut again rapidly. More cats began to appear; some crouched on doorsteps, some perched on green-tiled windowsills, each and all studying their progress.

A large black tomcat leapt down from a wall. The lead guard halted and waited for it to cross his path. Finn thought that an accompanying guard saluted it. Black cats were connected to good luck in some places, or so he'd heard.

Finally, they came to an open square or marketplace lit by lanterns hanging from poles. There were stone tables and benches scrubbed so clean they shone like ice. Finn thought this was probably where people came to buy and sell their bread and fruit. It gave him a small sense of comfort, that real people lived here. A small sense of relief. It was short-lived.

The lead guard released Finn from his waist hold, but kept a firm grip on the back of his neck. Another man in white with soft red boots emerged from a doorway to release the boys behind him. They were ushered into an alley by yet another guard and disappeared. Finn did not go with them.

Flanked by his silent, white-robed captors Finn was guided up a wide stairway and under a key-shaped arch by the burly guard, where he was briefly released into the custody of another strong hand, which gripped his neck to guide him through a patio crowded with ferns and sweet-scented greenery and then through a blue door. The door closed on the outside world.

Finn's new guard, who was not armed, so possibly not a guard, tapped on an inner door. It was opened by a very bent, very old man with pale blue eyes in reddened eye-sockets. He had long grey hair and a nose like a squashed blueberry. The old man raised a glass lantern to Finn's face and touched his white hair with a wrinkled finger, then pursed his lips, took a deep breath and said in Finn's language, "Yes, he's a Volsung."

The guard put a hand back on Finn's neck and propelled him forward and the old man led them up a narrow, higgledy-piggledy stone staircase to a large room. The old man entered, lit a beeswax candle on a chest, and then closed the shutters to a square window. There was a ceramic cup beside a lidded jug on a small brass-topped table. The only other furniture were two low chairs and a wide bed, with what looked like a down-filled mattress. Finn was gently shoved into the centre of the room. The two men left the chamber, shutting the door behind them. A lock turned with a clunk, and Finn was alone.

Chapter 14

Finn awoke next morning, half-dressed, lying in the soft bed. He had no memory of removing his empty sword harness, salt-stiff boots, jerkin and trews, or getting under the lavender-scented linen coverlet, but he had slept well and felt refreshed. Sunlight lit the room.

Someone had been in; the candle had been extinguished and the shutters opened. He got out of the bed and tip-toed over to the window on bare feet, his calf muscles screaming at every step. The marble tiled floor was cool. He opened the green-glass panes of the window, anxious to know where they had brought him, but all he could see were flat rooftops. As he gazed out, he became aware of a gentle humming, crooning sound. Doves or pigeons: there were pigeon lofts on the flat roofs below. The sound was comforting, but his feet were cold.

Finn stumbled back to the bed, then paused to strip off his filthy shirt, because he could see the bed had clean white linen, and everything in the room, floor included, was spotless. Closing his eyes, he tried to go back to sleep. For a while, he tossed and turned, then hunger got the better of him. He sat up and looked at the table, which bore a pitcher, a cup, a hunk of brown bread on a tin plate, and a bowl of fruit.

The Doomsong Voyage

Wrapping the white coverlet around his shoulders, he got out of bed, tripped over his boots and collapsed on the floor as his leg muscles buckled under him. Pulling himself onto a chair, he poured a cup of water from the lidded jug. Then he ate the bread, alternating hands to massage his thighs. Climbing a steep hill and taking so many steps after weeks at sea had turned his leg muscles to stone. Still hungry, Finn examined the fruit in the bowl. There was an apple, two oranges and some curious finger-like fruit with blotched yellow skin. He broke one off the hand-like bunch and sniffed it. It smelled like nothing he'd ever tasted and looked like nothing he'd ever seen. He bit down on the end and spat it out as a squirt of soft flesh went up his nose.

Abandoning the strange fruit, he rubbed the apple against his blanket and bit into it. As he did so, he noticed his travel pack by the doorway. His heart lurched with hope. He dropped the apple on his plate and went to the pack. Not stopping to consider how or why someone had brought it into his locked room, he pushed his right hand into his much-travelled, oiled-leather sack to get at his second set of clothes and froze with shock as he touched the hilt of a sword.

Doomsong — if this was Doomsong — was wrapped in his spare shirt. Unwinding it carefully, he took hold of the hilt and held it up to the light. Gradually, the dull iron weapon began to glow. The pommel resumed its sunburst, the melded, Dwarf-forged blade resumed its colour and the runes reappeared. Finn nearly wept with relief.

But why, if he was a prisoner, or to be sold as a slave, had they returned his sword? Was somebody on *Guillemot* in cahoots with white robed, red-booted slavers? Who? Wolfman? Who else might do such a thing?

But no; slavers wouldn't allow anyone to keep a weapon. Nor would they provide such pleasant accommodation.

Then he remembered the old man touching his hair, recognising him as a Volsung. What was going on?

Finn crossed the wide room, picked up his old, rough-textured woollen tunic and trews and put them on, then debated whether to put on the back-sheath harness or leave the sword in his old pack, hoping his captors would forget about it. Yes, he thought, do not draw attention to Doomsong.

He pushed the sword and sheath into his crumpled sack and then returned to the open window. Staring out between the bars, looking down this time, instead of outwards, he could see a white wall, partly covered by a climbing plant with white, star-like flowers. A large ginger cat sprang up onto the windowsill, sidled in through the bars and dropped down to the floor. Finn turned, surprised, and watched it saunter to the chair he had vacated, jump onto the seat and then take up an alert position on the table.

"Where have you come from?" he laughed, sitting down again.

The cat studied him then brushed her head against his shoulder. Finn smoothed back her delicate ears. "You are very pretty," he said, for this was definitely a she-cat.

The cat brushed against him again. A key turned in the lock to the door behind them. In a series of neat, silent moves the cat hopped from table to floor, then up and through the window bars, and disappeared.

A lean-bodied man entered the room, wearing an embroidered red waistcoat over a voluminous white blouse with silver and gold thread in the cuffs. Under his soft, silvery white turban he had sharp features and eyes so dark they looked black. There was a long, curved dagger tucked into a red leather belt at his waist.

"My name is Adeef," the man said in Finn's language. "Get dressed. I have come for you myself."

"Come for me?" Finn asked, confused by the man's aggressive appearance and his mild tone.

"Yes, come."

Finn wanted to ask a dozen questions at once, but all he managed to say was, "Where?"

"Wherever I take you," the man replied. "People go where I tell them."

Finn bit his lower lip, looked into the man's black-brown eyes. "Please, sir, I do not wish to be rude or impertinent, but please, where am I?"

"In the High Alcazar of the Independent State of Barbalus," Adeef responded, then added quickly, "Do not ask why. That will be explained. *If* you are who we think you are. If not," he lifted his narrow shoulders, "we always need galley slaves. For now, all you need to know is that I am the Grand Visior to the Emir and you do what I say." A thin smile scythed across his narrow face, "Do you understand?"

Finn nodded. "Yes. Except, what is a *vis-i-or*?

"A *vis-i-or* helps to arrange and control an emir's household and, when necessary, domain. My role, as Grand Visior, is to supervise and oversee all matters pertaining to the Mighty Hammil, Emir of Barbalus. A visior's role is to predict what may happen, interpret what needs to be done and ensure relevant arrangements are made. In war and peace."

Finn's throat went dry: Adeef had made the word 'arrangements' sound ominous. Trying to keep his voice from croaking, he said, "Was it you, sir, who arranged for me to come here?"

"In a manner of speaking. Come."

Adeef placed a firm hand on the back of Finn's neck and propelled him down the higgledy-piggledy staircase to the patio, where a bald giant in an ankle-length white robe was waiting. Adeef released his grip and the giant's hand closed around Finn's neck. If this was this the way they controlled prisoners' movements here, Finn thought, it was surprisingly effective.

The white-robed giant propelled him through an archway. His grip was softer and gentler than Adeef's and the previous evening's guards. Gentler, perhaps, but forceful, inescapable. Panic rising in his chest, Finn tried to twist around to speak to Adeef. "What do you want me for?" he shouted. "Why am I here?"

"You will see," Adeef replied, then strode away in the opposite direction.

Finn was led into a bath house, where small boys in loin cloths were slipping and sliding across a green-tiled floor playing a game with a lump of yellow soap. Older boys were standing around a large wooden tub, grinning. Before Finn could take in what was happening, the man behind him lifted him by the scruff of his neck and the seat of his trews and threw him into the tub.

Finn fell, face forward, fully clothed, into warm water. The water was deep. He surfaced gasping for breath. The small boys screamed with laughter and gathered around the tub. One threw in the soap. The giant placed a hand over Finn's head and thrust him under the water again. Finn resurfaced, spluttering. Then hands of every skin shade from blue-black to pink-white pushed him back down, again and again, until tiring of his near-drowning, some of the older youths jumped into the tub and began pulling off his clothes. His shirt tore in two as they yanked at the sleeves. Another two jumped in, to help with his boots and trews.

Finn fought back, but the boys won, and with a whoop of triumph, they sent the soggy trews out of the tub to slither across the wet floor. Two boys jumped out and more water was poured in, and something Finn had not seen before, a round, loaf-like shape that soaked up water and grew larger.

Fearing it was alive, Finn reached out to poke it, but a boy with long black curls reached it first, rubbed it over the soap and began to scrub Finn's face and chest. The sensation was not unpleasant, but far too personal. Finn grabbed the soft object and began scrubbing his body and then his legs and feet, removing weeks of brine, sweat and grime for himself.

Adeef appeared out of the steam. The older bath-house boys slid back against the tiled walls.

"Dress in these clothes," Adeef commanded.

A small slave held out a set of neatly folded clothing. The white-robed giant took a roll of thick linen from a shelf and moved to the tub. Finn climbed out of the murky water and dried himself, then dressed in the clothes: a pale blue, long-sleeved silk tunic over white pantaloons.

Finn slicked his long wavy hair off his face with hands whose nails shone pink for the first time in many weeks and couldn't keep from smiling. He felt better, better in himself – despite the surroundings and circumstances – than he had for a very long time. Possibly, ever.

The giant clicked his fingers, and another small slave produced a length of black ribbon. Finn tied back his hair and straightened his shoulders, enjoying the sensation of wearing silk next to his skin for the first time. There was no means of seeing his reflection, but he knew he looked good – tall, well-made... and barefoot.

The giant snapped his fingers. Rope-soled shoes were produced. Finn pushed in his feet. They were the right size but felt very strange. Then, accompanied by young men of his own age, he followed the giant out of the bathhouse. No neck-hold this time. But no chance of escape, either.

Finn was led through a maze of corridors, then up a wide, white marble staircase to stand before iron studded doors. Tall, red-turbaned guards flanked the doors, each holding a long spear across his body, as they had at the gates below. These spears were more ornamental, decorated with gold, but the points were bright steel and very sharp. One rapped at a door, which was immediately opened from the inside. The giant guided Finn into a high-ceilinged oval chamber and then released him, bowed low, and backed out. The doors were closed with a soft thud.

Finn stared around him in awe. The chamber, or temple, was magnificent. Better than anything he had described in even the most exotic of his tales. The floor was as broad as a summer meadow with a geometric mosaic in green, white and gold. At the far end of the oval space was a black marble dais. On the dais was a vacant, gem-studded throne and a purple velvet footstool.

A ray of light illuminated a green jade statue. He recognised the soft nature of the stone, for traders brought items carved from jade and marble and alabaster back to the Cold North from their adventures in Arabia, from the warm lands of the South and dangerous cities of the Far East. This, however, was larger than anything he had seen. A seated, stylised cat, its neck long, its head heart-shaped with neat little ears. Around the walls were other cat sculptures and statues, some of great felines with square jaws, some of house cats curled in sleep, some were stalking with a front paw raised, other, leaner felines were paused forever, low to the floor, ready to pounce.

Grand Visior Adeef entered from a side door. From another door, hidden behind the dais, entered a very fat, sallow-skinned man robed in white and gold. He was followed by a line of men-at-arms in red turbans and a group of women in embroidered floor-length gowns of pale, golden silk. The women and girls arranged themselves in order of height or age on either side of the throne. The obese man was clearly the emir or ruler.

Adeef made his obeisance, bowing low and then touching his forehead with one hand and his heart with the other. Moving to Finn's right, and using his left hand, Adeef propelled him to the centre of the chamber nearer the dais. For a very long moment there was absolute silence. It was broken by a low growl, a long, rumbling growl that sent a shiver down Finn's spine. A sleek-bodied feline lying across the dais raised its head and twitched its tail. This cat was not a statue. It was large, long, and covered in dark spots. And very much alive.

The creature studied Finn with unblinking amber eyes, then rose to its feet, stretched and sat upright at the king's knees like a house cat. Except it snarled, revealing fangs like a wolf. Worse than a wolf. The sight and sound turned Finn's guts to jelly. This was a creature to be feared. Yet, the soft-looking fat man on the dais was stroking its head. Finn watched the man's hand, wondering what talent or power the gods had gifted him to have command over such a creature.

Five human giants entered from a rear door and came to stand behind the emir and the women. Each wore baggy green pantaloons and silver-thread sleeveless jerkins. Their upper bodies were oiled; their chest and arm muscles bulged. Personal bodyguards, Finn assumed. As if any were needed with that great cat at the ruler's knee. Arms folded, they gazed across the room. The tableau on the dais looked complete, yet still nobody spoke.

Finn's gaze wandered to the women and girls arranged at an angle to the throne. The tallest two, wives perhaps, stood to either side of the emir. From eldest to youngest, each had fair or auburn hair and kept her hands clasped demurely at her waist. A latecomer, a young man, appeared at the door behind the dais. He had long, deep copper auburn hair. Something about him reminded Finn of Katranina.

It was not Katranina – how could it be? And this was a boy, a boy who caught Finn's gaze and acknowledged him with a small tilt of the head. Addressing the emir, the boy gestured at Finn and said something.

The emir beckoned Adeef to him. Adeef went to the dais, spoke a few words in the guttural language the guards used, and returned to Finn's side. "The Mighty Hammil says you are welcome in the High Alcazar of Barbalus."

"*Welcome!*" Finn spluttered. "I was captured."

"Tss," Adeef hissed, "show respect."

"But—" Finn started.

"Tss," Adeef hissed again, adding under his breath, "Pay attention!"

The Mighty Hammil spoke. His voice rumbled around the chamber, not unlike the great cat's growl, and Finn gulped, realising what Adeef was saying about 'respect.' "What's going to happen to me?" Finn gasped.

The side of Adeef's mouth twitched. "Listen and pay attention, you fool."

"My Grand Visior tells you to 'pay attention!'" The Mighty Hammil's voice rolled around the chamber again. Giving Finn a benevolent smile, he said, more quietly, "You are not a captive. If that is what you fear, you may leave, once you vow with your head, heart and soul to fulfil a task."

Finn gaped with astonishment. The Mighty Hammil was using the common language of the North. Wetting his lips, afraid, but not wanting to show it, Finn tried to sound positive and stronger than he probably looked. "And if I do not... vow to this task?" he replied.

"Then you will leave in another manner." The Mighty Hammil smiled as if it were amusing.

"What is this task?" Finn asked. Adeef rammed a sharp elbow into his ribs. "Sir. I mean, what is required of me, please, sir?" Finn croaked.

"Tell him, Visior," the Mighty Hammil commanded, then then beckoned the auburn-haired boy to his side and murmured in his ear. The boy saluted and marched away, then returned almost immediately with a ceramic bowl of sweetmeats or delicacies.

While this was happening, Adeef spoke directly to Finn in urgent, hushed tones. "The Mighty Hammil wishes you to locate the man known as the Northman of the Middle Sea – among other things."

Finn glanced at the great cat at the Mighty Hammil's feet. "And this Northman," he replied quietly, "does he have white hair?"

"He does."

"And is he a sea-raider?"

"He is. Do as asked and you will be safe."

As if prompted, the great spotted cat growled. A low, terrifying sound, and Finn thought that whether he did as he was asked or not, he was far from safe. "How is it you are so fluent in my language?" he whispered to Adeef.

"I travelled and traded in the North at one time, as did our Mighty Hammil before…" Adeef paused, "… the Mighty Hammil became what he is." His face was giving way to a private opinion, which was instantly replaced by a blank expression, Adeef continued, "Merchants travel and must learn many tongues and customs."

Finn studied the Grand Visior's profile: there was a story here. The emir had been a merchant who'd acquired enough power to rule an independent state. Finn wanted to know how, but as Adeef had indicated, this was not the moment. Instead, he said very quietly, "You know my language."

"From our dealings with Northmen. Yes, we have – used to have – a treaty whereby they respected our vessels and left us in peace for a percentage of each major cargo. The Mighty Hammil also has wives from the North, as you can see."

Despite his nerves and the sense of danger, Finn took it all in, wanting to ask about the treaty and why, if Adeef and the emir had knowledge of the North, they couldn't approach Goran the Volsung themselves. Instead, he said, "And when I find this sea-raider, what must I do?"

"You are to bring him here. I will discuss arrangements with you later. Go to the dais, bow low to the Mighty Hammil, touch the toe of his shoe and promise to fulfil this task. Then back out with your eyes on the floor."

The great spotted cat sniffed Finn's shaking hand as he reached towards the emir's silk slippers. Trying to stay calm, knowing it was unwise to show fear with any predator, Finn closed his eyes and prayed to Frigg that he should live to tell the tale, for this spotted cat was a skilled predator, of that he was sure. Trained, perhaps, to catch captives trying to escape.

The Mighty Hammil spoke a few more words in the language of the High Alcazar and waggled a plump, beringed hand. Adeef pulled Finn to his feet. "Thank the Mighty Hammil for supporting your quest."

"My quest? Who told you about that?" Finn gabbled.

"Tsss." Steel-strong fingers closed around Finn's neck. "Keep your eyes down."

"He is not a very fine specimen of a Volsung, Visior." The Mighty Hammil spoke over their heads. "We expected a warrior. We are disappointed."

Adeef hastened to the dais, disturbing the spotted cat's serenity. The cat yawned. Adeef took a pace backwards, speaking a few urgent and angry-sounding words to the emir, nonetheless. The Mighty Hammil took another long look at Finn and then, chin wobbling, nodded agreement and waved a be-ringed paw in dismissal.

Adeef clasped Finn's neck and together they reversed out of the chamber.

As Finn straightened and separated from the Visior's clasp, Adeef spluttered something that Finn mentally translated as 'stupid old fool'.

Chapter 15

Finn was conducted through the palace's many passages, politely this time, no gripping hand on his neck. As they walked, he tried to get information out of Adeef. "Why does the Mighty Hammil think Volsungs are warriors?" he asked.

"Because they were. There are sagas telling of their deeds." Adeef turned his head to see Finn's expression, "A Volsung slew a marauding dragon. Single-handed, according to the legend."

Finn caught his breath: did Adeef know he now possessed the sword that supposedly killed that dragon? "It's only a story, an ancient tale at that," Finn replied. "I recount it myself. Did I not mention I am a tale-maker? Just a humble wandering, feeble-bodied tale-maker, walking from village to village to earn a crust of bread. The Mighty Hammil is right to be disappointed. I am no warrior. I'm no use to you at all, really."

Adeef halted. "Feeble-bodied? I think not. Nor unintelligent."

"But look at me." Finn raised his arms in supplication, realising as he did so how his arm muscles now bulged from hauling on ropes and shifting cargo. Despite the meagre rations and scant sleep, he was no longer the scrawny-armed, puny youth who had scrounged shelter with his cousins every winter. Adeef would have seen this in the bath house, so there was no point in using that old excuse.

As they walked on down another brightly lit corridor, Finn considered how these two factors changed or affected his options. He was seen to belong to a legendary warrior clan, and he was no longer treated like the beardless youth who had boarded *Guillemot*. Despite still being as good as beardless, thanks to his very blond colouring, he wasn't going to sidle out of whatever task they had in mind for him in that way.

So, there were two basic alternatives – go along with what they wanted with good grace, then run or wriggle out of it at the first available moment; or agree and make life as difficult for them as possible so they ditched him. Except that might result in unpleasant consequences: death or a slave galley. Trying to decide on the lesser of the two evils, another thought struck him. "Grand Visior," he said clearly, "if you want me to do something for you, or the Mighty Hammil does, why did you capture me and treat me like a prisoner?"

"We lacked certainty. I was informed you—"

"Informed?" Finn halted. "Who informed you about me?"

"A visior has informers, spies. How else can we advise our rulers? Come along; yours is the next chamber. You have a charming view. The rooms are yours until we depart."

"*We* depart?"

Ignoring him, Adeef gestured to one of the guards who had been following them. The man stepped past them and opened the double doors to an opulent suite of rooms.

Finn had never seen such luxury. Floor to ceiling, the salon was decorated in scarlet and gold. Deeper red patterned rugs covered marble tiles and bright tapestries with geometric designs hung at the walls. The air was filled with a sweet, intoxicating scent Finn could not name. He crossed to the inner chamber. It contained an elaborately carved and satin-canopied bed. Apart from that, the room was bare. Finn went to a small door at the rear of the bed chamber. There was a wide window seat with a hole in it. He peered into the hole. It smelled like a cow shed. "Ah, that's what it's for."

Returning to the salon, Finn went to the window. The gentle sound of crooning drifted up or down or from around. "People keep a lot of pigeons here," he said absently.

"My Secret Service," Adeef replied from across the room. He had good hearing. "Pigeons are excellent couriers."

Finn did not understand what Adeef meant. He put his head against the iron bars to see better. "Why are there bars on the window, if I am not a prisoner?" he asked quietly.

"Windows are barred to keep out thieves."

"What sort of mad thief would climb all the way up here to steal from armed guards or the Mighty Hammil?"

"Is that a rhetorical question?" Adeef countered, re-arranging the flowers in a glass vase set on a gilded chest. They had petals like red and yellow turbans.

"Rhetorical?"

"A question that requires no answer. That being the case, I shall leave you to enjoy your new conditions. Farewell."

Finn raced across the room, skidded on a loose rug and grabbed Adeef's arm to right himself. "No! You said you'd tell me why I am here."

Adeef looked at Finn's hand on his arm. "Only the Mighty Hammil tells the Grand Visior what to do."

"Yes, sorry." Finn snatched away his hand and then placed himself between Adeef and the doorway. "But, please, you must see I need answers. Why am I here? How did you know I would even be in Berjer, or wherever we are?"

Adeef sighed and gestured at a divan. "Take a seat."

Finn sat. Adeef began to pace the room and then, speaking as he moved, he said, "The High Alcazar – which is where you are – has or had a treaty with Goran the Volsung whereby Goran would refrain from raiding our fleet, which sails from the Levant twice a year with rich cargoes of silk and spices. He also agreed to protect our vessels against other pirates, in return for our diplomatic protection *on his behalf* with the Byzantines and the emirate of Cordoba, both of whom would prefer to see Goran in a gaol, or under the ground, once and for all. Basically, Goran received a generous annual reward for protecting and not stealing our cargo shipments, and we protected him from his enemies – the people who owned the goods he pirated."

"That seems like a fair deal. If these people are powerful and his enemies."

"It worked well enough. Until his sea-rovers moved into the slave trade... " Adeef took a deep breath. "...and captured my daughter."

"For the slave market?" Finn was genuinely appalled.

"I assumed so, but then I learned she is still on Goran's island."

"Have you tried to ransom her?"

"Of course I have! But no price is high enough. I send emissaries and they return empty-handed. The last one did not return at all."

"He's called Ice-Heart, for a reason, then," Finn murmured.

Adeef turned and gave him a weak smile. Finn returned the smile and continued, "I'm very sorry about your daughter, but I don't see how I can help. I'm a nobody. Not even a proper Volsung, according to your emir." Finn suddenly looked up at Adeef. "Did your Mighty Hammil break the treaty because of your daughter? Or did Ice-Heart break it before?"

Adeef's eyebrows rose in surprise. "In this, you do not disappoint. I said you were not as unintelligent as you try to appear."

"I'm not trying," Finn sighed. "But really, did an effective arrangement, which is what it sounds like, fall apart because of this abduction?"

"Yes, is the short answer. Goran had also been taking more than his fair share of our goods before his men forgot themselves. Our cargoes became too tempting for him. I cannot be certain, but I doubt anyone acted without his say so."

"Ah, well, Northmen can be a bit flexible about rules and promises. Don't expect anything from them – us – me included – and you won't be disappointed. I'm a chip off the old block in that respect."

"That is precisely what I was hoping," Adeef replied.

Finn frowned. "What I'm saying is, that I'm no more to be trusted than Ice-Heart."

Adeef glared at Finn, unblinking, his brown eyes black with anger. "Don't try that ruse on me. I am not Grand Visior for being soft in the head."

Finn closed his eyes and tried to relax on the over-stuffed divan, waiting to be given his orders, his new Fate.

"My informers tell me," Adeef began, strolling back to the window, "that you are of special importance to Goran, whom you seem to know, is also named Ice-Heart."

"Hardly. He doesn't know I exist."

"Then it is time he acknowledges you."

"As a member of his clan? Oh, as a relative. For an exchange of prisoners. Pff, I doubt that'll work. I'm of no value to Ice-Heart."

"That is not what I was informed."

Finn scrunched up his face. "What? No, I mean who? Who told you that?"

"You did. A moment ago. You have just told me you are 'a chip off the old block'. Is that not true?" Adeef let his words hang in the air.

Finn shook his head. "No, no. I didn't mean that. If I were a clan leader's son, even a by-blow, or a nephew, I would have been treated a lot better than I was when I was a child."

"But you are a Volsung?" Adeef insisted, peering at him under hooded eyelids.

"I am *of* the Volsung clan, yes. There will be a family relationship to Goran somewhere in our line, but no more than that."

Making no reply, Adeef continued to peer at him. Eventually, he said, "Either way, my plan remains unchanged. We sail in a few days' time."

"How many is a few?" Finn asked quietly.

"Five, six, seven days... whenever I decide is best."

"But there's a trading knarr waiting for me in the harbour."

"I shall send word: they need not wait," Adeef replied and left the chamber.

Finn's head began to spin. What did these people know that he didn't? Who had told them he was looking for Ice-Heart?

On the other hand, if this was a way out of the High Alcazar, he'd go along with it, and, as in Plan A, run or wriggle out of it at the first opportunity. As long as he was near the harbour. He knew enough about boats now to steal something small and row down the coast. Except they'd catch him, of course.

Unless he could get to the harbour before Seavogel left. Hope re-entered Finn's thinking. He slipped off the divan and began pacing the room as Adeef had done. Maybe, if he was a *favoured prisoner,* he could get outside for some exercise later, or early tomorrow, and find a way out. He re-crossed the long room to see if his door was locked, bolted or barred. It wasn't, but there was an armed guard outside. Finn gave him a feeble smile and closed the door and then sank to his knees with relief; his smelly old travel pack was there on the floor.

Undoing the drawstrings, Finn pushed his right hand into the sack. The sword was still there. A sword, anyway.

Joy was instantly replaced with doubt – had they replaced Doomsong with another weapon? Finn tugged the sack open, removed the harness and gently eased the weapon from its sheath. No golden pommel glowed; no bright, rune-run blade shimmered. Fearing the worst, Finn lifted it to the light. The grip began to warm in his hands. Hints of colour rippled down the blade then faded again. Finn stared at it, grinning with relief. It was the same ugly, rusty old thing he seen before, shorter than any warrior's blade should be, but this was Doomsong, entrusted to him by Master Odo until he could find its True Owner.

The rightful owner, leader of the Volsung clan. Unbidden, a fragment of the last conversation floated into his mind. 'My cousins would have told me'... *or would they?* Finn wondered. Was this why Tait and Augal had bullied and teased him, fed him the scraps from their plates? Not because he was an orphan, but because one day he might be more important than they were? Was this why Master Odo had chosen him to find Goran?

The idea lifted Finn's mood, filled him with excitement, anticipation, hope, then dropped him hard on the sharp stones of reality. *If* – and it was only an 'if' – he were closely related to Goran, that was precisely why Tait and Augal had treated him so badly, because Goran named Ice-Heart had abandoned them – his clan. Goran, *and his relatives*, had no right to expect preferential treatment. Goran, as Ice-Heart, commanded respect only among low-life pirates and slavers. And if the hints dropped by Harp-Legs were true, Ice-Heart had also abandoned his chosen woman and her child.

Finn tucked Doomsong back into the sack, pulled the drawstrings tight and hugged it to his chest as another link in his chain of reasoning clicked horribly into place.

Adeef's prisoner exchange was not going to be successful because Finn was of no importance to Ice-Heart, no value to anyone. As Tait and Augal had made so very plain. Unless he completed the task Master Odo had set him. Which he couldn't do as Adeef's prisoner. So, the sooner he got away from the High Alcazar, the better.

Chapter 16

Finn's next meal was a good deal better than barley bread and water. It arrived on a huge brass tray. Chilled soup made with crushed almonds, a platter of cold chicken, and a wooden dish of green leaves and brown seeds that Finn could not identify. There was a variety of decorated sweet pastries. The tray, which appeared to be bigger than the boy carrying it, was set upon the table. The boy emerging from under it was bony, with thick brown hair cut with the help of a pudding basin. He was no more than ten or eleven years old.

Finn glanced at the open door behind him, wondering if it was worth a try. "Don't even try," the boy said in the common language of the North. "There's a guard by the door, another on the stairs, and two in the patio. Adeef has put sentries all the way down to the gates. You've got a decent meal here, though." He held out a hand palm upwards and waggled his fingers.

"You want payment?" Finn queried.

"Money, coins, a small token of your gratitude. I put extra pastries on that plate." He reached across the table, selected a delicacy and gobbled it down. "Delicious," he mumbled, cheeks bulging with minced dates in honey.

"I don't have any money," Finn said. "I had a purse, but that was taken when I was captured, which is odd – they left me my travel pack and…" Finn winced at his foolishness, "… my clothes."

"Pity," the boy said, selecting a larger pastry. "I was hoping we could do a little business together."

Finn laughed. "You're a bit young for that."

"I'm small, but quite old." The boy looked Finn in the eye and added slowly in a deeper voice, "And I'm *very* clever."

"I'm sure you are. You know my language, for a start."

"Oh, everyone knows that. This place is full of Northmen, and women, of course. My mother's mother was born in the Cold North."

"Really? Why is she here, and the women I saw with the emir?"

The boy shrugged, "Cuz they are good-looking and strong, I suppose."

"But they are thralls?"

"Thralls?"

"Captives, slaves."

"Oh, yes. We all are, one way or another."

Finn digested this information along with a tasty bit of chicken and let the boy prattle on.

"Anyway, they use the language of the North, and if you want to keep on their good side, chatting to women about personal matters in their own tongue goes a long way."

Finn smiled at 'personal matters,' a tactic that had kept him fed and warm during many treks across frozen land. "So, if you are all enthralled, why do you need payment? What can you do with coin in this place?"

"Trade. I run a business: buying and selling, and lending, of course."

Finn sat down at the table and sampled the chilled soup. "Buying and selling what?"

"Secrets, mostly."

The soup bowl halted in mid-air. "You mean, you learn secrets, and sell them?"

"Correct." The boy folded his arms across his chest in an accomplished imitation of Adeef and adopted a nonchalant stance, swaying slightly from side to side. "Personal and bath-house trifles come free, usually. Sometimes I pay for more private details. Sometimes I steal useful bits of evidence," he drawled with a slow wink. "I'm quick on my feet, and I know all the hidden passages, so I can get in and out of chambers pretty fast when I have to."

"That's handy. Given that I am in need of coin and erm – a favour – myself. Is there a secret I can trade with you?" Finn was only half joking. If the boy knew of hidden passageways, perhaps he knew a way out of the Alcazar. "What's your name, by the way?"

"Zongolo Elzebar Ulf Chervary y Bragi. I was a little prince until I was captured."

"Of course you were. You look exactly like a little prince."

The boy's eyes narrowed. "Some people call me Zongo, but only the people I like. And you are Finn."

"Yes. I won't bother to ask how you know that."

"You should! That's the reason I'm here."

"Buying or selling?"

Zongolo grinned. "I was selling, but you've got no coin. Shame."

He started to leave. Finn set down his cup and reached out to him. "Wait. I need to know something important. I can't pay for it now, but I'll find a way to reward you somehow."

Zongolo made a drama of placing a finger to his lips, tiptoeing to the open door and poking his head round it, then tiptoeing back to stand as close as he could to Finn. "You want to know why the Mighty Hammil wants you to find a pirate?" he whispered.

"Yes."

"He doesn't."

Finn raised an eyebrow. "Ah. But the Grand Visior has told him he does?"

"Coo, you're nearly as quick as I am."

"Hmm." Finn drummed the edge of the polished table. "So Adeef is in control here."

"Tsss!" Zongolo hissed. "The Mighty Hammil will have your head for treason at insult like that."

"But Adeef *is in control* of what happens to me?" Finn said quietly.

"Yes. And the next bit I tell you is worth your weight in gold."

Finn wanted to laugh but the words sent a chill down his spine. "Go on."

"If Adeef doesn't get what he wants, you'll be eliminated. That'll be Adeef's favourite assassin's job."

Finn gulped. "Assassin? You mean people who kill...?"

"Don't tell me you don't know about trained assassins?" Zongolo rolled his eyes. "'Fur-skinned asses with axes' they call Northmen here."

Finn ignored him. The information was no more than he'd worked out for himself, but knowing he'd be in Adeef's galley with one or more trained assassins made his heart pound. He closed his eyes, "All-father protect me, I'm done for."

"Probably," Zongo responded, selecting another pastry.

Finn's mind began to race. Master Odo had sent him to the Middle Sea to find Goran the Volsung to save his people from starving, meaning that Finn couldn't risk losing his own life before he found Goran, and he couldn't risk Goran getting killed by Adeef's assassins, either. Which, even if the exchange of prisoners was successful, was probably what the Might Hammil and/or Adeef had in mind as revenge for breaking their treaty and/or capturing a beloved daughter.

Zongolo prodded Finn in the shoulder. "What you going to give me, then?"

Jerked back to the moment, Finn thumped the table, suddenly very decisive: he needed to get out of the Alcazar, and fast. What had he got that would purchase information about secret passageways? He had no secrets to sell. Nothing of any value apart from Doomsong, which he could never trade. He shook his head, giving in to despair, "I've nothing to offer you."

Zongolo studied him. Two dark, calculating eyes in a child's face. "There is something," he said quietly, glancing meaningfully at the open door. "You must promise to take me with you."

"Oh! Oh, all right. I'll tell Adeef I want you as – as what – a body servant?" Finn smiled at the boy. "Would that do?"

Zongolo leaned in closer to whisper something, but as he did so, the ginger cat trotted into the room and leapt onto Finn's lap, purring so loudly Finn couldn't hear what the boy was saying.

Finn gently pushed the cat off his knees, and she began to wind in and out of his legs, purring louder than a hive of bees.

Zongolo said something louder, and Finn looked up. "What did you say? Treasure?"

"Hammil isn't bothered about Perla – the girl. Or the treaty. He wants Ice-Heart's treasure *and his island*. To increase Barbalus's power and territory." Zongolo kicked a rope-soled sandal at the cat to shut her up.

"Don't do that!" Finn put out his hand to protect the cat. "You'll hurt her."

The open door slammed against the wall. A guard filled the frame and jabbered something. Zongolo left without another word and the cat slipped out behind him.

Zongolo returned to collect the empty tray later in the day. "I can get us out of here," he whispered urgently, rearranging the plate and bowl with a noisy clatter on the tray's metal surface.

Finn's eyes lit up, "You can? How? When?"

"Sentries change their shifts at sunrise, we'll get out at dawn while they're changing the guard. They always stop for a chat. We can slip by them then."

"But that means there'll be double the number of guards ready to grab us."

"Not if they don't see us. Not if you're dressed like a servant and we go down with the laundry."

Finn's excitement cooled. "You don't need to take risks on my behalf."

"We had a deal, remember? You take me with you. You'll need me to guide you, anyway."

"Yes but..." There was truth in that, but even assuming this Zongolo could acquire a servant's outfit it didn't sound like much of a plan.

Finn bit his lip, did he need to risk more trouble, given that he'd be leaving soon anyway? And — now he thought about it — might it not be easier to get away from Adeef in the harbour? Beorn Wolfman might be there, and he was good with a sword. Finn bit his lower lip harder; was it Beorn's voice he'd heard when he was thrown into the hut? The doubt made him reject any hope of Beorn lending a hand. Even if *Guillemot* had sailed without him, though, he could get a passage on a boat returning to the North.

An image of a one-eyed Wanderer with a wide-brimmed blue hat pulled over his face flashed into his mind. No, he couldn't do that. He'd agreed to fulfil an important, very important task for someone who nobody would ever dare disobey, not if they even half-guessed the Wanderer's real identity. If Adeef was to be feared, Master Odo was to be dreaded.

Finn looked at the boy, shifting from foot to foot, waiting for an answer. Another thought occurred to him. "Zongolo –"

"Call me Zongo, it's quicker."

"Zongo, if you know a way out, why are you still here?"

"Because!" the boy hissed angrily. Then, changing his tone to a childish whine, he said, "Because I can't chance it on my own. I'm only little, you see, and there are wolves and bears up in the hills."

"But if you're all captives here, you could rebel together. Start a revolution."

"We aren't *all* captives. Some are Hammil's children and grandchildren or nephews and nieces being trained to set up other Alcazars. Some servants are happy here. And the guards are treated all right; some even like it."

"But you don't?"

"No, I've got a future. I'm going to be rich and have a big house of my own, and I can't do that if I'm a servant, even if I was born here."

"I thought you said you were a prince."

"So?" Zongo challenged. "What's that to you? I might be. My mother could be a princess from the North, or somewhere else. My father's a sentry. I don't want to end up like him. Not when I see Hammil's shipmen bringing in silks and precious gems and lovely things from foreign places."

"Shipmen? Do you mean traveling merchants?"

"Not merchants, like those who buy and sell. Shipmen go on ships and bring..." He shrugged his shoulders. "...things back. For the Mighty Hammil. And his wives, and family."

"Well, there's your answer: wait until you're older and become a shipman."

"It's not allowed. Servant and sentry class aren't allowed to leave or better themselves, and the goods that come in aren't traded, so I won't get any coin from it. Besides, Hammil sells difficult children. I have to be careful."

Finn gaped at him. "Children are sold? Then we should try to get as many out as possible."

"Far too risky. Kids talk, gossip. They're all stupid."

"Perhaps once we're out we can find a way to release the children here. Find someone to help us and—"

"Yes, yes, good idea," Zongo replied, far too fast.

Clearly, Zongolo would say anything to get what he wanted. Finn liked him less and less, but he was offering a way out of captivity, or something far worse. "All right," he said, "what have I got to do?"

"Nothing much. Be ready before sunrise. I'll bring the clothes. Then you just follow me."

Zongo left the room with a spring in his step, carrying the tray, but Finn felt none of his excitement. Moving to the open window, he noticed the ginger cat on the tiled sill. She gave every appearance of having overheard and understood their conversation.

"Hey, cat," Finn said, but as he reached through the bars to stroke her, she arched her back and hissed at him.

Chapter 17

At sunrise the next day, Zongolo entered Finn's suite with a mop and bucket, slopping water at every step. Leaving the door open, he began to swing the soaking mop from side to side over the marble tiles from the entrance inwards until the salon floor was awash with soapy water. Finn watched in silence through the open bedchamber door. The boy and his bucket eventually reached the end of his bed. Turning to stand with his back to the connecting door, Zongolo kicked out a foot behind him to close it, then, placing a finger to his lips first, he began pulling items of clothing from under his voluminous white blouse. "Put these on over what you've got," he whispered. "It'll be chilly up on the hill."

"Up on the hill? I need to go down to the harbour, not hike up a hillside."

"We'll get there; trust me," Zongo said, magicking a pair of scruffy rope-soled shoes from the waist of his pantaloons.

Finn dressed in the silken finery of the previous day, then pulled Doomsong from under his pillow and strapped on his shoulder harness.

Zongolo's eyes lit up. "A weapon! A sword! But don't use it; that'll get us both killed."

Finn bit his tongue, pulled the white blouse over the sheath and his silk tunic, then stepped into the baggy,

146

unbleached linen pantaloons. "Guards will see me for miles wearing all this stuff," Finn said.

"Do you want to get out of here or not?" Zongo snapped, stamping a foot.

"Yes," Finn replied, although he was having serious doubts. He had never slept in such a wonderful bed. Never imagined such luxury.

"You've got to look like a servant. This is what we wear in the kitchens. Guards don't notice slaves and servants."

"But they might this time."

"Worst that'll happen to me is a thrashing. My father's a sentry."

"And me?"

"That's your look out. I'll say it was your idea, anyway."

Trying not to fumble with nerves, Finn tied the cord of the pantaloons into a double knot. "All right, now what?"

"Start mopping the floor backwards the way I came in. Keep your head down. When you're through the main door carry on mopping backwards as far as the second set of steps, then pick up the bucket and go down to the laundry yard. I can make some excuse and nip into the laundry." Zongolo quickly removed Finn's bedcovers and bundled the sheets into his arms so high that nobody could see his face.

Finn was nearly at the entrance to his suite with mop and bucket when Zongolo squeaked, "Stop! Wait!"

"What?" Finn mouthed across the salon.

The boy began tapping his head. "Your hair!"

Finn nodded and began to pull his loose hair over his face, but then realised what Zongolo was afraid of. Dropping the mop with a worrying clack on the marble floor, he tiptoed back to his bed chamber for his travel pack. "It's all right," he whispered, poking around for a roll of white cloth that he'd borrowed from Tait's wife's sewing basket, thinking it might serve for bandages, should he be injured on his travels. Close to nervous laughter, he wound the fabric around his head and tucked the end under his left ear.

"That's a rubbish turban," Zongolo grinned. Then squeaked again as Finn hefted his travel pack over his shoulder. "You can't take that!"

Finn scowled, this was not going well, and they hadn't left his chamber. With an angry sigh, he dropped his only remaining possession and returned to the mop and bucket. "Come on," he whispered, "let's go."

"All right, but if the guard on duty says anything to you, give him a stupid grin. Don't speak." Not waiting for a response Zongolo led the way out of Finn's chambers, just as a guard appeared at the end of the passage to replace the sentry on Finn's door.

The two men greeted each other with a joke, ignoring the servant who mopped around their feet and the boy carrying dirty linen down to the laundry. Once down the steps and in the yard, Zongolo dropped his bundle by accident and took his time picking it up, waiting for Finn, who had never mopped a floor in his life, to reach him.

The moment Finn's feet touched the last step, Zongolo hissed, "This way," and hurried into a very narrow alley. "Leave the bucket here," he said, "and stick the mop handle across the gap."

Finn wedged the sodden mop head and the long handle across the entrance to the alley while Zongolo stuffed the sheets into the bucket.

"Now what?" Finn asked.

"Now, we run!"

Zongo was fast on his feet and nifty at taking turns in a maze of alleys. Jogging at a good pace, they soon arrived at a large shell-shaped basin fed by a mountain spring. Above the ornamental spout there was a door the shape and size of the base of a barrel. Zongo scrambled up into the basin, pulled open the round door, and being small, wriggled straight in.

Finn hesitated. Being much taller and broad-shouldered from weeks at sea as an oarsman, it was going to be a very tight squeeze. But if this led to one of the secret passageways the boy had mentioned, it was worth a try.

The doorway disguised the entrance to a natural water chute in the smooth rockface. Putting his head and shoulders into total darkness, Finn halted and nearly backed out.

"Come along," Zongo's young voice called from above. "This tunnel leads into the hill."

Lacking an alternative, Finn levered himself upwards on his elbows, getting very wet in the process. After a few moments he said, "This is madness. We're going up a stream, not down a hill."

"There's an opening further up, come on."

Finn had no option but to follow. Turning around was impossible, and slithering back down with the water seemed foolish, so he carried on, levering himself upwards, using his feet like a frog.

Eventually, the tunnel opened, and daylight lit a narrow ravine. Rocks stretched up on both sides, so high Finn now had to stand sideways and crab-step his way up the hillside. "This is madness," he repeated. "We shouldn't be going *upwards.*"

Zongolo was too far ahead to hear him. Not, Finn thought, that anything he said would make a difference. The boy was using him as a means of making his own escape.

The ravine suddenly widened, and the sun burst out from between dark clouds. Finn waited until his eyes adjusted to the bright light, and then continued sideways along a ledge no wider than his feet, on a cliff face above steeply sloping, open terrain. Leaning his back against the damp rock wall, Finn tried not to look down. It was a sheer drop, and the ledge felt very smooth beneath his well-worn rope-soled shoes. Side-step by shuffling side-step, he edged along the open section onto a wider ledge, then onto a stretch of stony ground.

To his surprise, Zongolo was waiting for him at the start of a goat track. "This way, I think," the boy said, beckoning Finn to follow him.

"You 'think'?" Finn was furious.

"Well, I've never done this before, have I? Obviously!"

"Obviously," Finn sneered, although he did feel a minor sense of relief that he wasn't alone.

The track led through a rabbit-nibbled clearing with lichen covered boulders and clumps of sharp-bladed grass. Lightning split the sky, sending a blue streak through gathering clouds. A long way below, and many leagues across country, Finn could see the sea. Thunder rumbled overhead, reminding him of the great spotted cat at the Mighty Hammil's feet and why, whatever happened, he would never return to the Alcazar, if he could help it. Zongolo sprinted on ahead, following an animal track, and disappeared behind high clumps of broom and stunted trees.

Trying to keep up, Finn stumbled over a bare strip of quartz and fell to his knees. As he got to his feet, a heavy grey cloud obscured the morning sun and a deep, male voice said, "Quite dramatic, isn't it?"

Adeef was perched on a large, square-shaped boulder, not ten paces away. "Fitting weather for a boys' adventure," he drawled as they approached, "or one of your interminable northern sagas, but convenient timing. My plans have been moved forward. We need to go down to the harbour."

The 'we' evidently included Adeef's men-at-arms, each bearing a long, curved sword, who were standing around the sheltered plateau – waiting. Horrified, terrified, Finn reached over his shoulder to pull Doomsong from under the servant blouse. The men-at-arms took a step closer.

"A brave attempt," said Adeef, "but pointless, like your blade. You'd better sharpen that iron stick if you intend to use it as a weapon. Not that it will ever serve against trained men with quality steel blades. Not here, anyway."

"I could stab you in the heart," Finn retorted, stung by the truth.

"And stay alive for two beats more of your own? Possibly. Assuming your blade can break the threads of my shirt."

"I knew trying to escape was foolish," Finn sighed.

"It demonstrates a certain determination, which is no ill thing."

Catching sight of Zongolo, frozen in the act of running like a scared rabbit, Finn was tempted to say it was the boy's determination not his, but Adeef forestalled him. "Put it away," he said, indicating the iron stick in Finn's hand. "You won't need it. Yet."

Finn gazed at the dull weapon, relieved yet disappointed that it did not glow in his hands, then lifted it over his shoulder and tucked it, with some difficulty, back into its sheath.

Adeef watched with folded his arms. His thin lips sliced a smile for the merest instant. "Sit down, Finn of the Volsung. Get your breath back," he said, pointing to a vacant boulder.

Finn slumped down on the rock, then eased his shoulders and neck, which were stiff after squeezing up the water pipe like a rat.

"Better?" Adeef asked. Finn nodded. "Good, now, start to finish, tell me how you got to Berjer."

"To Berjer?" Finn was surprised by the question. "I was on a trading knarr called *Guillemot*," he began slowly, searching for a means to omit any reference to Master Odo, which even on a mountain top in a thunderstorm sounded fantastical, even to a life-long tale-maker. Or could he use that? The fact that he invented wild adventures, and was now attempting to live one for himself? That might work as an excuse. Except Adeef wanted to know about the voyage from the North, not the hike up the hill.

Making no reference to what had happened in The Old Salvation, Finn recounted the bare facts of his voyage, leaving out any mention of dragons (which he might have imagined) or slithering Grendels (which had definitely been real). "Shipmaster Seavogel put in at Berjer to trade, and I came ashore to have a look around." At this point he went very quiet, reliving the short time he was on the quayside, buying a basket and fruit.

"Is there something else you want to tell me?" Adeef inquired.

"Yes. No. Possibly." In his mind's eye, or his mind's ear, Finn could hear a voice outside the hut where he'd been dumped by his captors – Beorn Wolfman's voice. Was this relevant? Was Beorn connected to the High Alcazar? There were plenty of people from the North there. Was he sure it was Beorn, though? No. "I came ashore," he ended lamely, "and I was captured by your men and brought up here."

"And was that a neatly plotted means to infiltrate the High Alcazar, or a fortunate mistake?"

"A fortunate mistake!" Finn leapt off the boulder and stood straight and tall. "I'm on an important voyage to... do something important. I don't have time for diversions or nasty, time-consuming interruptions like this." Finn hoped his tone was sharp and sarcastic. "Why would I even want to enter the High Alcazar?"

"I can think of various reasons, but then, I am an experienced spymaster," Adeef responded. Standing up, he slowly paced around the boulders and then in one quick action, clasped Zongolo by an ear. Leaning very close to the pinched ear, he whispered loud enough for Finn to hear, "Is there anything *you* should tell me, boy?"

Zongolo gulped. "No. I only do – did – what I was told."

"But you fancied a 'diversion,' a change of air."

"I – I – I was only doing what I was told, Grand Visior." Zongo's voice was squeakier than usual.

Adeef released the child and returned to his pacing, then swiveled around in front of Finn, "Do you still intend to find Goran the Volsung?"

Unsure if or when he'd mentioned this to anyone in the Alcazar before being presented to the Mighty Hammil, Finn mumbled, "Yes, if I can."

"Yet, you do not wish to help us renew our treaty with him, or..." the fierce looking visior spoke as if they were exchanging pleasantries over a mug of ale. "...the other matter I mentioned? May I ask why?"

"Because you – or I – might not find him. If I do not find him, or he avoids me when I'm on my own, that is one thing, I simply sail back to the North...." He bit back the words 'without him.' "But if your planned exchange fails, and he doesn't want me, and you don't either..."

"A possibility, yes. And sound reasoning. Might you consider returning to me in the High Alcazar, if, as you fear, he rejects you?"

Astonished, Finn blurted a single word. "Why?"

"Because young people with thinking skills are not easy to find."

Finn blinked, uncertain how to react.

"No matter." Adeef flicked a hand. "Keep it in mind, though. As an option. If you survive."

As Adeef spoke, an eagle screamed high above the hilltop. Finn looked up. The sky was clearing as the storm moved on. Was it Skiila? Had she found him? His face muscles relaxed with relief.

Adeef followed his gaze. "Eagles. There are many in this area. They have extraordinary eyesight. My hunting birds can detect the smallest prey leagues above the ground. Remember that, boy," he added sharply, turning to Zongolo.

Shading his eyes, Finn scanned the sky. A local bird, or Skiila?

Ignoring him, Adeef went to the edge of the plateau and studied the hillside below, then signaled to his men, who sheathed their weapons. Beckoning with a very similar action he said, "Come along, Finn of the Volsungs, there is a fine vessel waiting for us in the harbour. No point returning to the High Alcazar now."

Finn looked around, wondering if Zongolo had managed to run off. He hadn't. A guard had him suspended above the ground by the scruff of his neck.

"Let the little rat return the way he came," Adeef said, referring to Zongo's limp form. "He's served his purpose."

Listening to Zongolo whining about rough treatment, Finn had to accept that Kat had been right about his willingness to be taken in. He'd let a smart-talking child convince him it would be easy to escape. It had to stop, if it wasn't already too late.

Instead of heading back to the water chute or making his way back to the Alcazar by an easier route, though, Zongolo fell into line behind Finn, as one of Adeef's guards led the way down the hillside.

"What are you doing?" Finn asked over his shoulder in a low voice.

"Coming with you."

"As Adeef's spy? I don't think so."

"I can be your body servant."

"You're loopy if you think that," Finn scoffed.

"Maybe. But I'm still clever."

Chapter 18

The track through wide-topped pine trees zig-zagged down the eastern face of the hill. The short-lived rainstorm had released a thousand odours topped by the warm barley-malt scent of damp summer grass. On any other occasion, it would have been a very pleasant morning. Sunlight filtered through the canopy; birds hopped unseen among branches protesting at the invasion of their territory. Finn stayed alert for any sign of a goat or badger track crossing their path, where he might risk making a run for it, but soon gave up. Adeef's men would find him within minutes and it could only make things worse than they already were.

A stocky guard, born and bred in the area, if not the Alcazar, led them around the hill to the southern slope, then onto another path that curved among well-tended olive terraces down to an old Roman road, where a cart and a lot of armed men were waiting. This time, Finn was seated between Adeef and the driver, not thrown in like a sack of turnips. Zongolo nipped over the back board, unnoticed or ignored, to hang on as best he could. The rest of the journey down to the harbour was conducted in silence.

Adeef's escort halted on the quay beside a high-sided galley, twice the size and far more sophisticated than Seavogel's knarr. Finn climbed out of the cart, trying to see if *Guillemot* was still in the harbour, but Adeef guided him by the neck towards a gangplank too quickly to see anything at all.

"It's beautiful," Finn murmured looking up at the galley. He had spent much of his youth crossing to and from islands and the mainland in the grey Baltic Sea; he'd mixed with mariners on short voyages and in taverns, but he'd never heard tell of anything like this. A white-garbed, red-turbaned crew lined the rails, awaiting orders.

"Welcome to *Gliding Swan,*" said Adeef, releasing Finn from his grip at the base of the gangplank. "She is named for my first wife. A little more poetic than *Guillemot,* don't you think?"

"I suppose so. But I can't go aboard. I *have to* get back to *Guillemot.* I'm sorry about your daughter, but honestly, truly, I do have a very important task to complete."

Adeef raised a warning finger. "Your cargo tub waits no longer. Word was sent."

Finn's heart sank. "No, please. It's difficult enough. Shipmaster Seavogel has a cargo to sell, and he's supposed to be helping me. I think."

"That is no longer your concern," Adeef snapped. "We sail earlier than I planned, thanks to your foolishness, but *Swan* is ready. Always ready. Please, go aboard."

Curious onlookers were gathering to see why guards from the High Alcazar were on the quay. Finn stared about him, hoping Seavogel was among them. Anyone. Even Katranina. But there were no friendly faces. Then he saw someone vaguely familiar. An angular youth in bright clothing was lighting juggling torches. It was very early in the day for harbour-workers and merchants to pause for entertainment, but what drew Finn's attention was how the torches were being lit. The colourful youth was breathing on them.

Looking across the gathering crowd, the juggler caught Finn's eye and sent a bright blue flame into the air.

Finn gasped. This meant something. A message. A signal. What?

Then a voice in his head said, 'not what – *why*?'

Without another thought, he was pushing through the crowd, ducking and diving beneath wicker trays of pastries, around stubborn mules and nippy donkeys, between fishwives with baskets, under a rope and over a barrel, then in and out and around everyone and everything a second time, but not once, in all his dash, did he see the fire-breather again.

A small boy with brown hair grabbed his shirt. "Where you going?" he demanded. Zongolo. In the moment Finn halted to shake the little traitor from his sleeve, the fire juggler stepped out of the crowd, right in front of him, and sent a whoosh of flames directly at Finn's face. Finn jumped backwards just in time to save himself.

No friendly faces in this crowd; quite the opposite. Finn ducked down, doubled over and tried to hide behind a mule-cart. He'd rushed into another foolish mistake, and now he needed to rush out of it, fast.

But *why*? Katranina was right, as always, why had someone – and not for the first time – tried to harm him?

Somebody grabbed him from behind. Finn's heart nearly stopped. A large, calloused hand grasped the back of his neck. An Alcazar man-at-arms. Offering no resistance, Finn was propelled along the quay to be dropped at the Grand Visior's feet like a dead rabbit.

Saying nothing, the Grand Visior snapped his fingers at a guard behind him, then signaled to others to block any means of escape. Finn watched as if it were happening to another person. His only chance of getting away was to dive into the water. But he couldn't swim.

As Finn boarded the *Gliding Swan*, Zongolo jogged up the gangplank behind them, causing Adeef to swing round with a curse. "Not you, brat!" A guard grabbed Zongo by the scruff of the neck.

"I'm Finn's servant," Zongo whined. "You said, Master. You said I was to stay with him."

Angry, Finn turned, and started to laugh at the boy squirming like a puppy in the huge guard's hand, but then saw his pleading expression and stopped. Whatever, whoever Zongolo was – and he was an irritating traitor – he wanted to escape the Alcazar for a sound reason. Uncertain how to react, not wanting his company but not wanting him to suffer, Finn finally glimpsed a familiar face on the quay.

"Beorn!" Finn waved from the high deck. "They're taking me somewhere." He stuck out his arms and placed his wrists together as if shackled, hoping Beorn would get the message. Hoping Beorn would stride up the plank like a seasoned warrior and rescue him. Instead, Beorn shuffled backwards and disappeared from view.

"Enough!" Adeef hissed at Finn. Turning to a guard, he said, "Take him to his cabin, and lock him in."

Finn was dragged up a broad, highly polished companionway to the upper stern deck, then shoved into a cabin barely larger than Norna Silveryarn's hut. As the door shut behind him, he gasped in surprise. Fine panelling lined the bulkhead around a narrow bed. Daylight from a round window lit a brass ewer and wash basin set upon a shelf. His berth was compact, but a hundred times more comfortable than Norna Silveryarn's.

Finn removed his servant garb and unstrapped the harness holding Doomsong. Pulling the short sword from its sheath, he raised it to the light and watched as a thin ray of sunshine caught the golden sun on the pommel. He let out a whoop of joy. There was magic in the sword after all. Doomsong knew how and when to disguise itself. A blunt old iron stick, Adeef had called it. Hah! Some stick!

Once out of the harbour and into deep water, Finn was escorted to a table under a canopy. Shading his eyes from the glaring sun, he looked out to sea, hoping to catch a glimpse of a squat trading knarr with a black-varnished bird's head. The only boats out in the water looked like local fishermen, so he went to the top of the stern companionway to study the galley. Not as tall as the trireme he had seen in the harbour on arrival, *Gliding Swan* nevertheless had three decks and deep holds under bow and prow, where, no doubt, captives could be kept in chains.

The Grand Visior was on the main deck talking to a short man who, Finn thought, might be the galley's captain. Adeef had said the *Gliding Swan* was his, but obviously he was not the captain or *skipper*, as they said in the North. Below the main deck were rows of oarsmen. Who, Finn feared, he would be joining if they didn't locate Ice-Heart, or if Adeef's trained assassin didn't get him first.

According to what he'd heard from sea travelers in Baltic taverns, oarsmen on warships weren't chained, so they could fight for their master if they were boarded by an enemy or pirates. It meant they had a chance to escape in a skirmish, except their outcome would be to row for the raiders or drown.

Gliding Swan's elegant form, her polished rails and decks, screamed the word 'prize,' although she had three masts with triangular sails, which would make her hard to follow in a good wind.

Adeef beckoned Finn to join him.

"She is a beautiful vessel, is she not?" he said, as Finn came to his side.

"She is," Finn responded, deciding to be polite and find out if they were heading directly for Goran's island. Before he could ask, however, a cat crossed the deck, and instead of saying anything sensible, Finn said, "You have cats aboard."

"Of course. Fat cats mean a clean ship."

"Is that why there are so many cats in the High Alcazar?"

Adeef's greying eyebrows lifted in surprise. "Are you also a cat-worshiper?"

"A cat-worshiper? Hardly. Where I come from, cats get turned into hats and mittens. Especially ginger ones. Who worships cats?"

"Many people in the Land of Pyramids." Adeef pointed eastward over the starboard rail. "They revere cats there. Cats are an important part of their daily life, and death. Why do you ask?"

Adeef's arm movement had caused the sleeve of his embroidered blouse to roll up. There was a small knife strapped above his wrist. Finn noticed the knife, then remembered hearing that a pyramid was a funeral mound and regretted asking the question, if the answer led in that direction. "Just curious," he said. "It's not important."

"On the contrary," Adeef's thin lips became a tight slit. "It was perceptive of you." He turned to study Finn's profile, then tapped the rail as if he had come to a decision. "Apart from the Mighty Hammil's leopard, what makes you think you saw cats *inside* the High Alcazar? Or are you referring to the strays kept to kill vermin in the street?"

Finn gave an embarrassed shrug. "I have an over-active imagination. I am a tale-maker: I often see and hear things differently from how other... people see them."

Adeef rubbed his angular, blue-shadowed chin with long fingers. "You were not aware of this feline influence at the High Alcazar beforehand?"

"Before I was captured? No. I'd never heard of the Alcazar."

"The *High* Alcazar," Adeef corrected. "There are other Barbalus Alcazars on the Middle Sea. Berjer is the first and principal fortress, so it is called the High Alcazar. The Mighty Hammil's mother was from the Land of Pyramids. She was said to be like a cat."

"Like a cat? How?" Finn asked.

"She had grace, poise, she could be affectionate, but only with her family. And utterly ruthless. Vicious even. The Revered Father of the Mighty Hammil admired these traits greatly. The strays I mentioned, street-dwellers, are also respected. It is believed, across the water," Adeef flung out his arm again, "that cats are or become the vessel of the soul. Some say that if you are buried with a cat, you have the possibility of living again."

"In feline form?"

"As to that, I could not say."

"Oh, well, it's good for the cats. They must feel nice and safe over there, not risking their skins like the ones in the North."

"Yes and no." Adeef tugged his sleeve over his knife. "There is a steady trade in tomb cats."

"Tomb cats?"

"Cats bred for tombs. Quality felines are raised to adulthood, then their necks are wrung and they are mummified for the tomb. The wealthy pay well for them."

Finn grimaced. The conversation was heading back in a funerary direction. There was a moment of silence.

"Come, let us eat," Adeef said.

Up on the stern deck, they sat at the table set with silver platters and small, two-pronged instruments like miniature pitchforks. Adeef poured sweet wine into an engraved goblet and handed it to Finn, who took a small sip, then drank some more, failing to notice that Adeef had replaced his own goblet with a beaker of lemon-water.

Emboldened by the wine, Finn said, "An over-active imagination is a valuable asset in my line of work." As he spoke, he visualised the beautiful ginger cat that – or *who* – had twined between the bars of his window. "It's curious, though, isn't it, how *ordinary* cats can also have human qualities or traits."

Adeef looked away. "Is it? I try not to indulge my imagination. There may be something in what you say."

"In the North, wise women, who some name *disir* or *norns*, have cats with special powers."

"There are no witches in the High Alcazar." Adeef snapped his fingers at the guard. "Witchcraft is for the simple-minded."

Two cabin boys staggered up the companionway, carrying lidded tureens, which they placed on the table along with a basket of small bread-like squares. One of the boys winked at Finn. It was Zongolo.

Finn turned to Adeef. "When you found me on the hill, was it because Zongolo was told to take me up there, or was it his idea?"

Adeef's scimitar smile crossed his face. "Spies are spied upon; a necessary arrangement. Predicting what may happen is the basis of my success. What the Greeks and Romans called politics, leading to effective diplomacy."

"Where I come from, effective diplomacy happens at the end of an axe."

"The North is primitive. Not ignorant, but vulgar and remarkably naïve."

Finn watched green buds being ladled onto his plate. *'Naïve'*, he thought; *that definitely applies to me.*

"Politics and diplomacy are how I helped establish the High Alcazar and now plan to extend our territory with as little bloodshed as possible," Adeef continued. "What will you achieve in your life, Finn of the Volsungs, at the end of an axe?"

"Nothing. I've only ever used an axe to chop wood," Finn replied. "But I might have to start soon, if I survive to find one. I tried using words and failed. They'd have taken notice of an axe."

"Vikings are simple-minded brutes," Adeef said, and turned his attention to his plate. "But you are a Northman – not a Viking. What is the difference?"

"I was traveling with a peaceful merchant, who trades in the Middle Sea. Vikings started out like that, seeking merchandise and looking for fertile land to settle, but now they just raid, loot, and steal treasure."

"So, you are a Volsung Northman, and Goran Ice-Heart is a Volsung Viking. Interesting."

While they ate, mariners began tying lines of brightly coloured fabric triangles and small bronze bells to the main mast rigging, then across the main deck.

"Boats will see and hear us from leagues away with all this," Finn said, pointing at the decorations.

"That is the idea."

Finn thought it was a bit silly and finished his green buds. He had never seen or tasted anything like them before. The sauce was both sweet and sharp, and delicious in every way. Adeef went to the top of the steps and called out to a deckhand to hang more ribbon streamers along the bow rails.

"You will have every pirate on the Middle Sea after us with all this decoration and silver on display," Finn said between mouthfuls.

"That is the idea," Adeef replied. "Have some more artichokes."

After Zongolo removed the empty tureen, Adeef said casually, "We should discuss what may happen when we reach the pirate island, if they do not find us first."

Finn swallowed rather too fast, coughed and drank more wine to clear his throat. "Are you going to exchange me for your daughter directly, or do you plan to use me to resolve the treaty issue first? I can't see how, but you're the one who understands diplomacy without an axe, not me."

Adeef gave him an appraising look. "You really should employ your thinking skills more often. Except in this case, you are wrong. You are not a prisoner, Finn. You are a valued guest. Exchanging a prisoner for Perla, my daughter, would be an insult."

"But you know Ice-Heart..." Finn was about to say, "and you know he can't be trusted," but stopped himself.

"I do not *know* him; I know of him. I sent emissaries to address the treaty issue, and to negotiate for Perla. And I do accept that sometimes the edge of an axe or the blade of a sword speaks louder than words."

Finn leaned back. Wine was making his mind work faster but his words come slower. "The treaty before the girl? Or your daughter after a fight?"

"I intend to avoid a fight at all costs. That's why you are here. Ice-Heart won't want to risk losing one of his own clan – or a relative."

"I wouldn't be too sure of that," Finn replied, swigging down the last of his wine. "He's not called Ice-Heart for nothing. Are you sure your daughter is with him? Maybe he's sold her."

"She is with him."

"How do you know that?"

"The same way as I learned you were coming to the Middle Sea, through my Secret Service. Homing pigeons, Finn," Adeef sighed. "Fast and reliable, even in bad weather. My intelligencers tie messages to their legs and send them home."

"You must have people who travel everywhere – with pigeons," Finn giggled.

"It's not an original idea."

"No? Well, seems clever to me. So, what happened to your daughter? How did Ice-Heart get her to start with? Don't tell me he got into the Alcazar."

"Perla was taken while she was on the beach with her servant, collecting shells." Adeef's tone conveyed exactly what he thought of that activity. "I have tried to ransom her for one whole year, without success."

"But you've got armed men. Why didn't you send them to get her, after your emissaries failed?"

"The risk is too great. Attacking a pirate stronghold where they have every advantage would be unwise."

Finn nibbled at a salty bread square, hoping the All-father would ensure Goran Ice-Heart accepted him willingly, which would be a huge advance in every respect. He could give Goran his message and they could sail North immediately, together. "Which island are they on?" he asked.

"Ibiza, or as some call it, Eivissa."

"And you've got an informer there, with pigeons." Adeef inclined his head.

That was how Adeef had located him; he had an informer in the North. Maybe someone who'd been aboard *Guillemot.* "Grand Visior," Finn said, "is one of your spies a juggler and fire-eater?"

"Not that I know of," Adeef said, getting to his feet. "Now, it is hot and time for the mi. We may have some rather violent visitors later, or in the next day or two. I suggest you get some rest.

Chapter 19

Three sleek Norse-built longships began following *Gliding Swan* on the first night as she passed Malaga, jingling and glittering in the dark like a Yuletide festival. Adeef was informed. Nobody mentioned it to Finn, but watching the turbaned crew and the Barbalus guard move into pre-arranged positions, he drew his own conclusion.

When day turned to night on the third day, and the summer sky turned black as a guillemot's beak, the three longships closed in. Weary from three days on high alert, the crew cursed the pirate's tactics. Instead of ramming their prey, which would damage the prize ship, the sea-wolves were nipping the heels of their chosen victim until they were too weary to fight back, too drowsy to resist boarders. Adjube, *Gliding Swan's* captain, who appeared to never rest, shouted and scolded and even ordered Adeef to stay ready. Adeef smiled with satisfaction and gave Adjube a surprising order to pass on to his crew. Finn was told to stay in his cabin until called for.

Finn's guard either forgot to lock his cabin door, or didn't see the need. Finn wasn't sure if this was a good sign or not. Eager to know what was going to happen when Ice-Heart's pirates – if they were his pirates – boarded the galley, he sneaked out onto the upper stern deck and crouched behind the rail, watching and waiting. The moon moved across a cloudless night sky. And nothing happened. Unable to keep his eyes open, Finn crawled back his cabin and fell fast asleep.

One of Adeef's look-outs spotted the pirate's signal as the rising sun tinted the watery horizon pink and orange. Taking their time, waiting for the sun to rise higher, the pirate oarsmen kept pace with the high-sided galley and then moved directly under the prow, believing themselves unseen and unheard.

Once in position, bow-women, dressed from neck to toe in protective grey leather, ranged themselves alongside the rail, where they had a clear view of anyone popping an unwary head over the side of the tall galley. Standing legs apart, riding their sea-steed with practised grace, they watched and waited, as the galley's men-at-arms watched and waited above them.

Something woke Finn from deep sleep. Rigging clicked and clacked; the gentle moan and groan of a wooden vessel at sea had not changed, but there was a heavy atmosphere, an uncanny silence. Finn splashed water onto his gritty eyes, pushed his long white hair off his face and tied it with the new black ribbon, then slowly, purposefully, he strapped on Doomsong, eased open his cabin door and crouched behind the stern deck rail again, watching and waiting.

Goran Ice-Heart boarded the *Gliding Swan* first, just as the sky turned the colour of fire. He had judged the moment and position to perfection. His crew shimmied up ropes hooked onto the galley's high bow deck.

If Adeef's men saw them, they were blinded by the morning sun. Finn shaded his eyes and watched Ice-Heart, at the other end of the galley, raise his left hand and whistle a signal. The boarding party transferred knives from their clenched teeth to their hands, while more men and a few women arrived behind them, armed with scimitars. Once he had his pirate crew in position behind him, Goran Ice-Heart whistled again.

A chosen few of Adeef's men watched with their swords ready, waiting for their own signal. Finn, his heart racing in anticipation of a merciless fight, gripped the rail as three of Ice-Heart's biggest, strongest raiders moved onto the second step of the bow companionway in front of their leader. Nobody else moved. Everybody was silent.

With a sudden gush, wind filled the galley's sails, and as if this were a signal, Ice-Heart's crew went into action. His infamous Barbary Apes and Byzantines, his Turks and renegade mariners from a dozen other lands, leapt down the steps and began chasing a few of *Swan's* crew around the deck in a mortal game of catch-as-catch-can.

It was a trap; Finn could see that. *Swan's* oarsmen were in place, ready to row, not fight, and there were at least a dozen armed guards below decks, presumably waiting for the next signal.

At the moment when Goran Ice-Heart appeared to be alone on the bow deck, Adeef came to stand behind Finn, motioning with his hands for him to stay crouched down. Standing with arms folded to show he carried no weapon, the Grand Visior tilted his head in silent greeting.

Goran's laughter floated above the merry sword dance on the main deck. "Adeef of the High Alcazar," he called, "I am honoured. Who else would provide such an entertaining welcome?" Goran hooted with apparent delight, but his eyes roamed the deck for the hidden assassins.

Finn waited for Adeef to grab him by the neck and offer him for Perla, but the moments dragged on as the bladed game of tag continued below them. What was going on here, he wondered.

Goran took a few steps backwards, kicking open cabin doors for hidden assailants, then stood legs apart with folded arms, exactly like the eagle-beaked Moro behind Finn.

The two men watched as Ice-Heart's pirates pursued the crew, who kept eluding them. Goran finally signalled to his boarders to stop wasting their energy. Adeef gave a hand signal that Adjube relayed to his crew, and little by little, grown men and women stopped chasing each other around the masts and came to a halt.

Once all was quiet on the middle deck, Goran leaped down the steps to stand with his back to the main mast and locked eyes on his Barbalus adversary above. "Well," he shouted, "here I am. Do you intend to parley, or shall we cut a few throats and steal your silver?"

"We parley, Pirate," Adeef replied. "On *my* terms. Lay down your weapons; you have no need of them. I bring you a gift."

"By the All-father's beard, you do," Ice-Heart retorted. "And what sort of gift is our most respected Grand Visior offering me this time, besides his ship?"

Not waiting for a reply, before Adeef could get Finn onto his feet, Ice-Heart put two fingers to his lips and whistled a new command: 'Let battle commence.'

Finn took a deep breath and stood up straight and positioned himself, on the top step of the bow companionway. Nobody noticed.

Adjube sounded another signal and Adeef's men rushed up from the hold with swords at the ready. Ice-Heart's crew cheered at the prospect of blood.

The noise alone was terrifying. Grown men screamed, trying to escape capture or being thrown overboard. One of *Swan's* older mariners lay crumpled against a mast, his head broken open. Others lay, clutching injured arms and legs, while Adeef's guard leapt left and right with steel flashing in the sunlight, in a very different game of catch. *Swan's* deckhands joined in the hand-to-hand combat for their lives against a practised rabble whose dirty tactics showed no mercy.

Finn stood at the top of the steps, frozen with fear, unable to move. Then he could. Pulling Doomsong from its sheath, he heard himself shout, "Stop. Stop fighting!"

Doomsong glowed in his right hand.

Despite the mayhem, the clashing and shrieks, one of the sea-raiders saw or heard him and skidded to a halt on the blood-wet deck. Then another and another. A huge marauder halted, blade in the air, and stared up at him. Then another and another. The fighting came to a halt.

"What would you have us do, Captain?" one of the pirates called out, addressing Finn.

"Stop fighting, as he says!" bellowed a voice from amidships.

All movement ceased, save that of a tall, white-haired man standing by the main mast, who pushed his short sword into the wide belt at his waist and stared, like his raiders, at his mirror image on the upper stern deck.

"Well done, Finn," Adeef said with a wry smile of satisfaction.

Finn neither saw nor heard him, his eyes fixed on the older version of himself below: Ice-Heart.

The sea-rovers looked from one white-haired Northman to the other. The one in baggy white pantaloons was younger, perhaps less commanding. Yet it was his voice that had caused them to stop.

Ice-Heart asserted himself a second time. "Come down!" he shouted, pointing from the young Northman to the deck below.

Raiders shuffled around, forming a half-circle at the base of the companionway. Finn tucked Doomsong into its harness and did as he was bidden. As he reached the bottom step, a deft-handed Greek pirate grabbed the hilt of the sword and drew it from the scabbard. Taking one look at it, he laughed out loud. "The boy's brought a spade to dig his own grave, Cap'n," he shouted, and threw it up into the air, then made a pantomime of catching it and being dragged down by its weight. He tossed it up again, and the ugly-looking blade was caught by another raider.

"Funny shaped anchor this is. Here, Troll, see if it's any good to you," he yelled, tossing the sword to a giant in pink satin pantaloons, who took one look and sent the dull blade over a few heads to an acrobat, who tossed it high and turned a somersault before catching it again.

Finn watched with stomach-churning fear and the weird sensation that this had happened to him before, in some way.

"Heave it overboard," someone shouted. "See how fast it sinks."

"No!" Finn screamed, at exactly the same moment as Ice-Heart.

The blade was now hurtling across the deck from one side to the other as the pirates dodged between masts and lines, faster and faster until, in what seemed a single fluid movement, Goran the Volsung caught it in mid-air and leaped up the companionway to stand beside Adeef on the upper stern deck.

And the weapon glowed.

The exquisite, Dwarf-crafted, rune-written, once-broken and dragon-damaged blade pulsed back to life.

Goran looked at it and smiled. His crew drew a collective breath. Adeef's mariners gaped. And a young tale-maker from the far Cold North sank to his knees. "No, please. It's mine. It's mine."

Chapter 20

"What's your game, Grand Visior?" Ice-Heart demanded.

"No game, my violent friend," Adeef replied. "Merely an exchange of valued guests. This boy – I believe you know who he is – for my daughter. We sail to your island. You bring her to me, and you can have your – what's your expression – kith and kin? Plus, you keep the sword. I'm pleased to see I wasn't wrong about that."

For a long moment, the only sound was the clinking of rigging. An oarsman coughed. A small boy with brown hair put his head above the hold, took one look at Ice-Heart and dipped down again.

The silence continued. Ice-Heart glanced down at the young man kneeling on the blood-slicked deck below, then at Adeef. "You want to exchange your precious black pearl for this ninny? I don't think so. I'll keep the sword though, as a gesture of good will."

"Keep it, it's nothing to me. But know this, Ice-Heart, I shall be coming for Perla, and your treasure, and your island! You won't escape me, *Viking*!"

"I've never tried to, *Moro*!" Ice-Heart's face lightened with a wide smile. "And you're welcome to come for your precious Perla. I'll show you around the island myself – if you survive long enough to get ashore. Come! Pay us a visit. My archers are always looking for moving target practice."

Before Adeef could say another word, Ice-Heart gave three sharp whistles and leapt down the companionway, joining his crew to knock out every Barbalus on the deck and collect their weapons, which they hurled over the side onto their longship or into the water. When their fun was over, Ice-Heart whistled the retreat and the rabble began scrambling over the carved rail, removing rope ladders and lines as they went.

While his rovers made their exit, Goran Ice-Heart tucked the legendary Doomsong sword into the belt at his waist, then grabbed Finn by the harness on his back and heaved him bodily over the rail, ready to drop him two decks down onto the galley's oars. Holding onto Finn with one hand, he looked up at Adeef and said casually, "Any last requests?"

Adeef shook his head. Goran dropped Finn over the high sided galley.

"No!" Adeef called out. "This is not what should happen."

"Never is with me, Visior, I thought you knew that," Ice-Heart laughed, swinging a long leg to straddle the middle deck rail. "Stop by for a cup of sherbet next time you're passing my way. You know where I am. Your pretty Perla makes a fine serving wench, by the way. Almost as if she were born to it, eh?" he added with a knowing wink.

Checking his new sword was safely at his side, Goran raised a hand in farewell and slid down the hull to balance on an oar and then, stepping neatly from one paddle to another, he raced forwards to his waiting *Wave Steed*. The sleek longship surged forward the moment two Viking giants pulled him onto the deck.

Whether by accident or careful timing, Finn fell, headfirst, between two of *Swan's* huge oars, straight into the

Middle Sea. Death immediately closed in around him. Knowing he was doomed, he made no effort to stay afloat.

Greyness stifled his breathing. Greyness filled his eyes. Greyness was suffocating him. Until the greyness was broken, and something or someone grabbed his shirt and tugged him to the surface. Finn never learned who it was.

When he opened his eyes, the sky was blurry and blue. He began to splutter, rolled onto his side, choking out salt water and wishing he were dead.

They left him to recover, or not, there on the deck of a Norse-built longship. Nobody came to help him. Gradually, Finn's breathing returned to normal and he managed to get into a sitting position. His first thought was that he was very thirsty, then that he was hungry, then that he had achieved what he'd been sent to do – almost – and it was a hundred times more frightening than he'd imagined. Sitting there, apparently ignored, he watched Goran's crew pull away from *Gliding Swan* with the distinct sense that he'd escaped a bad situation for something far worse.

Eventually, a tattooed sea-rover brought him a beaker of sweet water. Finn gulped it down, then coughed and retched it up again. The sea-rover laughed, slapped him on the back and said something like, "That'll teach you not to waste water."

Finn reached out with the empty beaker to ask for more and felt Ice-Heart's eyes on him. Moving around the single square sail, Goran came to his side. Riding the waves as the longship hurtled forward, he said, "Nasty experience, was it?"

Finn tried to speak, but his mouth was too dry. Ice-Heart crouched down beside him. "Ah, well, you're still breathing," he said, patting Finn's shoulder, "and I've got the sword, safe and sound. When you're feeling better, you can tell me how you found it."

Finn shook his head, "No, it... I..."

"Sshh. Calm down, there's plenty of time," the fierce pirate murmured softly, patting Finn's shoulder again.

"Adeef," Finn gasped out. "He – they want your island."

"So he said," Ice-Heart chuckled. "Won't happen while I'm there. Now, the question is, do I want *you* there?"

"Please, please, I've come a long way to..." Finn started to cough again.

"I'm sure you have. Men, women, stripling lads like you, they come from all over to join Ice-Heart and make their fortune. Don't fret, you can stay with me until I find something useful for you to do. Unless you're as useless as you look now. Well, you might manage to get away before we throw you out. My island's got high cliffs. Did you know that?" Ice-Heart raised an eyebrow and gave Finn a toothy smile that didn't reach his eyes.

Standing up, Goran realised his crew were all watching him. "Never heard tell of the Doomsong sword?" he shouted. "Course you have. The best prize I'll ever take, this is. I might even give up pirating for a while, to celebrate." Nobody spoke. "Oh, don't worry, you'll get your share of the loot next raid. Troll can take you. About time he started to use that big head of his."

With that, Goran, named Ice-Heart, ambled up the narrow deck of his longship and settled down under the prow with Doomsong cradled in his arms like a babe.

Chapter 21

"There's no room for malcontents and moaners on this island. Those who want to leave are free to go. Right now."

Finn had only been on the island for a night and a day, but he knew this was a hollow offer and heard the menace behind Ice-Heart's words.

The pirate captain, whose moods swung faster than a slap in the face, swiveled around. A long-bladed knife glinted red in the firelight. "Those of you whining about not getting any loot off the Barbalus *Swan* can go. Those of you tired of the life here are free to leave. You won't be stopped."

Seated on the dusty floor by the entrance to a wide-mouthed cavern, Finn pulled his knees up to his chin and watched the man he'd come so far to find stroll with barely controlled fury around the cauldron hanging over the central fire-pit. Doomsong, Finn noticed, was no longer at his waist.

The cavern was oval in shape, larger than any dwelling he had ever entered, and higher. The floor was rough and uneven, with odd, shallow dips. To one side, there were a series of natural rock shelves, which served as Ice-Heart's crew's bunkhouse. Some had cushions and blankets; some had only sheepskins; some were screened by improvised curtains nailed into the rock face.

Moving to the entrance of the cave, Ice-Heart waved his knife into the night and then swiveled around again: "There you are, my lovelies, the world awaits those who wish to leave. Off you go, with my blessing." The high roof of the cave gave his voice a sinister echo. Nobody moved. Ice-Heart took a step to one side, coming closer to Finn and widening the gap for anyone who dared exit. The corner of his mouth turned up in a sneer and he said, "Come along, who wants to be first? The offer is open to all, except *you*." The blade pointed down at Finn.

Finn shook his head and started to say, "I'll stay," but Ice-Heart's attention had shifted. Deeper in the cave, there was a murmuring. A veteran sea-rover named Hal Short-Butt, joint-pained and old before his time, shuffled towards the night sky. His woman, worn thin from stitching wounds and from worry, followed him.

Ice-Heart danced across the mouth of the cave, to lean with exaggerated ease against the opposite side of the entrance. Finn watched, sensing how everyone held their breath.

An old-timer named Kalv, who had taken pity on Finn and stayed at his side for most of the day, leaned forward. "Leaving Ice-Heart is more dangerous than staying," he said in a low voice. "Those with any sense slip away during a raid or disappear when we over-night on land somewhere. And he's in a foul mood tonight."

As the elderly couple edged through the entrance, heads down to avoid the pirate's piercing blue eyes, Ice-Heart gave the man a kick that sent him tumbling down the steep hillside. The woman squealed and nearly fell, running to reach him.

A girl holding a sack of kindling to her chest hunkered down beside Finn and Kalv. "They have no shelter for the night, but they are free," she sighed.

"Better to wait until dark and get away then, while he's in his villa," Kalv said, cocking his head in Ice-Heart's direction. "If you can pay for a local fisherman to take you off the island. They're all scared of upsetting Ice-Heart, so that ain't easy."

"You could wait for the fire to die down and get away if you really wanted, couldn't you?" Finn said, looking at the girl, who was probably about his age or a bit younger. Something about her dull brown hair and round face on a small-boned body reminded Finn of a hedge sparrow. "Someone in the town or harbour would take pity on you, surely."

She shook her head. "Kalv is right; they daren't offend Ice-Heart down there. I have no coin and nowhere to go, anyway."

"Same goes for most of us," the Kalv muttered, "and it's not called 'Ice-Heart's Island' for nothing. Locals are terrified of getting on his bad side. You planning to make a run for it?"

Finn shook his head. "I can't, I've got something important to do here." *When the time is right,* he added to himself. Would the time ever be right to give Goran Ice-Heart Master Odo's message?

With this in mind, Finn watched Ice-Heart stride back through the smoky cavern and into a narrow passage at the far end. He had a fine dwelling on the other side of the hill, they said.

Finn turned to the girl still crouched beside him. He'd noticed her before but had no need to speak to her. Not that anyone bothered with a thrall, and this one rarely spoke. "What's your name?" he asked.

"Seren."

"Have you always been a thrall here?"

She shook her head. "I was a thrall in Hibernia before."

Curious, Finn watched her return to the fire-pit with the kindling. She had a hard life, but he could understand why she'd made no attempt to escape. To be out in the wild with no shelter, no means of getting off the island, what chance would she have of finding her way home?

Where was Seren's home? Hibernia? Was that her home? Somewhere many days journey across the sea, if she ever reached it. Home to a life of drudgery, for Seren was no princess, so a life no different from what she had here, where at least there was shelter and a full cauldron each day. Better to accept what you had and make the best of it.

The couple who'd just left had been very unwise. If, as Kalv said, the old man had been with Ice-Heart for years, he'd had plenty of opportunity to escape. Unless he hadn't wanted to leave without his woman. Perhaps he was misjudging the man, Finn thought. Perhaps he'd wanted to be sure his woman got away, as well. Not so foolish then. Lucky man, lucky wife. Would anyone ever choose him for a life partner? Probably not; what could he offer?

Suddenly, Ice-Heart was back in the cave again, helping himself to a bowl of fish stew. The knife was no longer in his hand but the tension in his shoulders made him no less dangerous. Seren hurried to serve him. "Ah, our very own Audumla," he drawled, handing her the deep wooden ladle. "How are you today, my dear little cow-face?"

Keeping her head down, Seren replied, "Well, master."

"Good, good. A happy cook makes a tasty meal, eh?" Ice-Heart began pacing around her, light-footed as a wolf. "Our Seren of the Britons," he began sweetly, too sweetly. "You are a good little cook. You should serve me in the house."

Head down, Seren stirred the stew. "As you wish, master."

Finn realised he was holding his breath, like the girl, waiting for what was to come. To his surprise, Goran bent down beside her to say, "You shall have a proper bed to sleep on, in the old slave quarters. But a pallet bed is better than the rock floor, no?"

Seren nodded. "Yes, master. Thank you."

"And what else can a girl like you do? Could you prepare meals on board when we go a-raiding?"

Seren looked up, her eyes bright. "Oh, yes. I understand the winds, and tides as well. If it's needed?" her voice fell to an apologetic whisper.

"Do you, now? Winds and tides? So, single-handed, you could steal my longship while we are busy on land, eh? She's a sly one, eh, boys?" Ice-Heart threw the comment out to his company, then tossed away his bowl with a clatter, stood to his full height and bounced on the balls of his feet as if weighing up a difficult matter. "Do we take the risk, lads? Not that she'll be the only woman on our adventures. They can handle bows and arrows and knives, but a cook on longer trips, that would be useful. Especially when we're lying in wait on land."

A ripple of disquiet ran among Ice-Heart's crew and camp followers. A group of boys came together, muttering angrily. A stocky redhead got to his feet. "Captain, *we* should be considered before her. We've been with you longer."

"Can you make meals from damp grain and skinny rabbits? She can."

"But we'll be raiders with you soon, and we need to learn about..." The boy closed his mouth. Ice-Heart had raised a warning finger.

Seren moved away from the fire-pit and straightened her back. She barely reached Goran's chest. "I am a good cook, Captain," she said, loud enough for all to hear. "And I learned the ways of the sea from my father and brothers, long ago."

The gang of boys muttered angrily among themselves again. Finn studied the way they gathered around a redhead built like a bullock. These boys probably bullied Seren, maybe tried for her favours in the dark. If Seren had given them the slip, they'd be angry and out for revenge. He suddenly felt very protective of this slight, homely girl. As, for some reason, did Goran the Volsung. For, instead of playing for attention, he said, "The thrall girl will sail with us until the next full moon, unless I sell her in the meantime."

Ruffling Seren's dull brown hair, Goran resumed his posturing and strode towards Finn. "And in this meantime, I'd better deal with you."

Finn got to his feet. "Captain, I'm here to... that is, I have to..." The single warning finger silenced him.

"You will also sail with us. I need to see what you're made of before I decide whether to sell you."

Giving Finn no chance to respond, Ice-Heart returned to the cauldron, took a clean bowl from a shelf and held it out for Seren to fill. "It's very good," he said, sniffing at the stew. "Oregano, or is it thyme?"

"Oregano and rosemary," Seren whispered. "They grow on the hill."

"Clever girl." Goran smiled at her and returned to Finn with the bowl. Every pair of eyes followed him, waiting to see what was going to happen to the suspicious-looking newcomer.

"There are you are, boy," Ice-Heart said, astonishing everyone in the cave. "Eat up. What's your name again?"

"Finn. Of the Volsung."

"Of the Volsung, yes, Adeef tried that on yesterday. Maybe later we'll take a stroll, and you can tell me all about your Volsung connections, and I'll decide, maybe, later, whether to believe you or not."

Swallowing hard, Finn took the bowl in silence.

"What's the matter, cat got your tongue?" Goran laughed.

"Seems like it," Finn responded. Then he relaxed and said, "I'm a tale-maker by trade. I normally talk for a living...."

But Ice-Heart wasn't listening, he was strolling out of the cave into the night. In the silence that followed, Finn thought he could hear him whistling as he descended the steep path to the cove, where they'd hidden the longships.

Finn sipped his stew and then, looking up, he noticed a woman staring down at him. A young woman was chained to the wall of the cave on a shelf of rock at the opening to the narrow passage. Was this Adeef's daughter?

Dressed in a knee-length black tunic with gold stripes and tight, shiny black trews, she looked strange and exotic. Something about her reminded him of a tale told by a traveller in The Old Salvation. The traveller had visited distant hot lands, where there were leagues of sand and no trees, and returned to the North along the treacherous river route from the Black Sea. He told a story about a beautiful and very clever woman named Shera-razada – or something like that – who saved herself from death by telling a king strange tales with hidden messages.

This young woman looked clever, and dangerous. Her body-fitting tunic rippled as she moved. Nothing like the modest white cotton worn by the women of Lisboa and Berjer. Perla – if this was Perla – wore her 'value', as Harp-Legs' women called it, as a statement. Even in the sweat-reeking, smoke-filled cavern, she proclaimed her worth, her price. A princess held for a queen's ransom, chained to a wall like a wild animal.

Finn watched her now, unsure of her status: Adeef's daughter, or a princess to be ransomed? As if sensing his gaze and pity, she flexed her fingers in her wrist manacles and tugged her wall chains to the limit. Leaning forward she arched her spine and hissed. Finn shifted backwards, as if she could reach him, then gave a nervous laugh, grateful she was chained. Grateful she was manacled and not him.

He sighed; manacles might soon be around his own wrists. Goran Ice-Heart was someone to fear, commanding and aggressive and unpredictable, his hair as white and wavy as sea foam, his mind as sharp as sharks' teeth.

Finn moved to the fire-pit. "Seren, why is she chained up?" he asked, indicating Ice-Heart's hostage. "I can't see her getting very far on her own."

"It's a game," Seren replied in a whisper. "Perla attacks the master, or attacks one of his men, and he chains her up as a punishment. Then he lets her go again. He's got a new scar today; did you not see?"

"I'll make sure I give her a wide berth, then," Finn said, pulling a face.

Seren looked into his eyes, smiled and returned to ladling stew into bowls for the crew.

Sometime later, Goran strode back into the cave. Standing in the wide opening, backlit by moonlight, he called out, "We sail the day after tomorrow. We'll be out two or three days off Frankia, depending on what we catch. If we're lucky, we may get a cargo out of Roma or Aleppo. Sharpen weapons and get yourselves ready. No wine tomorrow. None. Understood?" There was a general rumble of 'Yes, Captain.' "And you," he said, pointing at Finn, "will come as well. You can show us *your* sailing skills."

Not giving anyone chance to comment, Ice-Heart leapt up the natural stone steps at the rear of the cave, and making a dumb-show of it, sidled up to Perla. The beautiful, sleek, purple-black young woman cursed him in a deep, guttural language, then lunged forward, for the chains were long enough for her to leap on his neck and bite him, if he drew nearer.

"Ah, no, no," Goran laughed, dodging out of her reach and waving a small key in front of her. "Unless you want to stay here all night?"

The woman gave a small shrug and relaxed against the rock wall. Goran unchained her without another word and led her by the hand into the narrow passage to his quarters. Perla followed without a murmur.

Goran Ice-Heart did not return for the evening stroll he'd promised Finn. Instead, at Kalv's insistence, Finn told a cavern of cut-throats the story of Audumla the cow.

While Seren collected empty wooden bowls, Finn gathered his audience, as he'd done at his cousins' fireside, as he'd done in a hundred taverns and hundred more far-flung homesteads, and began the tale.

"As you probably know," he said, beckoning with a hand for the rowdy boys to sit nearer where he could control them better, "at the dawn of time everything in the Cold North was covered in ice and snow. The first living beings there were created out of melting ice. The very first to breathe a frosty breath was a giant in human form named Ymir.

"Like our Troll," someone shouted. Everyone laughed.

"One night, one long, freezing, starless, moonless winter night, while Ymir slept like a bear in a deep hollow, a man was born from his right arm and a woman from his left. Or the other way around. Nobody will ever know for sure. Then a cow came into being. Her name was Audumla."

Seren looked up and smiled, spilling left-over stew on a rover's lap and making those around him chuckle.

"Well," Finn continued, "as Audumla licked ice to quench her thirst, a man emerged from the melted drops that fell from her warm tongue. The man's name was Buri. Then came Bor. Bor was the father of Odin, Vili, and Ve.

"Now, each of these three brothers, Odin, Vili and Ve, had supernatural powers, and they began a power struggle for land with the race of Giants, and they killed Ymir, who was very old by then. It was still a tragedy.

"They saw it as success, though; so then Odin, Vili and Ve discussed and debated the best way to people their land, which they named Earth. They wanted people and creatures who would forever be under their power.

"As the brothers were talking about this, they looked down on the rotting body of the dead giant Ymir and saw grubs appear. Fascinated, they watched as fat, yellow and white grubs..." Finn wiggled his thumbs. "...grubbed under Ymir's huge ribcage, down into the loins." Finn paused to dramatize the grubs' progress, "then under and over his long, long spine; burrowing and tunneling through flesh and bone like caterpillars on a cabbage. And the three brothers said, all at the same time, 'These will do.'

"So, they activated their powers and tried to turn these busy grubs into human beings, except it didn't go as they hoped. The short, squat creatures burrowing through the dead Ymir stayed short and squat. They started to grow upwards, though. Then they grew arms and legs, and round heads and round eyes and bulgy noses, but they didn't grow big enough to be the beautiful people Odin, Vili and Ve wanted. What they had created was a race of Dwarves.

"Now, Dwarves look ugly to us – there's no getting around that – but Odin, Vili and Ve gave these busy creatures sharp minds and clever skills to make up for having squat bodies. But what were they going to do with them?

"Then Odin said that, as they were created out of Ymir, whose gigantic body was returning to its origin, becoming soil, rocks and stone again, the best thing for the Dwarves was to stay underground. And this is why the clever, grumpy Dwarves live in caves, tunnels and deep underground caverns—"

"Like us," sneered the redheaded bullock of a boy.

"—and make the very best gold helmets and steel swords. And all thanks to Audumla," Finn finished, searching out Seren and giving her a wink.

"Is that it?" asked one of the youths. "Is that the story?"

Finn tilted his head, "I thought you'd know about Odin, and his spear Gungnir. Do you want to hear about that as well?"

"Yes," responded most of his audience.

Seren brought Finn a brimming cup of lemon water, then perched herself on a narrow ledge at the side of the cave, in such a way that she could jump to her feet if Ice-Heart returned. Finn sipped his drink, waiting until she was settled, then started again. "In gratitude for making their race, it is said, the Dwarves made Odin a spear named Gungnir. It was shaped in the sparks and heat of their first forge, from magic metals that can only be found underground. What they made for the other two brothers is not told, but as blacksmiths, they did – perhaps still do – forge the sharpest swords and the surest shields. It was they who made Thor's hammer, which makes the sound of thunder. It was they who made the..." Finn halted, took a deep breath. "...the wondrous blades of legend."

Finn brought the story to an abrupt end, filled with a terrible sense of nostalgia and loss. His body ached with a need to get home. Home to fingers numb with cold, to distant white horizons and blue icicles hanging from rooftops; home to a land that was strange and dangerous in ways he understood. And his eyes glistened with tears for a very personal loss. If Kalv and Seren noticed, they said nothing.

Later, much later, on his rock-hard shelf of a bed, Finn woke from a vivid dream of a Dwarf lifting a sword with a golden pommel from bright flames, as the mountain above him shook and rumbled... *Where was Doomsong?*

Goran knew what it was. How? What had he done with it?

Finn sat up as Katranina's voice said, 'Not how or what; Finn must ask why.'

Why did Goran not ask him about the sword?

Because he wanted Finn to forget about it. Well, he was wrong about that.

Finn lay back on his stone-cold bed. He had to find Doomsong and get home as fast as he could, with or without Goran. But not without the sword.

Chapter 22

Finn spent most of his next day on the island, sitting under a wind-twisted olive tree, gazing at a perfectly calm blue sea under a perfectly cloudless blue sky. He was not shackled and he was free to leave the cave, but he felt no freer to do as he wished than Seren. There were no armed sentries as in the Alcazar, but archers, some with evil-looking crossbows, were stationed on rocky outcrops to deter foolhardy treasure seekers or rivals coming up, or thralls from going down.

Goran's raiding crew spent the morning sharpening weapons, jesting and ragging each other. A few had set up wrestling teams. The fights were noisy, jovial and brutal. One man had his arm broken; one was injured so badly that he was carried to his rock-shelf bed.

Around midday, Goran arrived, called to various men and women, and signalled Finn to join them. They followed him down to the cove, where the longships were pulled up on the strand; they crossed the beach and waded around a rocky promontory to a smaller inlet.

"Will we be able to get back?" Finn asked, as the sea water reached his waist.

"Full tide isn't much above the height of a man along this side of the island," Goran replied over his shoulder. "Ebb, flow, we can usually get in and out without much fuss. This beach is protected from high winds. A safe haven for my sleek *Dreki*. See?"

Finn saw. A beautiful galley was careened on the narrow beach and a dozen or more slaves and crew were scrubbing her hull with spring water that flowed down the cliff behind them.

"I call her *Dreki*," Goran said. "She's as good as a dragon. Swoops down on her prey to steal their gold, and flies back here to hide it with my treasure. Nobody can find her, not even your sneaky friend Adeef, and he's tried often enough." Goran's smooth, high cheek-boned face was alive with joy and mischief.

"The only dragon in the Middle Sea," Finn said, admiring the galley. "Or are there real dragons here as well?"

"Not like the ones in the North. They've got something nastier in Serkland, in Africa. Serpents that fly out of trees to strangle anything that breathes: men, goats, anything. And worse, if that's possible, serpents that hiss poison at your eyes, to blind you before an agonising death. They make your little vipers look like fish bait."

Finn gave an involuntary shudder. "I hope they can't get over here." He cast an anxious glance at the scrubby trees and bushes clinging to the rock face above them, but Goran wasn't listening. He was striding over the gravelly sand to *Dreki*, calling out instructions as he went.

When he turned back to Finn he said, "*Dreki* requires a lot of maintenance. We use her for big raids, when we know what we're going for. Longships are handy for land *razzias*, but I don't risk them for big prizes far from land. Your friend Adeef was an exception. He put himself in my way; too good an opportunity to miss. Being small in comparison and low in the water can have advantages."

Finn grimaced. Adeef had put himself in Goran's way for a reason, and his plan had failed. "What are you getting her ready for?" he asked.

"There's a fleet sailing this week from the Levant. That's the eastern end of the Middle Sea. It'll be carrying rich pickings, and there's another galley, possibly two, on a regular run, taking a cargo from Aleppo to the Barbalus in Berjer. And, even better, if we can find her, there's a Serkland cargo galley sailing in the opposite direction with goods from the Timbuktu camel caravanserai. They come prepared for trouble, but we may be lucky."

Finn grinned at the sound of the name. "Tim-buk-tu," he repeated.

"A place and name to remember, Finn. They send salt, gold and myrrh up to the coast for traders who work the Middle Sea. The fleet I'm going for first, though, will have silk, precious gems, and ceramics from distant Cathay. Ever heard of Cathay?"

Finn nodded. "I'm not entirely ignorant. I've been traveling the North for years and years. I do know a few things."

"But not what a camel train caravanserai is?"

"Not exactly. A camel is like a big horse, isn't it?"

"It's got four legs and can carry a pack or a man on its back." Lookinhg Finn in the eye, Goran said more slowly, "You don't know anything about blazing hot deserts or camels, but you know enough to bring you all the way from the snows of the Cold North to join me here?" He leaned closer, peering at Finn through thick black eyelashes. "I wonder why?"

Why? Finn nearly grinned. This was the moment....

But no. This was not the moment. He had to find Doomsong first. If he delivered Master Odo's message, and

Goran laughed and refused, which Finn thought was more than likely, then the sword was lost to him. Goran coveted precious objects, like Harp-Legs and a thousand other Vikings raiding for treasure. He wouldn't give up Doomsong.

Finn returned Goran's suspicious gaze and said, "You are right, I came to the Middle Sea for a reason, only Adeef got me first. You rescued me."

"Did I?" Goran's eyes narrowed again.

"These cargo vessels you mentioned," Finn responded, moving closer to *Dreki's* keel, "aren't they too big and well-guarded to board?"

"Yes and no. That's why *Dreki* has an iron beak." Goran pointed up at the galley's triangular prow.

As Finn studied the pointed prow, reinforced to ram and hole larger vessels' hulls, Goran said, "Sixteen benches, two or three to a bench, to pull us in and get out fast. I've got an even bigger galley down in the harbour. It would take an experienced crew to steal that one, so she's safe enough there."

"Aren't you worried your men might mutiny one day and take her?"

Goran laughed out loud. "Not while I make them rich. You should stay; join them, see some of the wonderful world we've found. I might even take you into Serkland. Fascinating place. I get good prices for thralls there, too, especially pale-faced girls. They like male slaves big and tough, though, so you'd be safe enough, until I put some more muscle on you."

Goran's tone had become friendly and jocular again, but Finn was wise enough to understand the threat in his words. Measuring his own choice of words, he said, "Does that mean you'll be staying on this island, then? As your permanent base?"

"Why not? We've got most of what we need for a good life here. Farmers inland, fisher-folk in the villages. Coastal traders and merchants live by the port, over on the other side. This half – more than half – of the island is mine. Natives keep their distance, 'specially when I'm down in the harbour. Lock up their daughters, they do. And the boys, in case I nobble them to row – or to sell."

Goran gazed at his galley like an indulgent father, then shouted something at one of his crew in Middle Sea mariner argot. A young man lazing against a rock jumped up and raced back to the barnacle-cleaning line. Goran sprinted around the hull after him and Finn followed.

"It's got to be clean, idiot, completely smooth to avoid drag," Goran yelled angrily. Turning back to Finn, he said, "A week they've been at it, and they're still not finished." Then, pushing into the line himself to scrape off barnacles and green-weed, he roared, "Put your backs into it! Your skins are in is as much danger as mine if we don't get away fast enough!"

While Goran's attention was elsewhere, Finn climbed aboard the tilted galley to admire its design. Making his way to the covered stern area, he looked down the long middle deck and tried, without any difficulty, to envisage what it would be like to be part of the crew, and then what it might be like to live here on the island, permanently. If Goran thought that was what he was aiming for, there was no harm going along with it, until he found Doomsong.

Much later, as Goran led the way up to the cave, Finn said, "What do you do with the prizes you take – the gold, silks and spices?"

"Keep what I need and share the rest between my free crew. Keeps them loyal. Some goes to the locals to keep them sweet, and quiet."

"Quiet?"

"There's a price on my head. And a few rivals along the coast would like to see me out of their way. Skippers and traders will arrange a little night raid to eliminate a nuisance. Easier to buy them off than fight. What would happen in the North, boy, if I raided there?"

"You'd get an axe in your skull."

"I would. Fortunately, they aren't so bloodthirsty here. They prefer dungeons, where rats and starvation do the dirty work for them. You weren't kept in the Alcazar's underground, then?"

The question came so fast, Finn barely had time to register Goran's tone. "No."

"So, they got you for a slave?"

"Yes."

"And let you keep a sword?"

"No. Not to start with. Adeef thought he could use me." Finn hesitated, "As bait, for you. To exchange for his daughter, Perla."

Goran hooted with laughter, then snapped, "You or the sword?"

"What?" Caught off guard, Finn wasn't ready for the question.

"You heard."

"Erm – well, in exchange for me, I think. How do you know about the sword?"

"There's a legend. An old Wanderer told me about it when I was young." Goran halted under the rough branches of a half-dead almond tree and turned to look out to sea. For a moment there was silence.

"What did he tell you?" Finn whispered, curiosity getting the better of his fears.

Goran bit his inner cheek, tilted his head from side to side as if trying to avoid a memory. After a moment he said, "It was when I was about your age, maybe younger. I was hiking into the mountains to join a battle, to fight as a mercenary. An old Wanderer – *the* old Wanderer – stopped me as I was passing through a woods. He said this was where Sigmund lost his life, and his famous sword." Goran bit his cheek again, started to say something else, and then changed his tone and said, "I thought it was a stupid story at the time." Shifting his weight onto the balls of his feet, he swung around and gave Finn one of his unnerving, searching looks. His mouth twitched into a crooked smile. "That is the sword, isn't it?"

"Yes. That is what I was told. But what did the Wanderer – Master Odo – what did he tell you about it?"

"What did he tell me? Wouldn't you like to know."

"Yes! Please, I would."

"Ha!"

Goran Ice-Heart strode on without another word until they reached the track that led to the cave, where he halted again. "Right, you go back in there, for now." Finn started to move, but Goran suddenly grabbed him from behind. "That Wanderer, he told me something else you'd do well to remember. Or perhaps you already know. You say you're a tale-maker; d'you know what it was?"

Finn's mouth went dry. He opened his mouth to speak and closed it again.

Goran pushed his white hair back off his face. Taking his time, he said, "It was believed by many, generations gone by, that a Volsung – a true Volsung of Sigmund's line – eventually brought suffering to friend and family alike."

Finn bit his lip, unable to form a reply.

"Do you understand?" Goran asked.

"I think so," Finn whispered.

Finn ate his evening fish stew on the rough ground outside the cave, then moved inside to escape the night insects that had taken a liking to his fair northern flesh. Lounging against the cool stone wall, he watched to see who was free to move as they wished and who were thralls like Seren or captives like Perla. Was it worth trying to rescue Adeef's daughter and return her to Berjer, or better to ignore her? Assuming he survived the next few days at sea. Assuming he could find Doomsong before he left the island – tried to leave the island.

Struggling to get comfortable that night on the wedge of stone he'd been allotted, Finn examined the warning he thought Goran had given him: that he should not expect any favours, least of all from a Volsung pirate.

If anything, the warning helped clarify the plan that had been forming itself in his head since he'd seen *Dreki* and heard how settled Goran had become on the island. Locating Doomsong – rescuing Doomsong – was a priority.

Goran had had the sword in his belt that first night when he'd left them in the cave and gone through the tunnel to his dwelling place. What had he done with it? Was it with his other treasure somewhere underground, or in his private dwelling? Finn put a hand under his head, checking that the harness was still there under his Barbalus silks. Keeping the sheath was important Gradually he dozed off to sleep, then woke with a start, and the words 'True Owner' shouting in his head.

Finn rolled onto his side, willing himself to sleep in the smoke-filled, never-silent cave, but his mind raced on. From the moment he'd set out on *Guillemot*, he'd envisioned holding Doomsong up to the light so Goran Ice-Heart could read the runes. Once Goran had seen the legendary sword, he'd pass on Master Odo's message, word for word. More or less. And formally hand over the sword. Without Doomsong, how was he going to pass on the message about a clan leader's obligations? Not that he was going to succeed in persuading this pirate king to return to the ice and snow and help people he had ignored for years.

Chapter 23

Despite his midnight worrying, Finn woke later than most people in the cave, instantly aware they were talking about him. Ice-Heart's crew were suspicious of him, probably due to his appearance, although not even Kalv had asked him who he was outright. Trying to ignore them, Finn climbed off his stone shelf and went out into the trees for his morning routine. He returned while the cooking fire was still unlit and, for once, the air was clear. It was the first time he'd been able to really see his surroundings.

A few boulders created uneven steps up to the crack in the far wall, where Goran Ice-Heart came and went. Finn wandered over to the steps, then gasped in surprise. On the wall was a drawing of a herd of horses racing towards him. He put out a hand to trace the shape of a head and a bristly mane, and then noticed other animals above and below: deer with pointed antlers, oxen, and strange creatures with a single horn between their eyes.

"As you can see, we are not the first residents of this cave," Goran said, leaping down from the narrow gap onto the ledge above Finn. "Nor am I the first to live in my hilltop palace. Would you like to see it?"

Surprised, Finn said, "What is a palace?"

"A palace... how can I explain a palace? Imagine a mead hall built of stone, furnished with soft beds and silk hangings. Ah, but you were in the High Alcazar; you have met what people of the Middle Sea consider normal comforts."

Finn looked at Goran's face, unsure if he was expected to answer or not. Goran raised an enquiring eyebrow, so Finn said, "Yes. Their homes are more comfortable than ours in the Cold North."

"*Yours* in the Cold North," Goran corrected. "Not mine." Not waiting for Finn to reply, he continued, "You have not travelled further east from here; did you plan to?" Finn shook his head. "Perhaps you should. If you go far enough it's possible to reach another sea, the Black Sea, they call it. From there, you can travel upriver to the lands of the Kievan Rus. And from there, all the way back to your small island – and smaller life."

"I know; Seavogel told me about that."

"Seavogel? Shipmaster of *Guillemot*?"

"You know him?" Finn asked, surprised.

"He's a Volsung; of course I know him. You sailed from Minnaholm on *Guillemot*?"

Finn was surprised again. "You know Minnaholm, my island?"

Goran shrugged. "An inspired guess. Seavogel is from the mainland."

"Is he? I didn't know Seavogel was a Volsung." Finn's thoughts became tangled.

"A bald Volsung. Most people up there and on the islands are from our clan. Only a few of us with white-white hair are from Sigmund's line, though." Goran's mouth twitched. "As you, and a few here, well know." Finn took a deep breath, but Goran didn't give him time to speak. "A palace – *palais* as the Franks say – is a gilded dwelling with every comfort. The

Romans built mine, although it is not large. You have heard of the Roman Empire?"

"Of course." Adeef had mentioned it, too. He must learn more. Attempting to conceal his ignorance, Finn tried to smile. His initial fear and wariness of Ice-Heart had lessened while they were on the beach cleaning *Dreki*, but it was back now.

The older Northman raised a dark eyebrow again. "Is there something you want to tell me?"

"Yes, I do! About the sword."

"Ah, that. Come with me."

Hopeful, nervous and excited, Finn followed the Viking along a narrow underground passage. At one point it forked, and another passage led downwards. Goran stepped upwards, onto an open ledge and then into another passage, which finally opened into a dark chamber lined with shelves. In the soft light from a hanging lantern, Finn could see leather buckets and huge ceramic jars.

"They kept their wine and olive oil down here," Goran said.

"Who?"

"The families who lived here before. Come and see my villa. All the splendours of Byzantium and none of the intrigue. I make sure of that."

Goran led the way up a stone-cut stairway into another storeroom, where the air was warmer and smelled sweet. Bulging sacks of grain were stacked on a ledge along one wall; on the other side were dozens of smaller ceramic jars and bottles. "Wheat from Egypt, almonds and honey from my gardens, sweet wine from Malaga. And cats to keep the mice away," he added, scooping up a tiny kitten and dropping it into a basket with a pile of suckling kits and their exhausted mother. "I haven't found a solution to the flies and biting insects yet. Any suggestions?"

Finn wasn't expected to answer. Goran was striding out of the storeroom into a tiled patio, similar to those at the High Alcazar, except this one had a fountain spouting from the mouth of leaping dolphins. The water falling into the shell-shaped basin glinted a dozen colours in the morning light. "Pretty, isn't it?" Goran said, "As is she." He indicated an extremely pretty girl sitting on a tiled bench, swinging her bare feet from side to side. "That is Vita from... somewhere. She rarely speaks, so I have no idea who she is. She's the laziest thrall I have ever encountered, but as thralls go, she's pleasing to the eye and suits the surroundings, don't you think?"

The questions and comments came so fast Finn stopped trying to answer and simply admired his new surroundings. Set around the square patio were stone benches covered in gold, green and white tiles that reminded Finn of the High Alcazar again. He wondered briefly where Adeef was now. Was his ship – which had been left unscathed – sitting out in the bay waiting for Finn to rescue Perla?

He turned a full circle, trying to look out to sea, but the patio was surrounded by a dwelling with rooms opening onto the fountain area. A silent male thrall in loose white clothing arrived, carrying a tray with a basket of fresh bread, two glass beakers and a jug. The boy was about his own age but much shorter, with a deep olive-toned skin and cropped black hair.

Goran indicated a table. The boy set down his tray and took a few steps backwards, his arms straight at his sides. Goran slid onto the bench and poured a thick liquid from the jug. "Orange juice," he said. "Cold and sweetened with cane sugar. Try it."

Finn sat opposite, lifted his beaker and sipped. His eyes opened in surprise. He licked his lips and drank again more deeply.

Goran smiled. This time without malice. "This, Finn of my Volsungs, is something else you cannot enjoy in your land of ice and snow."

"That's actually why I'm here," Finn started, seizing the moment. But whatever he was going to say was lost as Vita from Somewhere padded across to stand at Goran's shoulder.

"Back to work, hussy!" Goran laughed, sending her scampering through one of the open doors.

"About our ice and the cold in the North..." Finn began again.

"And aren't I glad to be away from all that," Goran replied. "Now, tell me what a Volsung was really doing on a Barbalus war galley?"

"I was captured," Finn sighed. "Wasn't that obvious?"

Goran sniffed. "Captured, and kept in a dungeon?"

"No, I was locked in a room."

"Why?"

"Why was I captured?" Finn blew through his cheeks. "Honestly, I don't know. To be a slave, I suppose, to start with, but then..." Finn shrugged.

"Adeef saw a way to use you elsewhere."

"Yes, that's what I said yesterday."

"And fixed up a way to get you in here as a spy."

"No. Although, listen, you do have a spy here for Adeef. He sends messages, with a pigeon, I think."

"No longer; man and messenger have been dealt with." Ice-Heart gave Finn an empty grin, drank some of his orange juice, and then said quietly, as if speaking to himself, "Adeef lures me into an amusing little trap on *Swan* with a Volsung youth aboard, then lets me go without a decent fight. What I want to know is, why?"

"Because his daughter Perla is here, and he wants her back. And something to do with a treaty. The Mighty Hammil..."

Goran snorted, "Mighty in girth, that's all."

"Well, he – they – want to renew your treaty."

"What treaty? The deal we made over Barbalus cargoes? That ended when Adeef tried to double-cross me. What's your reward for getting Perla off my hands?"

"No reward was mentioned. I don't think he intended me to rescue her – he wanted to make an exchange. Because I am a Volsung from your clan."

"And he knew that because of the sword?"

"No, how could he? How could he know about that?"

"But he let you keep it."

"Because he thought it was a blunt old iron stick...." Finn set his glass beaker on the table and took a deep breath, "I think Adeef was told, or believes, I'd be of some importance to you. But I wanted to come here, to find you, anyway. To – to ask you – that is, to tell you that – that you are..." Finn let his words stutter to a halt as Ice-Heart's glass beaker smashed onto the stone table.

"So that's the way of it! Well, you can forget it – *boy*." Hands raised in anger, his face dark with fury, Ice-Heart was on his feet and crossing the patio. Pausing at an open door, he turned, "I've changed my mind about breakfast. Get back to the cave with the other parasites and make yourself useful."

Chapter 24

Dreki was anchored out in the bay when Finn and the leather-garbed archers made their way down to the cove early next morning. Seren was already there, transferring food, cooking pots and kindling from a hand cart into a rowing boat. Another dinghy pulled into the shallows to ferry the archers to the galley. Apart from quivers and bows, the women were carrying blankets and sheepskins to help them through the nights they'd spend on deck or on land.

Finn was wearing the cotton servant clothing Zongolo had given him, which was ideal during the day but not when temperatures dropped at night. He hoped someone with an extra blanket or sheepskin would be generous or willing to share. He was about to ask, but Ice-Heart called from *Dreki*, chivvying them into the small boats, and everyone was too busy to chat once they were aboard.

The oarsmen moved the galley into the open sea and the skipper, a scarred Serk named Duhl, gave the orders to hoist the triangular lateen sails. Finn, trying to escape notice, watched dolphins race alongside, aware that he was enjoying every moment, which felt wrong.

"Some think the Middle Sea is a great lake," Goran said, coming to Finn's side at the port rail, his anger of the previous day forgotten. "It is not, and it can be treacherous. Tonight, we put in at a cove and sleep on land. We've been spotted by two vessels belonging to the Aleppo fleet, so we'll lie low for a night and a day to wear them out, keeping watch and confusing their timing. I know where they're heading."

The skipper altered course for the north-east coast of old Hispania, and *Dreki* tucked into a cove with black sand and enough black rocks to make Finn wonder if Goran had been wrong about the absence of dragons in the Middle Sea. Seren and a much older thrall named Melda prepared their supper over a small driftwood fire, and it was eaten in near silence. This being the way of things when Ice-Heart was out hunting.

"Sound carries loud and long over water," he said in a low voice, bringing his food to eat beside Finn. "No talking or laughing. That's an order. My crew understands the strategy – lie in wait and raid at speed. Always keep the element of surprise."

"In every single thing that you do," Finn muttered without thinking. Goran frowned, then gave him a surprisingly genial wink.

After the meal, he threw a blanket at Finn, then rolled himself into a bundle of furs to await the dawn. Finn slept in snatches. Each time he awoke he felt eyes on him. Was the crew wondering how to use him, or how to be rid of him?

They sailed the next day, looting an unwary coastal trader as they pulled around the headland. It was a small galley laden with dried fruit, grain and amphoras of wine. Goran left the trader with enough to feed his family, and *Dreki* sailed on.

They made fast going, trying to catch up with the Aleppo galleys. Goran soon turned back into Ice-Heart the pirate, pacing the galley and shouting orders already given by the skipper. Five days and nights they sailed, criss-crossing the Middle Sea like a hound quartering for a hare. Getting increasingly short-tempered, Goran told Duhl to change course and head due west towards the Pillars of Hercules.

"If we get there fast enough, we can go about and surprise them coming from the opposite direction, and maybe find the Serkland gold and myrrh galley while we're at it," he told Finn. "Those Aleppo galleys have changed their route to avoid us."

Finn gazed over the rail, the wind blowing his loose white hair off his face and felt like a king of the sea. He turned to Goran, still at his side. "You mean, if we get to the sea-gate straits fast enough, we can go about and surprise them head on?"

"That's it. If we don't have any rivals with the same idea. Ramming and boarding are hard enough, but when there's more than one galley, there's the danger another crew will come to the rescue, or we'll be chased for what we've taken. That's why we stay quiet at night. We're not the only wolves on the water. Others might hear us and follow or find our juicy prey first." Finn nodded, unable to keep a smile off his face. "You're enjoying this aren't you, boy?" Goran said, slapping him across the back. "Maybe I'll turn you into a sea-rover instead of a spy, eh?"

Finn tried to speak but Goran continued, "You'll know much of the ways of the waves, Finn, if you've come safely from the North to here, but there's more to staying afloat and alive in my line. In daylight your target can see you and try to run, and your rival can see you and sniff out your prey first, and at night anyone on the look-out can hear you."

"And they know you are sea-rovers on a raid because of *Dreki's* prow."

"Correct." Goran started to move down the deck but then called back, "The galleys we're after are carrying armed guards, so stay out of the action. Watch and learn and be ready to take an oar if necessary. I don't want you dead – yet."

It was another two days before they saw one of the galleys Ice-Heart was after. *Dreki* trailed it, keeping a careful watch for rivals until they were running fast on a strong easterly, within sight of a shoreline Finn recognised. Low-lying mauve and grey mountains parallel to the coast; a series of long, firm-sand beaches, close enough to swim to, if only he knew how.

Finn didn't have time to examine his feelings about that. Ice-Heart whistled his archers into place and told every deckhand to stay out of sight. Duhl gave the order to lower the sails, the pilot adjusted their course and the oarsmen came into action. Slowly at first, then pulling with all their might, they rammed the Aleppo galley amidships.

Within moments, Ice-Heart was screaming at his crew. He'd sighted another vessel heading towards them. "By Frigg and Hel," he yelled, "that snake Adeef's set up a coast guard. Cut, grab and let's get out of here! Not without my prize, though. I want every coffer that rattles. Forget the silks and spices. Get their silver coin. Archers, ready! Boarders, ready! You boy," he shouted at Finn, "stay out of it with them." He pointed at Seren and the other thrall, Melda, in the stern.

Finn had no intention of staying out of it; he needed to see what weapon Ice-Heart was using and grab it if he could. *Dreki* pulled back, and then rammed the galley's damaged hull a second time, sending Finn toppling onto his backside. He was up in a trice, staying as close to Ice-Heart as he dared.

"We've got her!" the pirate captain cried with glee, raising his sword in the air to signal the boarding.

The sword was short and curved and highly polished, nothing like Doomsong in either of its guises. Finn nearly sank to the deck again with relief. He didn't, because he got caught up between raiders leaping onto the reinforced bow and, in the excitement and organised mayhem, he was shoved up onto the Aleppo galley deck. Employing another sound strategy – to make as much noise as possible, to appear more numerous than they were – Ice-Heart's crew were raising pandemonium.

The boarded galley's armed guard and deckhands defended themselves well, but Ice-Heart's archers got to the upper decks unhindered and picked them off like rabbits, while his raiders made sure the wounded never stood on their own two feet again. It was brutal, sickening. Having no weapon, Finn sidled across the blood-slick deck to get into the galley's hold before he lost an arm or had his throat cut. As he started down the steps, Ice-Heart grabbed his shirt. "Get whatever caskets you can carry. Leave the heavier coffers for Troll and Walrus to bring out."

Finn wasn't the first in the hold. Others were already sorting through the cargo. "They've hidden the gems and silver," someone grunted, shifting wicker crates and oil-cloth bales.

Helping to move a carpet off what looked like coffers, Finn heard Ice-Heart give an order on deck that turned his stomach. "Foot-less or leg-less! Nobody walks off this galley except us."

'That's where his name comes from,' Finn thought, as someone near him shouted, "Found 'em!"

A casket was shoved into Finn's hands. It was small and so heavy he nearly dropped it. Clasping it to his chest, he climbed out of the hold and tried to get back onto the *Dreki* as fast as he could without looking at the mutilated Aleppo crew. Ice-Heart must have been watching for him. "You're safe now, Chicken Liver," he yelled. "My nasty boys and girls have done their worst."

His face burning with embarrassment, Finn struggled towards the boarding plank onto *Dreki*, but Ice-Heart caught him by the back of his voluminous white shirt again, then tapped the casket. "Ah, good lad! Get back aboard, we're off."

Whistling the retreat signal that pierced the groans and curses of the stricken crew, Ice-Heart waited until the last coffer was thrown onto *Dreki's* deck, cracking open in the process, and then leapt down, as his well-trained oarsmen pulled out from under the cargo galley's hull and out of the Barbalus coast-guard's arrow range. Finn braced his back against the bow strakes of *Dreki*, hugging his casket to his chest like a baby.

The next set of manoeuvres happened in a blur, as *Dreki's* accomplished crew moved her around the starboard side of their victim and pulled away east, as fast as their arm and back muscles allowed. Leaving Duhl, the skipper, to oversee their escape, Ice-Heart danced from one end of the middle deck to another, laughing and joking as if it were all a game. Passing Finn, he paused, "Hand me the casket," he said.

Finn handed him the casket and then moved nearer the stern and looked back at the Aleppo galley, wondering if there was anyone left whole or alive. He'd listened to tales of violence, of how Vikings landed on foreign shores and took what they wanted by sword or axe. This is what Harp-Legs' Vikings could do on land. And would do to their rivals *for* land if necessary. Silent and shaking, Finn hunkered down under the gunwale, the pleasure of being at sea tainted by so much blood.

As *Dreki's* sails were hoisted, while the deck hands were busy and Ice-Heart was opening his coffers, the thrall named

Seren pulled her rough linen tunic over her head, jumped into the sea and started swimming back towards the wounded galley.

Someone saw her hit the water and shouted, "Man overboard!"

"It's the girl thrall," an archer screeched.

Ice-Heart went to the upper stern-deck rail. "Frigging Hel, she can swim!" he cried. "Get her, Walrus, grab her before she gets away."

"Let her go," the burly Northman called Troll replied. "We don't need her."

"We don't need her blabbing about our hideaway to anyone, either. Walrus, get her!"

The crewman with a moustache like walrus tusks dived with barely a splash into the sea and swam with alarming speed towards Seren. Finn's heart raced as he mentally urged Seren to get to the galley, or better still, the Barbalus vessel and safety; fearing what was going to happen when Walrus got her. Would Ice-Heart slit her throat? Or would Walrus push her under?

Walrus caught Seren with ease, put an arm around her throat and returned to *Dreki* on his back. Troll pulled Seren up over the side and Walrus flopped on deck like his namesake. "She's fast, Cap'n," he gasped.

"Fast, is she? We'll see about that," Ice-Heart replied. "Put her in irons."

Troll carried Seren under an arm to the stern and shackled her ankles and wrists to iron rings set in the rail. No one went near her except old Melda. She brought Seren her discarded tunic and a cup of ale, and then a blanket. When day turned to night, and Ice-Heart made no objection, Melda fed her like a baby.

In the moonlight, relaxed on raided wine, Ice-Heart went to stand over Seren. "You can swim," he said. "How's that?"

"My brothers showed me," Seren croaked, her throat parched dry.

"Why?"

"They were fishermen."

"Britons catch fish by hand? I had no idea."

"Nets get caught sometimes."

"They showed you how to gut fish as well, did they?" Seren nodded. "So," Ice-Heart continued, crouching down to push a strand of dull, straight hair off her round face with a bloodstained finger, "I have been favouring a quiet little cook who could slit my throat with a gutting knife and steal the soul from my chest like a siren. Seren the siren. Shame you're so frigging plain; I could get a good price for you with those skills." He stood up, studied her face for a moment then winked and said, "I'll keep you, on one condition: you never ever sing in my presence."

'Siren song' it was called. Finn had learned about sirens from traders in the North. Half-woman, half-fish, or bird – depending on the teller – when a siren sang, a mariner lost his life and his soul. Finn had told versions of that story himself many times, with embellishments. Looking at Seren now, he was glad she was so homely and quiet; safer for her that way.

Later into the night, Ice-Heart sat down beside Finn. "You all right, boy? Got over your fright?"

Would he ever get over what he'd witnessed on that galley, Finn wondered. "That cargo," he said, "was it for the High Alcazar?"

Ice-Heart grinned. "It was."

"What happened? I mean, can you tell me what happened to the treaty you had with the Mighty Hammil?"

"That puffed up, fat oaf. That was no formal treaty. It was an agreement. No document or binding oath involved. Adeef promised me a good percentage, and I got nothing, bar a few frigging jars of olive oil. Why?"

Finn shrugged. "I just wanted to know what Adeef was referring to."

"You *are* his stooge, aren't you?" Ice-Heart's face was so close Finn could smell the wine on his breath. "What's he told you to do? Report on me and my fortress? Eh? Eh? You'll not step off it again, if that's the case. I'll have you shackled like that stupid thrall."

Finn tried to edge away, but Ice-Heart put a hand on his chest, pinning him against the strakes. "Why are you really here, Finn? Tell me."

Finn closed and opened his eyes, desperate to pass on Master Odo's message, to get it over and done with and then to escape Goran Ice-Heart's unpredictable temperament. "I was sent to find you."

"You were sent to find me? By Adeef?"

"No, by..." Finn wanted to tell all, but not like this. Not with Ice-Heart the pirate half-drunk on success, on his fine vessel, surrounded by his loyal crew, many of whom were watching them, listening to every word. And not without the sword, to justify the message.

"You've gone very quiet," Ice-Heart murmured, removing his hand from Finn's chest. He moved away, retied the black leather thong at the back of his head; his sharp blue gaze never leaving Finn's gentler grey eyes. "Hmm?" he said, his angular jaw crooked to one side.

Finn swallowed hard. "I tried to tell you, the other morning," he whispered. "But you wouldn't listen."

"Ah, no, no; I know what you were going to say, and that, my white-haired Volsung countryman, won't persuade me to go back to the Cold North."

"But you don't know what I was trying to say."

"Oh, I think I do. It's what they're all waiting to hear, isn't it?" Ice-Heart flung out a hand, indicating his crew. "It's what your Adeef was betting on. Well, that little game won't work. I don't give a tinker's cuss whose son you are. And nobody wheedles their way into my empire that easy." With that, Goran Ice-Heart jumped to his feet in a single movement and swung down the deck to share the looted wine with his favourites.

Emotionally and physically drained, Finn closed his eyes, and by some strange magic, fell asleep. When he awoke, a low, bone-chilling mist lay over *Dreki*. Shivering, Finn struggled down the swaying deck to find his blanket and something to eat. There was nothing left. Wrapped in the now-damp blanket Goran had given him, he moved to the stern rail, where Seren sat hunched up, her teeth chattering with cold.

Finn swung the blanket from his shoulders and tucked it around her, then sat down as close as he could, to share what little body warmth remained to him until the dawn. Seren said not a word; her tears spoke for her.

Chapter 25

Returning to the island after the raid a few days later, Seren was hustled up the hill between two archers to prepare their evening meal. Everyone was tired and hungry, and she could barely walk, but Ice-Heart sent her anyway. His crew wanted to celebrate – the invincible Ice-Heart had taken them raiding and they'd returned with coffers of silver coin and precious gems.

Not waiting for permission or orders, Finn disembarked and followed them up to the cave, then sat by the entrance waiting for somebody to tell him what to do. A few of the crew staggered in, carrying sacks and bundles; some came in to leave their weapons and blankets in the sleeping area. Troll and the swimmer named Walrus passed the track to the cave, heading around the hill to the front entrance to Ice-Heart's villa. Each had a heavy casket in his arms. Various oarsmen followed them, balancing sacks on their heads.

The rest of the crew, aided by the younger boys, who had been waiting for *Dreki* to return, stayed down in the cove, ferrying booty to the beach, and from the beach to the cavern, where, apart from the olive oil and wine, it was left on the grassy plateau in the open. The oil and wine were taken directly to the villa.

When two iron-hinged coffers were set down outside the entrance to the cave, everyone, thralls excluded, gathered around as if it were a Midsummer festival. Sitting cross-legged in something approaching a circle, they waited for their leader, re-living their contributions to the raids and their escape from the Barbalus coast guard; speculating on who should get what part of the spoils for doing what, and what, if anything, would go to the boys who'd helped clean the hull and sharpen weapons but stayed ashore. Talking ceased the moment Ice-Heart arrived. Unlike his crew, he had snatched time to wash and change his clothing.

Laughing and joking, accepting the first beaker of wine before the jug circulated, Goran Ice-Heart was the centre of attention, and soon, the heart and soul of a night-long party. When everyone had a beaker of wine, the toasts began: to Bolli for being first aboard, to Magnus for being last off, to Walrus for being a fast swimmer, and so it went on, until Ice-Heart flicked a sharp knife from the side of a doe-skin boot and raised it in the air. Silence fell, and the serious business, the purpose of their long excursion, began.

Goran pointed and Troll opened one of the largest coffers, using an iron jemmy designed for the purpose by one of the resident smiths. Inside were chased silver trappings for bridles and spurs with fancy buckles. "We'll have to get horses next time," a joker quipped.

"Nah, this lot'll go for decent money in Valencia."

"Malaga's better for silver goods."

A brief debate on the best trading cities followed, until one of the smaller coffers was opened. There was a collective gasp. This was what it was all about. The coffer was full to the brim with bright round coins and hack silver. One by one, the crew went to Ice-Heart to receive a coin or a handful, according to their length of service. And all the time, food and wine circulated and the noise level increased, until the small coffer that Finn had brought out of the Aleppo galley's hold was in the centre of the gathering.

Finn held his breath. He had received nothing so far; would Goran let him have any of its contents?

Pulling the chest to him, Ice-Heart knelt over it, prized it open and then teasing, took out one single item: a green gemstone the size of a pigeon egg. Holding it between his rough-skinned forefinger and thumb, he waited until there was an 'ahh' of appreciation, then put it back. Next, he pulled out a necklace of fiery white stones, then a collar of amethysts, a gold bangle, dangling beaded earrings, and so it went on, each dropped back into the chest, so everyone knew that whoever got the chest would be very wealthy – and marriageable.

Everyone also knew that the only person who would get the chest would be Ice-Heart, the Viking pirate king. So, when he said, "Mine, I think," they feigned disappointment, but not surprise.

Ice-Heart clicked his fingers at a male thrall, who lifted the coffer and headed into the cavern with it. Finn watched him as far as he could without making it obvious. The thrall knew the location of Ice-Heart's treasure trove.

Once it was clear Ice-Heart had finished sharing the loot, the feasting, the singing and dancing began. Quietly, individually, various members of the crew sneaked away to stow their treasures in their secret – they hoped – hiding places. Finn loitered by the entrance to the cave, watching, saying nothing, chewing a hunk of barley bread and drinking juice pressed from oranges, which to him was sweeter than wine.

Eventually, Ice-Heart grabbed him by the shoulder and steered him across the cavern to the passage. "You'll live with me now, boy. And you, girl," he snapped his fingers as Seren passing by with a bowl of dried fruit, "you two will stay in my villa where I can see you – day and night. Starting now."

Seren handed the bowl to the nearest thrall and hurried towards the passage at the rear of the cavern. As she left, Finn noticed one of the women archers grab her arm. "Find out who he is," she hissed. "We want to know."

Goran pushed Finn up the deep rock steps and through the passage, and then up the stairs to the villa patio, where Seren was waiting for instructions. "You, in the kitchen," Ice-Heart said, pointing to a door. "You'll sleep there as well."

Waiting to see that Seren went where she'd been directed, Ice-Heart then led Finn into a bath house. Coming from the Cold North, where removing clothes and washing in water was to be avoided nine months of the year, Finn marveled at the chamber designed specifically for bathing. Warm steam hovered over a marble floor. A lithe male Serklander led them to a deep bath, decorated with a mosaic of a fish-tailed siren seated on a rock.

Pulling off his clothing, Goran jumped straight into the water. Finn hesitated, memories of the soapy tub at the Alcazar still fresh in his mind. Reluctantly, he allowed the slave to help him remove his filthy servant garb and then cautiously entered the water, down the steps provided. The water was warm. He started to relax. Once he was sure his feet could touch the floor tiles and he could still breath, he put a hand on a step to steady himself and leant backwards until his hair was drifting around his head like an empty net.

"I didn't know bathing could be so pleasant," he said, but Ice-Heart was floating in the water, fast asleep.

Later that evening, so tired he could barely keep his eyes open, Finn sat at a table in the patio alone, wearing what he assumed were a set of Goran's own clothes. The sensation of the cool fabric against his clean skin set him thinking. The loose white cotton overblouse and wide-legged trews were identical to the servant garb of the High Alcazar. It was probably what most men living around the Middle Sea wore. In the Cold North, people wore layers of wool under layers of skins that had kept sheep, goats and cows, as well as wild animals, warm in the worst of winters. Here, people protected their skins from the burning sun with thin layers of cool cotton, fine muslin and wide-weave linen.

Goran's choice of clothing, his dwelling and lifestyle showed how much at home he was in the Middle Sea, and Finn knew in his heart that Goran was not going to return with him – *if* he was allowed to return. Even so, he had to try. Master Odo had sent him for a reason, and that reason was more important than any of the comforts Goran – or Finn himself – had found on his island.

As if to conclude his chain of thought, Seren set a dish of roasted almonds and cup of delicious-smelling broth on the patio table. She was still wearing her rough-spun tunic, and her face showed her fear and fatigue, but she managed a smile. "It is chilled soup," she said in his language. "You might not like it."

"I'm sure I will," he replied and took a long slurp. The taste was new and strong and strange, but he smiled his thanks, not wanting to look ungrateful.

Seren nodded, but instead of returning to the kitchen, hovered at his side.

"Do you want to sit down?" Finn asked, for the girl looked exhausted.

"I can't. Mustn't," she replied. Then said in a rush, "They want to know who you are and where are you from."

"I know," Finn chuckled. "But tell me first where you come from. And why on this mortals' earth did you try to get to that galley after we'd raided it? Why not get away when we were on land?"

"They can run faster than me."

"But not swim?"

"I didn't think they'd notice." She paused. "I didn't think at all. I just jumped."

"But you are not from anywhere on the Middle Sea. How would you get home?"

Seren shook her head and then checked to see if anyone was nearby, fearful of being caught slacking. "I was taken from Britain to Hibernia when I was very small. Pirates captured my mother. We were thralls, but people were good to us there. Until *he*... attacked our village."

"And your mother?"

"She died. Long before. Are you Ice-Heart's younger brother?"

"This is very good," Finn said, sniffing the soup, avoiding the question.

When he looked up, Seren had gone and Ice-Heart was crossing the patio towards the storeroom. Pretending not to have seen him, Finn selected a few almonds and began to count. How long before Ice-Heart returned? Had he gone through to the cave or was he checking whether his coffers had been stashed correctly? And if so, where? Because Doomsong could be in the same place.

Waiting another few beats, Finn went to the storehouse door to listen.

Ice-Heart's steel-strong hand gripped his left wrist. Finn gulped but kept his face blank. "Ah, young Finn of the Volsungs," Ice-Heart said, "spying on me again."

"No! I'm not here for that."

"But you are spying on me."

"Not at all. I'm here to fetch you...."

"For that ball of lard, Hammil, and his sharp-nosed fixer? No frigging chance."

"Not for them no, I'm here to..."

"See what I've got tucked away for *my* future – or to tell the Barbalus what's in my secret vault?"

"No, honestly, it's nothing like that. Let me finish!"

"Finish what?"

"My words. You keep tying me in knots and I have to tell you something very important."

"Oh, all right, let's get it over with," Ice-Heart sighed, extending an arm and inviting Finn to return to the patio and then ambling with exaggerated slowness to the table he had vacated.

Finn pushed back his hair, retied a new black leather thong behind his head, took a deep breath and went to sit on the opposite side of the table. "First," he said, "I need to know what you've done with my sword."

"*Your* sword! I can read runes, you know."

"Oh, good," Finn gasped with relief. "That's why I'm here. For what it says on the blade."

"You've read the runes?" Goran's voice dropped.

"Yes. I keep trying to tell you. If you've read the blade message you can guess why I am here, and..."

"I guess nothing. Guessing is for children's riddles. I am curious to know how *you* came by the weapon; that is all. Unfortunately, this is not the moment. I have matters to attend in the town."

"You've just said you'd listen to me."

"My mistake: I have other matters to attend. Down in the main harbour."

"But why won't you listen – hear me out? You are..."

A single raised finger, now wearing a spectacular sapphire ring, halted whatever Finn was going to say next. Ice-Heart moved away from the table and pointed across the patio. "If you want to take anything back to the High Alcazar, Perla is in that chamber over there. You can start persuading her while I'm out of the way. She's not chained, so keep your neck covered. Good luck. And if you survive the encounter," he added, heading for the pebble-lined path that led down to the harbour, "sleep well."

Finn watched him go and then walked slowly around the fountain, waiting for his heartbeat to return to normal and trying to decide what, if anything, to do about Perla. Still hungry, he finished the chilled soup and wandered around the fountain again, cursing himself for a weakling, for not tackling Goran about Doomsong there and then, and walked straight past Perla's chamber. The slave who had attended him in the bath house and supplied him with clean clothes was standing beside another door.

"My room?" Finn inquired, and when the thrall nodded, Finn stumbled forwards with a grateful sigh and fell into his new bed. He was so weary he didn't notice a ginger cat on the green-tiled sill outside his open window.

Chapter 26

Finn woke in a soft bed in a spartan room with a heavy weight on his legs. A large ginger cat was curled into a ball on his striped blue and white coverlet. He jiggled his legs. The cat stretched, rose to her feet and stretched again, making sure her claws dug unto his legs.

"Shoo!" Finn said, lifting himself onto his elbows. "What is it with cats these days? They're everywhere!" Thinking about the spotted feline in the High Alcazar reminded him of his first impression of Perla – a sleek, wild and dangerous black cat, and what he should have done the previous evening. With a sigh, he sank back into the down-filled mattress.

This cat, however, was tame. Far too tame. Strolling up the contours of his body, she stared into his face, then jumped soundlessly onto the floor and went to the door. Obeying her unspoken command, Finn got out of bed and opened it. Then hopped back in. He needed to decide what to do – stay as a guest (what sort of guest?) and become a sea-raider with a merciless pirate, who said one thing and did another? Or complete his task and persuade Goran (how?) to return North and fulfil Master Odo's command;? Or get away from Goran's island, find Seavogel and return to the North, to do what he could for his people himself.

One thing was certain; if Perla wanted to be rescued, she could wait for one of her own kind. He'd got enough problems of his own. Finn sat up and stretched, not unlike the cat. Here was one decision he could make – to stay well out of the Perla situation.

First and foremost, he needed to reclaim the Doomsong sword. Because if Goran Ice-Heart wasn't going to fulfill his role as clan leader, he had no right to it. He'd said he'd read the runes, so he'd seen the reference to the "true owner", and that was the person who would return North to help his people. Not a cruel, greedy, one-time Volsung with no thought but for himself.

The next thought formed itself slowly in Finn's head and then stuck like a barnacle to a keel. If Master Odo had entrusted him, Finn, an orphan Volsung, with the sword, *there was a reason for it.*

Was this what Goran suspected and didn't want to hear?

Was it possible...? Was the family similarity Goran himself had mentioned more than a matter of clan traits? Were they both descendants of Sigurd the Volsung, who had slain the dragon Grafnir with the Dwarf-forged Doomsong sword? Or the boy called Davor, who had defeated the great beast through a clever trick. He had also been a true Volsung. So, who was the rightful heir to the sword? Who was the "true owner" if the sword had glowed for him?

Unless, as Seren had queried, Goran was an older brother. Much older. The alternative didn't bear thinking about: Goran Ice-Heart was not someone he could admire or respect.

Finn's musing ceased with a knock at the door. Seren entered with a brown jug balanced in a wide ceramic basin. She had a length of soft linen over her arm. "I brought you fresh water to wash," she said. "Your breakfast is on the patio. Fruit and bread, and goat's cheese." She gave him a shy smile and left before he could say thank you.

As he dried his face and neck with the soft towel, Finn began thinking about how Ice-Heart had divided the silver and a few precious gems from the raided vessel among his crew, according to their custom. The free-born oarsmen, rovers and archers had each hidden their loot, hoping they had found a safe, secret location. Using thralls, who received nothing but a beating if they slacked, Ice-Heart had transferred his much larger share to an underground vault. But where was the vault, and what else might be in it?

The moment Finn finished his breakfast, he began to explore the villa, identifying the kitchen and bakehouse, the outhouses where carts and farm implements were kept, the stables, clean and empty except for a sturdy cart, a few broken oars and coils of rope. Eventually, taking his time, he wandered into the storehouse, where, if necessary, he could pretend to be returning to the cavern through the underground passage. That is where he suspected the treasure vault was located – down the passage that branched off the cavern tunnel. He'd barely reached the middle step down to the lower wine cellar when a voice drawled, "Spying on me again, are you? Well, come and take a good long look." Beckoning Finn into an underground room with an iron-barred door, Ice-Heart continued, "Go on, take a good look at my booty, because this is the last you'll ever see of it. You get nothing. Understand? *Nothing*."

Finn took a deep breath and remained silent, watching as the bath-house slave stowed a sack of what smelled like clove spice into the storage space. "Worth more than their weight in gold, some of these spices are," Ice-Heart said, tapping the top of another sack. "I sold some last night in town. Very good prices. Peppercorns, cloves and coriander seeds. People pay well for all this across the sea."

"Did we take sacks of spices off the coastal trader?"

"We certainly did. Unexpected easy pickings."

"I thought we'd only got dried grapes and sacks of grain," Finn said, inhaling a new aroma.

"Good, I'm glad you thought that," Ice-Heart replied. "That means they will, too."

"Your crew?"

"Who else?"

Ice-Heart cheated everyone. Finn was not surprised. Making good use of the moment, he registered every nook and cranny of the storeroom, looking for a door leading to a secret vault.

There was no identifiable entrance to anything.

"Where are you going?" Ice-Heart, demanded as Finn backed into the passage.

"I thought I'd get a bit of archery practice, if one of the girls can spare the time. I've never used a crossbow."

"Plan to make yourself useful, do you, or shoot me through the heart – if you can find it?"

"Many here could do that better than me," Finn laughed.

"And yet, they do not. Ask yourself why, Finn. The answer may help you decide."

"Decide?" Finn gulped.

"To stay and be Ice-Heart's friend; or to stay and be his prisoner. I have changed my mind about letting you go; you have seen too much. My scouts and archers, and boat owners down in the harbour, all have orders to prevent your getting off the island. Find something to occupy yourself with until I make my decision on how to use you. Not archery, though, and certainly not crossbow archery. How does learning to cook with your little thrall friend suit?"

Finn's mouth went dry. He tried to find something to say, to appeal to Goran's better nature, to use their family connection and physical likeness, but the man in front of him was Ice-Heart the pirate, who lacked a better nature.

"Lost for words, are you?" Ice-Heart sneered. "That makes it easier for both of us. Now, go and find Troll, the big chap with the ugly mug, and get yourself down to the beach to clean out *Dreki*. I've got things to do."

Finn clumped down the steps, heading for the cavern to find the Viking named Troll. Thick tallow candles in crevices and lumps of rock lit his way until the right-hand fork, which was very dark and had a sudden drop. Finn tumbled forwards, banging his forehead and scraping his elbows. As he was getting to his feet, taking care not to crack his head on the low ceiling, Troll came up the steep slope, carrying a small oil lamp.

"Has he sent you for something?" Troll asked.

Finn hesitated. He'd fallen by accident and his head was spinning. "Yes, but I forgot to bring a candle."

"Here, take this. I can do this tunnel in my sleep. What's he told you to get?"

Finn put a hand to the side of his head. "Erm – the casket of gems I took on the galley."

"It's not down there. It's in the villa."

Troll's deep voice matched his size and shape. Aware their words would carry up and along the tunnel, Finn hesitated again but then mumbled, "Ah, right. My mistake," and started to scramble back up the passage.

Troll's next words froze him like one of the shiny pillars that grew up through the cave floor. "You're looking for your sword, aren't you?"

Finn bit his lip. Say 'yes'; say 'no'? His spine outlined by the oil-fed flame must have given him away.

"It's not down there. I've looked," Troll said quietly.

Finn turned, slowly.

"There's a pile of iron blades, blunt old things from whoever lived here generations ago, but not the pretty one."

Finn gazed at the big man filling the low tunnel, trying to read his expression in the dark, not daring to speak.

"Is it... the *famous* one?" Troll asked in a dramatic whisper.

"Famous?"

"From the legend." Troll bent lower, pushing his bristly face towards Finn. "I'm a Volsung, see. My family's told that story generation after generation, about a boy from nowhere who took the sword named Doomsong and... what's the other name?"

"Truthteller," Finn whispered almost to himself.

"That's it. I mean, is that the one? I know it can't be, not really, but it glowed in Goran's hand, like it says in the saga, and... well, I wondered."

"It's a good tale, the saga," Finn replied.

"It isn't the sword they talk about, then?"

"I suppose it might be." Finn's mind clicked back into action, "If you find it, will you let me see it? Maybe it'll glow again – for me." Finn forced a laugh. Could Troll be trusted?

Not wanting to take a risk with someone who'd probably been with Goran since he left the Cold North, Finn began backing up the steep tunnel, trying to think of something to send the big man on his way so he could get down to the vault, because Doomsong could well be hiding among the old blades Troll had mentioned, and short of wriggling between his tree-trunk legs, there was no way to get past him.

Once back at the fork leading into the crew's cavern, Finn said, "Well, got to get on. See you later," and turned, as if returning to the villa.

Troll headed towards the cave. After waiting to see if he was lurking in the dark to catch him out, Finn shaded the light from the small hand-lamp Troll had given him and hurried back down the steep tunnel. A waft of air caught at the flame as he entered a wide chamber; either there was another entrance or a natural chimney. The flame flared again, lighting every farm boy's dream of treasure. Iron-clad chests shut and locked; coffers open with brooches and buckles and beaded jewelery spilling out. Larger coffers with helmets, chainmail shirts and fancy wristbands; breastplates stacked in a row like legless warriors; and against the far wall, rows of old weapons stashed four or more deep. Finn couldn't stop smiling. If Doomsong was here, and he had a feeling it was, the clever blade was hiding as an iron stick.

But which one was it? Holding the lamp in his left hand, Finn ran the fingers of his right hand over the pommels. None that he could see or touch had the shape of a rising sun. Had Ice-Heart pushed Doomsong nearer the wall? Had he even been down here? Finn tried again, running his right hand against the first row of hilts, then poking and probing with a forefinger between them, until – yes, a faint glimmer. Placing the lamp on the floor, he began to shift the first row of blades as quietly as possible, pulling at the next row until he could reach the one that had glowed.

It was heavy and noisy work, and at every moment Finn expected Ice-Heart to come hurtling in, but there it was: a golden pommel like a rising sun. Finn put his hand around the tang and pulled.

The lamp went out. Doomsong's soft yellow glow lit the cavern.

And a blast of hot, onion-charged breath said, "It's true then."

In answer, Doomsong shone brighter in the absolute dark.

"What do you know about it?" Finn asked, turning to face the Northman called Troll, now standing behind him.

"That the sword was said to be invincible in the hands of Sigmund, until Odin broke it in battle and claimed him for Valhalla and Ragnarök. Then it was found and remade for his son, Sigurd, who slew the dragon Grafnir with it. Except…"

"Except?" Finn asked.

"My old gran said her old gran told them it wasn't Sigurd who killed the dragon; it was someone else. Direct line from Sigmund, only not Sigurd. She said it was an eldest-son-to-eldest-son kind of thing. It's only magical for true Volsungs of his line. I think."

Finn blew through his cheeks. "That puts me in line somewhere, I suppose."

"You going to tell Goran?"

Finn sighed. "I'll have to, now you know I've got it."

Then, remembering his quest, and fearing the power of a one-eyed Wanderer named Master Odo more than that of a renegade pirate, Finn said, "Yes. I shall tell him and say why."

"Right then, I'm with you, Finn, me lad. You're a Volsung, so we're cousins, and cousins have to stick together."

Finn looked at the brutish features of his kinsman in the glow of the sword. "You may regret those words, Troll. But I need all the help I can get. Come, we must find Goran and explain. I have something very important to tell him – while I have the sword with me."

Troll's face scrunched up. He scratched behind an ear. "Ah, well, I dunno. Maybe that's not such a good idea. Maybe you should just try to get away. I can help you with that."

"No!" Finn said, full of determination. "Come on. We need to find Goran. I have a message for him, from the Wanderer, Master Odo."

"The Wanderer!" Troll grunted. "Why don't I keep my trap shut?"

Chapter 27

Trying to stay calm, half-hoping Ice-Heart was busy elsewhere, Finn hurried up the narrow tunnel then stuffed the sword down the front of his tunic and hastened towards the crew's cavern, where he collected the back sheath harness, looped it over a shoulder and strolled casually outside. The tip of the sword poked into his groin with every step.

Once out in the fresh air, Troll was at his elbow. "Watch it," he said, "there's archers and lookouts posted all over the place. If things go bottoms-up with Goran, get down to the main harbour after dark and I'll help you steal a boat. But not till tonight."

"Are you being honest with me?" Finn asked, suspecting he was being tricked or led into a trap.

"Honest 'bout what?"

Finn sighed. Troll was the largest and ugliest person he'd ever seen or invented for his tales; his face looked as if it had been formed from river mud, with a nose that had been squidged on badly and then flattened with a paddle. One eye was higher on one side than the other. A straggly red beard barely covered a mouth of rotted tree stumps and did nothing to filter the stinking whiff of of his breath. And he was either very dense or pretending to be.

"Honest about what?" the giant demanded again, squinting down at Finn. "I'm only trying to help. A boat in the harbour is your only chance. If Goran don't like what you're going to tell him and has one of his fits, which he might – don't take much to send him berserk, and once he gets like that it takes a day or more for him to get half-way normal again – things have a habit of dying or disappearing along the way. Got me?"

"Got you. Thanks for the warning," Finn replied, shaking his head. "But I really do have something important – vital – to tell him before I can leave."

"I'll come with you," Troll offered.

"No! No, I need to do this on my own. Thanks. It's very personal, see. But listen, if anything happens to me..." Finn's words started to get as tangled as his fears. "Just keep an eye out for the sword, and if Goran looks like he's going berserk will you hide it? Keep it safe?"

Troll's small eyes blinked various times under his bushy red eyebrows. "Me?"

"You're a Volsung. You know about Doomsong. Who else could save it?"

"Oh, me! Yeah. Right! So, I'll come with you."

Finn couldn't find a way to refuse. Giving Troll no time to say anything else, he jogged around the hill towards the pebble-lined path that led into the main entrance of the Roman villa. Seren was picking rosemary from waist-high bushes lining the path. A ginger cat sat nearby, watching her.

Finn gave Seren a vague smile, intending to walk on past without a word, then stopped. Tugging the sword from underneath his tunic, ready to face Ice-Heart with it, Finn saw the flaw in his thinking and had a sudden premonition of disaster.

Despite all he'd planned – to show Goran the sword and the runes and then pass on Master Odo's message – he changed his mind. Goran had read the runes; he knew what they said. So, he would deliver the message first, *then – if* Goran agreed – he'd fetch the sword and hand it to him. Not the other way around, because otherwise he'd lose it forever.

Fast as he could, he stuffed the short iron blade into the deep, green rosemary bush, covering his fine cotton sleeves with sharp-scented needles in the process. He wasn't sure what Troll had seen, or if it mattered, but he wasn't going to confront Goran with the sword in his hand before he knew which way the wind was blowing. That was, whether he was talking to Goran of the Volsungs, or Ice-Heart the pirate.

The girl watched him in silence. Smiling at her, he said, "Stay close by here if you can, Seren, please. If anything happens to me, take this sword to..." To whom? If anything happened to him, Troll would come for it, meaning it would go to Ice-Heart, anyway.

For now, though, he couldn't risk losing it again, and Ice-Heart was more than capable of agreeing to return to the North to get the sword back, and then staying on the island. And doing away with the messenger.

Troll's warning was a bit garbled, but Finn had got the gist, and Goran –named Ice-Heart for being heartless – was striding towards him.

"I sent you down to clean *Dreki*. What you doing here, boy?" he called from the villa's open gateway.

Finn straightened his shoulders, stood taller, and began striding, in exactly the same manner, towards the pirate. Reaching him, he grabbed an arm and drew him into the patio area to sit on a stone bench by the fountain. Troll followed, his mouth open.

"What's going on?" Ice-Heart demanded. "Who do you think you are!"

"A kinsman, apparently," Finn replied. "Which, I suppose, is why I am here." And before the pirate could say another word, Finn began the speech he had rehearsed in his head a hundred or more times since boarding *Guillemot*.

"The fact that the sword glowed in your hand means you are the rightful, true owner of Doomsong. This means you are our clan leader, and it's your obligation to return to the North and lead your people out of danger. A mountain is going to explode and... and then there'll be ash over all the land, and we won't see the sun again for years to come. Master Odo says he wants you to take our people to a new land. Across the whale road to Britain or down to Frankia or Hispania, somewhere with fertile soil, and warm weather. Only you, Master Odo says, can do this. You are the one to lead them away. Otherwise, they might not leave their homesteads. You are the best person and only one with the knowledge of other lands who can do this." Finn raced the last bit, aware that he might have missed some of important points, but he'd run out of courage.

For a moment there was absolute silence. Then Ice-Heart gave a chuckle that turned into a harsh laugh. "That is a good story, tale-maker, a good yarn. Though not to my liking. It shows me in a bad light."

"No, it doesn't. Quite the opposite. You're the hero of the North – or you will be."

"Not if I don't go. Assuming any of this cock-and-bull yarn is anything more than a story."

"It's completely true."

"Which is why it casts me in a bad light, for, as you must know, I shall not set sail for the North. Not today or ever, so it figures me as a weakling." Finn started to speak but Ice-

Heart raised a calloused finger. "Which means, Tale-maker, that I was right in my earlier decision; you cannot return to the North, either."

Finn leaned backwards with shock. "But the sword, it glowed in your hands and..."

"It did indeed. I am its rightful owner, apparently." Ice-Heart tweaked the leather harness off Finn's shoulder, "So I'll be needing this. Don't fret, Doomsong will be perfectly safe with me. Another reason why you can't paddle back to your flat islands to tell tales. If, one distant day I choose to pass it on to my chosen heir, he or she can return it, or not. In the meantime, the sword, and Finn the Tale-Maker, shall stay on this island."

Finn opened his mouth to speak, but no words came.

Ice-Heart gave him a wolfish smile, then turned to Troll. "Shackle him in the usual place. Food once a day. No light; no visitors."

Moving surprisingly fast, Troll shoved Finn's left arm up his back and marched him towards the storeroom. Grabbing another oil lamp and lighting it single-handed from a taper on a shelf, he then pushed Finn down the steps, then down some more, and into another sloping tunnel, until they were deep underground in near perfect darkness. Troll knew his way, ducking down to avoid banging his head where Finn's forehead had taken various sharp knocks. Eventually, they arrived in another low-ceilinged chamber. Troll placed the small lamp on a log of wood that served as a table and pushed Finn against a wall, where he slapped a hinged iron cuff around his wrist.

"Sorry," Troll grunted. "You're lucky, though. I was 'specting him to chop off your hands, or your feet. He does that when he's not happy." Troll picked up his lamp, held it near Finn's face. "Sorry, cousin. I'll send you some grub later."

"But Troll... you know where I put the sword. Get it. Bring it to me. Please, I beg you. Don't let Goran have it. Not now. *Please.*"

Troll looked him in the eye, sniffed, then left the chamber, taking the only light with him.

Finn slumped against the cold, damp cave wall. "Frigg!" he called into the hollow blackness, "Mother goddess, you, who knows our Fate, tell me, is this my Destiny?"

The beautiful Aesir goddess Frigg, who knew Finn's fate, lit no light, showed no concern.

Chapter 28

Finn had no way of knowing if it was day or night. His bones and muscles ached when he changed position so he thought he might have dozed for a while. He was hungry, thirsty and angry. Angry with himself for failing Master Odo, and for what might happen to his people in the North. Angry for not handling Goran Ice-Heart better, although how could you predict how he would react to anything? And angry with himself for not listening to Katranina, after the Grendel incident. 'The question Finn should ask himself is *why*?'

He could hear her light voice, as if she were beside him: *Why* has Finn been unable to deliver Master Odo's message? *Why* has Finn allowed himself to be trapped? Why is Finn afraid of Goran the Volsung?

"Because," he huffed into the rat-scratching dark, "because he's untrustworthy, cruel and a liar!" he shouted out loud.

And maybe, a small voice inside his head, added, *I can't be trusted, either. I haven't done what Hammil or Adeef asked. Haven't even tried.*

Why?

"Because I have been weak. Chicken Liver, he called me. But! But that has to stop. Because..." Finn banged his head against the rock behind him, flexed his hand in the manacle chained to the wall. "Because if Doomsong glowed for me, I must belong to Sigmund the Volsung's line...."

A scuttling sound drew his attention, a mouse, or a rat. "If I ever get out of here," he said quietly, speaking to his four-legged audience, "d'you know what I'm going to do?" His listeners paused, waiting for the answer. "I'm going to tell Goran why he must help his people again and drag him down to a boat if I have to."

Or, Katranina's voice whispered at the back of his mind, *Finn can help his people himself.*

Yes, I had worked that out for myself, thank you.

The mental conversation came to a halt with that now impossible solution. Worn out from weeks of physical discomfort and doubt, fear and tension, Finn dropped his head onto his bony knees and gave in to tears. He was still snuffling when a flicker of light crossed his eyelids and Seren's voice whispered, "Finn, your cousin has come."

Expecting to see Troll's ugly face, Finn gasped with surprise when Katranina appeared. "What are you doing here!" he croaked.

"Hello, it is Cousin Kat, and welcome to you," she replied.

"You are not my cousin."

"Kat might be. Does Finn wish to stay here arguing, or leave? Kat only asks because she has put herself in danger for Finn – again."

"Gods and worms; yes, sorry." Finn tried to get to his feet.

Seren reached out to help him. "Wait," she said. "I've got a key for the manacle."

It took a while. The locking device on Finn's wrist was rusty and the key refused to turn until Kat took over and breathed on it. Then the lock clicked open, and the manacle fell to the stone floor with a loud clang. All three froze, waiting for someone to appear.

Kat left the prison chamber and then returned. "No person heard us," she whispered, "but Finn must be very quiet."

Finn took a few steps in the dark to get his balance. The two girls – young women – waited, then Kat took charge again. "Finn must go up the tunnel in the dark. Alone. When he reaches a rock wall he must take this turning," she opened her right hand, "and continue to the main cavern."

"Then I go through it, and out onto the hill," Finn concluded. "Aren't you coming with me?"

"Seren will follow with the candle. Separate from Finn. Wait for her on the hill in the trees."

"Is it nighttime?" Finn asked.

"Yes," Seren answered.

"What about you, Kat?" Finn said.

"Kat has night eyes. Kat can make herself small to tangle men's legs so they fall, if they follow you."

"Can you? Oh, well, yes, all right then. But Seren, you go first with the lamp. Not me. If anyone hears or sees you, pretend you're trying to get back to your place in the cave. Wait for me outside. If anyone stops you or anything, I'll creep back here. I don't want you getting punished again, or worse." He turned to Kat, "Will you be all right by yourself?"

"Finn is thoughtful," Kat said in her flat, ironic tone and then, before Finn could snap a reply, added, "Kat shall not be seen. All cats are black in the dark," and dipped away out of the flickering light.

Finn blinked, then gave Seren a gentle nudge. "Go on, you first, and don't worry if you lose me on the way." Seren moved forward but Finn tapped her shoulder, "No, wait. What happened to my sword? Did Troll come back for it?"

"I moved it into some other bushes, lower down the hill. And then I stayed out of sight. He didn't come looking for me. I thought he would."

"Brave, clever girl," Finn replied, giving her a hug.

With a hand shielding the small flame from the oil lamp, Seren went up the steep tunnel and then took the right-hand fork that led into the cave. Most, if not everyone, were asleep. Finn suspected a few eyes followed their progress down the rocky ledge and around the fire-pit to the entrance, but nobody stopped or challenged them – a young couple sneaking out for some privacy on a summer night, nothing unusual in that. Except perhaps that it was Ice-Heart's white-haired guest and a thrall; but then again, thralls did what they were told.

Once in the open air, Seren blew out the light and left it behind a rock, then, by unclouded moonlight, they hastened through the scrubby grass and shrubs covering the hillside, round to the villa's pebble-lined path.

Katranina was already there. "Hurry," she said. "Ice-Heart is on the patio with Perla."

Finn crouched down, whispering to Seren, "Show me where you hid the sword."

Seren led him off the path in among the almond trees to an ancient lightning-struck oak. "In there," she said.

Finn reached into the hollow trunk and pulled out the Doomsong sword. It was in iron stick mode. Smiling to himself, he tucked it under his arm and gave Seren a warm kiss on the cheek. "Thank you, thank you."

Katranina watched through narrowed eyes, fingers waggling at her sides.

"What?" Finn demanded, sensing her mood. "I would have lost this forever if it wasn't for Seren."

"Oh, brave, clever girl," Kat mimicked. "And Finn will lose it again if he does not get down to the harbour *now*."

"Oh, gods and worms, how are we going to get away? Goran has the harbour watched."

"Goran also knows *Guillemot* is there," Kat said.

"Is it? Does he? That's wonderful. As long as," Finn closed his eyes and shook his head with despair, "his lookouts and archers don't sound the alert."

"They will not. Follow Kat," the ginger-haired girl said, weaving her way soundlessly through ancient trees and brambles.

Finn followed, twigs cracking under his feet. They had got some way down the hill when Katranina came to a halt. "The thrall is still with us."

Finn looked around. Seren was behind him. "That's all right. We can take her with us."

"This is not in Kat's plan. Kat will take Seren back to the villa. Finn will continue down the hill."

Kat hooked her fingers around Seren's thin arm and started to lead her away, pushing her into the worst of the brambles and high broom, scratching her face in the process. "Ow," Seren squeaked, trying to shield herself with her hands.

Kat led her further and further into the night-lit bushes and briars, towards the cliff edge. Moonlight glinted on white surf as the tide rolled into a cove far below.

Nearer and nearer they came. Kat side-stepping around shiny granite boulders and bare roots Seren could not see. Nearer and nearer to the soft rush and pull of the surf below, until there was a crackling and crashing sound behind them.

Finn was using Doomsong to light his way through the scrub, its glow illuminating the sudden drop, not yards in front of them. "Stop!" he shouted. "Kat, stop! This is not the way to the villa, and you know it. Let her go."

Kat halted, gave a deep, meaningful sigh and released Seren from her grip.

Stumbling in his haste, Finn grasped Seren's arm and pulled her into his chest. "That was mean and unnecessary, Kat. From now on Seren stays beside me."

Katranina's small mouth pursed with disapproval. "As Finn wishes," she hissed, dancing lightly up and over a rock, heading back towards the olive grove and the harbour path. "The thrall can share Finn's dungeon or death, as Finn pleases."

"Don't be so..." Finn's words died on his breath. Coming towards them with bright lanterns blazing were two men, the feral, white-haired Ice-Heart and big Cousin Troll.

Ice-Heart wrenched Doomsong from Finn's hand. "That is mine, by right of inheritance, according to the All-knowing All-father and your Master Odo."

This, Finn could not dispute. But he tried all the same. "Not if you do not accept your duty to your people, it isn't."

Ice-Heart's mouth twisted into a snarl. "Very well, I shall do my duty as a benevolent clan leader, and let you go. How's that for Volsung charity?"

"Volsung charity! What about your obligations? Master Odo sent me on this mission to find you, because your clan – and a lot of other people – need you to take them a safe place. Somewhere far from the ice and snow that will come after the mountain explodes, and even now destroys all they plant. Somewhere fertile and safe, where we can start a new life. You know of these places. You can take us; you know you can. If you weren't so selfish and... and... cruel."

Finn raised his hands to his face. What more could he say to make Goran Ice-Heart change his mind, his character and temperament? Then something Goran had said came back to him.

"It's true then," Finn said, glaring into Goran's ice-blue eyes in the moonlight. "What you told me: that people believed, generations gone by, that a Volsung eventually brought suffering to friend and family alike."

"That's what I said and what people believed," Goran retorted. "We are nothing to be proud of. Sigurd, the so-called dragonslayer, proved that long ago. It wasn't he who killed Fafnir or Grafnir or whatever the beast was called; it was a weedy by-blow tale-maker. Did you know that?"

"Yes, we all know that. What's that got to do with the fact that you were born with a responsibility to your clan?"

"What is true is what you see with your own eyes, boy," Ice-Heart said, as if quoting.

Finn's head shot up. How often had he told his younger cousins and nephews that? Who had he learned it from? "Well, I see a self-seeking pirate who's happy to bring suffering to his people."

"There you are then. I am not the 'best person' to lead anyone anywhere!"

"You *are* a weakling!" Finn hissed in anger.

Goran stepped backwards as if Finn had punched him. "I gave up my birth-right and the duties that go with it a generation ago. I'm no use to you. You can tell your Master Odo that. I've made my life here and I am not going back. Not for All-father himself."

"But hundreds of people need you!"

"They were happy enough to see the back of me twenty years ago."

"Why?" Finn asked. "What did you do?"

"I upset their way of thinking. Ignored their family-life rules. That's the worst of crimes to ditch-diggers. They're not called 'stick-in-the-muds' for nothing."

"But what did you *do*?"

"Ask you cousins. Their parents created a scandal out of a perfectly innocent... well, not innocent... but it was them kicking up a fuss, using something private and personal as an excuse to take my land; that began it all. And they succeeded. They got my family's island for themselves, and if they're going to be blown up on it or smothered in ash, it's nothing to do with me. I've got a bigger, better island here. They can go fry themselves, for all I care."

"But that doesn't change the fact that you are the Volsung clan leader."

In the fading light from the sword, Finn saw Goran tilt his head. "No, I suppose not," Goran sighed. "But I don't have to be the one to help them. You can do it, if you've got the guts."

Finn had come to that conclusion himself, but now the reality hit him. He opened his mouth to speak, but no words came.

Goran Ice-Heart cocked his head again, "What's the matter, cat got your tongue?"

Finn swallowed, nodded.

"So, there we are," Goran said, as if concluding a debate. "Go, now. There's a knarr in the harbour waiting for you. Did you know that?"

"But your clan," Finn said quietly. "What do I tell them?"

"Spineless land-lovers: they can take their chance same way as I did. Same way as braver folk: go a'viking. If they haven't got the backbone to leave, they don't deserve to survive your so-called disaster."

"Do I tell Master Odo that as well?"

"Yes. He has no power over me here. Not the frigging All-father himself." Goran gave Finn a sharp poke in the chest. "Go on. Seavogel's down there, been there since we got back on *Dreki.* Go on," another poke sent Finn sprawling on twigs and grit, "hurry back home with tales of wicked Ice-Heart, or wherever you manage to get to. Tell them they'll you'll be the hero of the hour." Then, as if his anger was spent, Goran stopped.

For a moment, nobody moved or spoke. The night, the land, the air that had been charged with anger began to relax. Finn took a deep breath, but before he could say anything, Goran said quietly, "It's your time now, Finn. Time for you to create a legend for yourself."

Without waiting for a reply, Goran turned, shoved Troll out of his way and strode as fast as he could back up the hill, taking Doomsong with him.

"Wait!" Finn yelled. "If I am to do this, I need the sword."

Goran laughed. "No chance! You brought it to me, remember. Doomsong is mine now," he shouted, raising the blade in the air, the blunted blade of an iron stick without a glimmer of a glow.

Finn and Katranina, Seren and Troll watched. "The magic has gone," Finn whispered.

Troll placed a wide palm on Finn's neck. "Sorry, cousin," he said, and loped off after his pirate captain.

Finn and his two companions stayed where they were in the moonlight until Katranina broke the silence. "Now Finn may go and do what he must. *Guillemot* is waiting and Finn will not be stopped."

Holding Seren's hand, Finn led the way back to the mule-track, then down to the harbour, where he halted. "I can't go back. Not without Doomsong. I'm sure, certain, having the sword is connected to having power in some way. Leaving without it…" Finn choked back his deep sense of loss. "I just can't."

Kat's mouth twitched with annoyance. "Finn should use his mind and think about what he has just been told."

"I know what Goran was saying, that I can take our people to safety, but without Doomsong I'm just Finn the tale-maker. Nobody will listen to me."

"Oh, well, if Finn believes he is a nobody…" Kat gave one of her irritating shrugs. "…then he is and has no need of Kat." Wiggling five sharp-nailed fingers in the air, she said, "Farewell spineless, ditch-digger with no future. Kat has a home to return to, while it still exists."

Seren stayed at Finn's side, not daring to speak. "I'm sorry about all this," he said, putting an arm around her shoulders. "You should go back to the villa."

Seren shook her head, "That is not where I should be."

"As you choose. I'll put you on *Guillemot*; Seavogel drop you, or us, off at a port somewhere. Would it be all right if we stayed together after that – for a while, anyway?"

Seren's eyes widened in the dark and she gave him a small peck on the cheek.

High above, out of sight among the first hints of an orange-flared dawn, warning of a scorching day, an eagle screamed her presence. Finn looked up, suspecting who she was, and would have smiled, had he been happy.

Guillemot was waiting in the harbour. In that strange heat haze of a morning not yet come, there was a shimmering light in the bow. As they reached the quay, Finn took Seren by the hand again, then dropped it in astonishment. The shimmering light on the workaday cargo knarr surrounded the most beautiful woman he'd even seen.

Draped in a silver cloak, with silver tresses falling over her shoulders, she said in a light, lilting voice, "Come aboard and be welcome, Finn of the Volsungs. We have been waiting for you."

Finn crossed the gangplank with Seren behind him. The knarr was ready to sail. Seavogel was at the mast with Katranina beside him; Thorsman and the rest of the crew were at their oars, ready to pull. And in the bow stood the beautiful woman he had seen only once before, calming the sea in a storm or making it worse, he had never been sure which.

Laughing, relieved and relaxed for the first time since leaving the North, Finn swayed down the deck to shake Seavogel's hand or to draw him into a hug.

Chapter 29

Guillemot was wave-ready, but Seavogel gave no order to sail. Throughout the long, hot day, the crew loitered on deck in an unnatural silence. Midday came. Seren and Finn found what shelter they could and ate the goat cheese, walnuts and dried fruit that the crew had acquired from the islanders, and drank water cooled in ceramic flasks hanging overboard. They slept the Middle Sea midday sleep and awoke fuzzy-headed. The crew barely spoke and Finn and Seren had nothing to say.

Seavogel stayed at the mast, his bald head covered in a straw hat borrowed from a donkey. Katranina lay napping on a bale of soft Egyptian cotton in the stifling hold. The shimmering woman who had welcomed Finn on board had disappeared – if she had ever existed.

Resting with his back against the lower deck strakes, out of the sun, Finn half-believed he had imagined the events since leaving Minnaholm. Nothing fitted with his daily routine there or his wandering from farmsteads to taverns across the Cold North. Had it not been for the quiet presence of Seren, he would have willingly admitted he'd made it all up, for a story. But that could not be so, for Seren was sitting beside him.

Heat hovered above them, held them down with its weight, pushed through closed eyelids to scald unshed tears, it poked through cotton fabric to burn chests and backs and arms.

Afternoon turned to evening, lamps were lit on the white walls and flat roofs of harbour dwellings. Thorsman, Beorn and two others went ashore and returned with sharp white wine, rye bread and fat red sausages. The crew ate together, making as little noise as possible, then returned to their places to wait for the order to sail, or to sleep through another day. Everyone watched Shipmaster Seavogel, but nobody dared question him.

Eventually, as a soft breeze blew across the harbour, carrying the scent of night-flowering blooms and blinding daylight gradually turned indigo, Finn joined Seavogel by the mast.

"He will not come, Shipmaster," Finn said quietly. "There is no need to wait."

"You would leave without Goran?"

"Yes."

"And without the sword?" Seavogel asked, nodding a greeting to Katranina as she joined them. "Did he give you a reason?"

"For not returning with us? Yes. Of sorts. He said he has a good life on this island, and that Master Odo cannot reach him here; that the All-father himself has no power beyond the North."

"And that's a bald lie," Seavogel huffed. "I've sailed as far east as the Black Sea and as far south as Serkland, Africa, and the All-father has been with me all the way."

"There's no point waitingy," Finn insisted. "If you're worried about not completing Master Odo's task, don't. It's my failure, not yours...." his words died on his breath. Something, someone on the upper bow deck had begun to shimmer. The woman with flowing silver hair was there again.

Finn pushed back his hair as if to see better. "Who is it?" he whispered.

"Who do you think?" Seavogel replied.

Katranina gave one of her pursed lip smiles.

"What?" Finn demanded, feeling her gaze on him.

Kat shrugged, "Not *what*..."

"Don't start that again!" he snapped and turned back to Seavogel. "About Goran – to be honest, I think our clan will be better off without him."

"Happen it will. He can tell us that himself now."

"Now?" Finn queried.

Seavogel's face scrunched up in a wrinkled grin as a he pointed to the upper bow deck.

Standing beside the silver woman was the Volsung named Goran Ice-Heart.

"You've changed your mind!" Finn called with glee, racing down the deck.

"He will not change his mind, Finn," the woman said, her voice soft yet crystal clear. "It is you who must change yours."

"Riddles," Finn huffed. "I hate riddles."

"Think, Finn," the silver woman continued as if he had not spoken. "Think about what you have achieved on this voyage. You have found the man you were sent to find. What have you found out about yourself in doing so?"

"That I've failed someone very important, and a lot of other people will suffer as a consequence if I don't..."

"If *you* don't...?" the woman prompted. "Speak without thinking, without doubting, Finn. What have you learned? Who are you now?"

"Well, I'm not the lazy person my cousins moaned about. Nor am I a coward. Although I have been frightened, very frightened," Finn admitted. "But I..." he paused, looked back behind him at the red-haired girl in tan leather trews, "but I have had help. I have been saved, more than once, I am certain, by a friend – at least I think she's a friend, unless she's another cousin – whose special qualities I think I am beginning to understand."

Finn laughed nervously, for he was speaking without thinking, as he'd been instructed, and what he thought he knew about Katranina was more than a little strange. "Without Katranina, I would not be here now," he continued. "And Seren." He looked across the deck to where the girl was standing, watching. "I'm not going without you," he mouthed.

"So, you are sailing back to the Cold North to do as Master Odo requested, taking a new friend, who will support you in the future," the silver woman said. It was not a question. She turned her beautiful face to Goran. "Continue," she said.

Goran Ice-Heart stepped forward and pushed the hilt of a short iron sword into Finn's hand. "You might as well have this," he grunted. "It's no use to me."

Finn put his fingers around the rough iron grip and felt it warm in his hand and change shape. The blade began to glow.

"Yes," Goran said, "that's what I thought. I take back what I said about the All-father not reaching me here. Odin is your Master Odo; you do know that, don't you?"

Finn smiled and nodded.

"Good, right, well, in answer to your question last night, you can tell him I *formally* renounce my place in our line.

You are now Clan Leader of the Volsungs, Finn, so it's you who must take them to safety."

Finn took a deep breath and caught Kat's green-gold gaze on him. "*Why*?" he said, looking Ice-Heart in the eye. "Why are you doing this?"

"Because, Finn, you are my son. Because I rejected you all those years ago and your mother probably died because of it. That's what everyone said, anyway. You are in direct line from Sigmund and Sigurd and the lost boy Davor, who slew the marauding Grafnir for Sigurd so many generations ago. And that's why Doomsong sings in your hands."

As Goran spoke, the sword glowed brighter. "See," whispered the silver woman, "see how Truthteller knows its true owner."

Nobody moved, nobody spoke. Then Goran slapped Finn on the back, and in a skip and jump leapt the rail onto the quay, where he stood facing the *Guillemot,* and with his right fist over his heart, he gave an elaborate bow, then turned and walked into the night.

Seavogel sniffed with satisfaction and set about checking his rigging. Finn stayed where he was, watching without seeing until another surprise brought him back into the real world.

Standing beside Norna Silveryarn's hut was an unexpected passenger. A lithe, cat-like woman in a striped black and gold tunic.

"Are we calling in at Berjer?" Finn asked Seavogel.

"Happen we are," he grunted. "Best you stay on board until we get back North, though."

"Best I do," Finn grinned. "Happily."

"Are you ready, then?"

"You're the skipper, Shipmaster Seavogel."

"Ah, but you are in charge now, Finn of the Volsungs."

Finn looked across the deck to the island. There was no sign of Goran. Folding his arms across his chest he looked in the other direction, at the open sea. "I'm ready, Shipmaster," he said with a smile. "I've been getting ready for this for quite a while now."

"In that case, *cast off*!" Seavogel cried, and a large new member of the crew leapt onto the quay to tug the ropes from their rings. It was Troll.

"He's taken over from that two-faced liar, Beorn Wolfman," Seavogel said.

"Was it he who got me caught in Berjer?" Finn asked.

"It was, and he'd been after you from the start. I found that out when he tried to set fire to *Guillemot*."

"What happened?"

"He brought some fancy juggler fellow on board, juggling ruddy flames on a wooden boat. Deliberate, it was. Would have burnt us to cinders if Thorsman hadn't pushed him overboard."

Finn bit his lower lip. "Shipmaster," he said slowly, "do you think it's possible he'd been sent by Loki? To prevent me getting here?"

"He was. According to Norna Silveryarn, he's one of Loki's followers. You'll have to look out better for those fire-loving mischief makers, from now on."

"Norna Silveryarn knew!"

"Keep your friends close and your enemies closer: never heard that before?"

"No, but I will from here on." Finn looked up at the sky. "And the dragons? The two dragons, when we first set out, were they sent by Loki?"

"Probably. We'll have to keep an eye out for them, as well, on the way back."

"Watch out and think about – I've learned that – thanks to Kat."

"Right then," Seavogel slapped a hand across Finn's broader shoulders, "let's get homeward bound. We've got a lot to do when we arrive."

"Pull!" he called to his crew.

Guillemot's oarsmen pulled out of the harbour and into the Middle Sea, guided by a Shipmaster who could read the stars and a pilot who could return home by the shape and scent of white foam on wave water.

The End

Author's Note

This novel is a work of fiction based on Norse myths and legends, and historical evidence. According to a Norse saga, the sword named Gram (Anger), Doomsong and Truthteller once belonged Sigmund of the Volsungs. It was broken by Odin in battle and reforged for Sigurd, the Dragonslayer. *The Doomsong Sword* is a re-telling of this story with a fictional hero named Davor, who is Finn's distant ancestor.

Story-telling or 'tale-making' was an important part of life in a land of long dark winters. People of all ages, in what we now think of a Scandinavia, had a profound belief in the 'other world,' in spirits of the forest, omens and *disir*, women whose special skills were later considered to be witchcraft. Imagine yourself in a grass-thatched dwelling, lit only by the weak flames in a smoky fire-pit; the wind howling like a pack of wolves outside.... Anything could happen.

The imminent disaster that sends Finn on his voyage is a based on a real weather event caused by the eruption of a volcano and what became known as "fimbulwinter". The sun did not shine, the land was covered in ash and ice, livestock died and nothing would grow, so humble farmers and their families needed to find a new, fertile homeland.

On a personal note, I grew up on an ancient Viking battlefield in North Devon, England. The battle was commemorated by a local landmark at Bloody Corner on fertile ground near the Torridge Estuary. The Viking invaders were led by Hubbe or Hubba. Whether or not this bit is true, the legend is they settled down and stayed.

© J.G. Harlond

Málaga, June, 2024

The Author

J.G. Harlond

Jane G. Harlond grew up in Devon and studied in Bristol, Portsmouth and the USA before finishing her academic studies with an M.A. in Social and Political Thought at the University of Sussex. She has lived and worked in a variety of different countries and is married to a retired Spanish naval officer. Harlond has two sons and five step-children, all of whom now have their own careers in diverse parts of Europe.

If You Enjoyed This Book

Please Visit

PENMORE PRESS

www.penmorepress.com

All Penmore Press books are available directly through our website, amazon.com, Barnes and Noble and Nook,, Apple iTunes, Kobo books and via leading bookshops across the United States, Canada, the UK, Australia and Europe.

The Chosen Man

by

J. G Harlond

From the bulb of a rare flower bloom ambition and scandal

Rome, 1635: As Flanders braces for another long year of war, a Spanish count presents the Vatican with a means of disrupting the Dutch rebels' booming economy. His plan is brilliant. They just need the right man to implement it.

They choose Ludovico da Portovenere, a charismatic spice and silk merchant. Intrigued by the Vatican's proposal—and hungry for profit—Ludo sets off for Amsterdam to sow greed and venture capitalism for a disastrous harvest, hampered by a timid English priest sent from Rome, accompanied by a quick-witted young admirer he will use as a spy, and bothered by the memory of the beautiful young lady he refused to take with him.

Set in a world of international politics and domestic intrigue, *The Chosen Man* spins an engrossing tale about the Dutch financial scandal known as tulip mania—and how decisions made in high places can have terrible repercussions on innocent lives.

PENMORE PRESS
www.penmorepress.com

THE EMPRESS EMERALD

BY

J. G. HARLOND

Stolen: A child, a priceless jewel, and an identity

Abandoned as a child in a Bombay orphanage, Leo Kazan's life takes an unanticipated turn when he becomes the protégé of Sir Lionel Pinecoffin, the city's District Political Officer in Bombay. Under Pinecoffin's tutelage, the boy, adept at learning languages and theft, is trained as a spy and becomes immersed in international espionage, revolutionary politics, and diamond smuggling. In 1918, during a visit to London, he has a brief but memorable affair with a young English woman Davina Dymond in London before leaving for Russia.

Separated, their lives take different turns. As he matures Leo begins to question his family history, seeking to uncover the truth about his parents. A pregnant Davina is married off and exiled to Spain, where she gives birth to Leo's daughter. They are fated to meet again in Gibraltar in 1936, their love rekindled. But a new war plunges Europe into crisis, the Spanish Civil War tearing them apart, leaving, Leo and Davina in a fight to reclaim their lives and their love amid the violent storms of war.

PENMORE PRESS
www.penmorepress.com

Local Resistance

by

J. G. Harlond

WWII in England, Cornwall smugglers, Intelligence agents, detective story, locals and war in the UK, German navy operations on the coast of the UK. Murder thriller. Espionage.

On a stormy night in March 1941, Maisie Rose Hawkins leaves her drunk husband, Stan, out in the rain—and he disappears. Detective Sergeant Bob Robbins and young PC Laurie Oliver are called out to investigate and discover that Stan's small fishing boat is gone, the rope sawn through. As Bob searches for answers, it becomes apparent that in this small Cornish village where everyone knows everything about everybody, nobody quite knows the truth.

Beneath the surface of village life, a fierce battle is being waged against wartime deprivations. Shopkeepers quietly evade rationing restrictions. Food inspector Archibald Bantry, charged with enforcing those restrictions, dies in a suspicious car crash. Various leads connect a sea cave full of smuggled black-market goods to the missing Stan Hawkins. And what seems like the work of local malcontents becomes more complex and dangerous when Bob stumbles on the truth in a disused copper mine, where a much deadlier affair is underway.

"Uncanny happenings and warm characterization. . . . The realities of wartime life in this novel combine with a lovely sense of place to create a distinctly Cornish mixture of secluded charm and the unsettlingly mysterious." —Robert Wilton, prize-winning author of the Comptrollerate-General historical thrillers.

PENMORE PRESS
www.penmorepress.com

Historical fiction and nonfiction
Paperback available for order on line
and as Ebook with all major distributers

Penmore Press

Challenging, Intriguing, Adventurous, Historical and Imaginative

www.penmorepress.com

www.ingramcontent.com/pod-product-compliance
Lightning Source LLC
Chambersburg PA
CBHW060705190726
48289CB00002B/549